Once on the Isle of Spice

ALAN ENJOY THIS
JOURNEY —
CLAUDE

Once on the Isle of Spice

C. C. Alick

ISBN: Softcover 978-1-7960-2246-9
eBook 978-1-7960-2247-6

Print information available on the last page.

Rev. date: 03/20/2019

To order additional copies of this book, contact:
Xlibris
1-888-795-4274
www.Xlibris.com
Orders@Xlibris.com
794224

Somewhere during gestation, the embryo became aware of the village called Jean Anglais and the people who lived there. The unborn child felt, saw and heard all their concerns. From a swirling tableau, encompassing past and present, the fetus grasped at floating morsels of consciousness. Finally, the pre-born sunk into an embryonic dream of a group of people standing and listening to an old man, understood that out of respect, those neighbors would remain silent, but annoyed at his interference. Everyone in attendance at the meeting wanted Papa LaTouche to hush, and allow the two well-dressed men from the capital to complete the message they came to deliver. The midday sun blazed down on the gathering, heightening the anecdote the old man was spitting at the two strangers, representatives of the government, whom had arrived by car to make clear, through word-of-mouth, the changes they anticipated for the island with the advent of internal governance.

They stood in a semicircle in the common area between the houses that defined the village. The villagers recognized the old man's trickery, so they kept gazing at the two strangers, waiting to see what would transpire. Would the two men disappear like smoke, evaporate into the ground like rain, or turn to two shards of rock? When nothing happened, they felt sorrow for the outsiders who they knew would be afflicted by a severe strain of the babbles, that affliction which caused words to slit and slide, and then dwindle, as if uttered by the dead. His old voice teased out the tale, one finger pointing up at Ogoun's Point, the mountain above the village, as he told of the time when God and the devil shared a cave near the top of the mountain. The telling grew vigorous as he put across why those cohorts often emerged from their abode to indulge in monkey business, causing the sun and the rain to descend on the people and the village in long shafts of wet light. In the end, the two outsiders drove away, amused, and wondering how they had managed to lose control of the proceedings. Some of the people in attendance questioned the authenticity of the two men, since they had never seen them before or knew their names. Where did they come from? Humans or spirits remained a major concern.

After the strangers had departed, everyone returned to their routines, carrying bundles of wood for their fires, working on their plots of provisions in The Valley of Bones, and harvesting sugarcane for the meager cash the owners would pay. The people of Jean Anglais held many premonitions, inklings transported from Africa in their blood. They had knowledge of how an unborn child could know all their business, how spiritual beings with the ability to crawl along the threads of yarns being told could materialize among the people in many forms: a man or woman blowing on a conch shell and selling fish, as a frantic youngster searching for deceased relatives, or how they would sneak under the skin of infants.

Pubescent kids and dogs are susceptible to the influences of such immortals they maintained, and adults should be on guard. If you are suspicious of any lurking figure, stare hard, the figure would disappear, but not before whispering in the ear of a nearby child or a dog. No one has ever persuaded a youngster to repeat the secrets whispered by the Wanderers and nobody has ever considered asking the dogs.

The unborn child absorbed the history of Jean Anglais and why it appeared on no map. The village was named after a former Gerondist, a French planter who had participated in a failed slave revolt and met his death at the hands of outraged British colonials. Where the community began shifted with time. People believed the magic of Jean Anglais extended beyond their vision and down into the earth, to a spot in Africa where night changed clothes and return as day. Long-standing residents of Jean Anglais could show you the area where this phenomenon repeatedly transpired, near an old mahogany tree at the crossroads where the colorful houses gave way to the bush and the cane, and the area known as The Valley of Bones.

A certain being from the often-told tales found a chink in reality and decided to utilize that crevice to visit Jean Anglais, concealed beneath the skin of the infant. No one knew of its plan, not even its host or the Obeah woman, Mama Viche. She received a slight glimpse of matters to come when dense clouds formed above Jean Anglais and The Valley of Bones. Throughout the night and into the next day, a steady rain fell, people thought of Noah and his ark. Water saturated the soil around the base of the old mahogany tree, and when the weather switched to a hard, lashing wind, the old tree tumbled to the ground. That same day, after the tree fell, hail bombarded the village. The lumps of frozen rain produced a loud racket on the galvanized roofs, buried the grass, knocked down limbs, and left what resembled heaps of tiny, white eggs on the black soil.

Mama Viche stood at her front window facing the bottom road, thinking about her pregnant sister Maureen, and surveying the storm damage. "Must be a sign," she said to Maureen.

"Such strange weather, don't know what to make of it," Maureen responded from the kitchen table where she sat with a steaming cup of cocoa tea, and chewing on slices of breadfruit with salt-fish in coconut oil. She kept rubbing one hand over her protruding stomach as if to soothe her expected progeny, the girl child she planned to call Alma.

The storm had raged and drifted away, leaving an awkward silence that was soon consumed by a volatile rumble. Utensils in the kitchen rattled. Mama Viche looked around and cringed as if anticipating pain. They both came to a similar realization. The vibration was coming from the earth, down the slope of Ogoun's Point. A dislodged boulder slashed through the undergrowth, missed all the houses and came to rest between a stand of fruit trees behind the house shared by the sisters.

Melting hailstones mixed with scattered knocked down leaves littered the surroundings. Some old residents of Jean Anglais asserted that this had happened only once before, a long time ago, on the day the devil had learned of God's plan to depart for heaven.

An abrupt sunbeam illuminated the surroundings, casting doubts on the brown puddles and the shifting sludge. Mama Viche and Maureen came out of the house and joined the other villagers. Some stood gazing skyward as if accusing God. Others followed the deep gouges carved in the soil by the passage of the boulder.

These people shared certain collective feelings, rudiments from ancient times floated all around them like rumors. They had no idea how they retained certain bits and pieces from the motherland or why they experienced collective dreams. Convenience betrayed them and accelerated the demise of their blended consciousness. Their presence on the land before they gave it a name, the food from the soil that nourished their bodies, the rain and sun that soaked through and fortified other living things; all these allowances held an enduring vigor that refused to depart in silence.

"Did we witness some miracles today?" Papa LaTouche spoke to no one in particular. The old patriarch ran one hand over his balding head and graying beard in one dismissive swipe as he continued to look skyward.

"Bad weather, sheer luck, and a warning, that's what happened here today," said Mama Viche. She stood with her sister and the assembled near the big boulder. "Look at this mess, see how close this thing came to my house? I warned those fellows, told them they shouldn't cut too many trees on that slope. They didn't listen to me when I gave words about disturbing the resting place of our ancestors."

No one responded to her admonition. They didn't want to get into a quarrel with her after the earlier incidents of backbiting and betrayal about who placed their homes in jeopardy. A fellow called Mano, the fiercest drummer in the village, the lover of the Obeah woman's sister, had taken the blame for the whole mess. The police had come to arrest him. The man took to the bush and stayed hidden for months. Some villagers took pleasure in taunting the authorities. People brought Mano food and water, kept a lookout for the police; they would blow the conch shell the moment they spotted any official-looking vehicle. Mano eventually surrendered at the beginning of the rainy season, and received a prison sentence. A collective effort to ignore the incident concerning the removal of the trees persisted. Mama Viche, the Obeah woman, bringing it up as they stood near the boulder behind her house didn't bode well. After all, no one died or was hurt.

"Who is that? What's he carrying?" Papa LaTouche pointed to a man walking up the road in the distance as if the rain, the mud and the confusion had nothing to do with him.

Swallow, a resident of Jean Anglais, strolled past his neighbors without any salutations. He approached the front of his house with a cardboard box tucked under one arm. The man placed the box on his porch, took out the contents, and began fingering some knobs. The villagers moved away from the rock the moment they heard a shrill voice accompanied by music. They hastened to catch a glimpse of what Swallow had brought home: a square, red plastic box with wires attached to a battery. Right away, they recognized it as a radio. Swallow claimed an English man had given him the radio and battery, but his neighbors assumed he had stolen both.

"Take that thing back to where you found it. You sure it was a man who gave you that thing? You sure it wasn't an evil spirit?" The Obeah woman removed a checkered bandanna wrapped around her hair, and she ran the fabric through the perspiration on her face.

"What you talking about, Mama? A man gave the things to me. Didn't look like no evil spirit."

"Okay then, okay. Don't listen. You know what evil spirits look like, huh? Don't expect me to deal with whatever when mischief comes calling." She spoke and raised both of her hands in the air as she rewrapped her head with the bandanna.

The woman wanted to shout at Swallow and the villagers about what she saw within the radio, how that box could entice them to pay less attention to their own stories, how the attraction of their existence could be blown apart by that foreign noise. But she kept her tongue locked behind her teeth. Two predicaments now occupied her thinking, the radio and her pregnant sister, both irritated more than her skin.

The grounded spirit came and took refuge in the first born child of John Augustine and his wife Joan, remained there silently, just observing the daily details of their lives. Conditions had settled down; the sun had retrieved most of the moisture from the soil as it made two journeys across the sky. Villagers had picked up and stacked the downed limbs. Nightfall appeared limp in that pithy interlude after sundown, chickens cackled, and birds issued a final chirp from the trees and brushes. John sat under the plum tree in his front yard; smiling and joking with a few of his male friends. No sign of the anxiety gnawing at his guts showed on his face. The men were tossing down shots of strong rum and chasing the liquor with coconut water. John moved off and lit a bottle torch; the breeze pushed the stink of the kerosene, bothering his nostrils and stinging his eyes. He held his breath to stall the irritation and hide his mounting anxiety.

The sex of a first child had never been a matter of importance to the residents of Jean Anglais, except for John. His firstborn had to be male and had to be tied to this scrap of land and this old house until death. Trying to fulfill the pledge he had made to his father took on significance. John believed half of what his father had declared about the future. A boy child to inherit the land made sense to him. But the old man's assertions about the demise of Jean Anglais and the connection to the spirits of ancestors trapped in a field of sugarcane in the Valley Of Bones only buoyed John's cynicism about the olden days. Those old people and the elastic world they inhabited.

As the news spread through the village that Joan, John's wife, had gone into labor, a few of her friends hurried down the dirt path to offer support. Knowing that the Obeah woman always handled the deliveries alone, the women took up stations near the front door of the house, as if to keep the men away from the mystique of the birthing process.

Inside the house, the head of the child had crowned at the mother's birth canal. Mama Viche noticed a loose bit of membrane wrapped around the head and face of the infant. The old woman understood the significance of a "veiled birth" and the threat this phenomenon could one day pose to her authority in the village. For a split second, as the mother strained to expel the infant from her body, Mama Viche considered suffocation, but she poked three holes through the veil, two near the nostrils and one near the mouth. She separated the child from the membrane, placed the bloodstained bit of tissue in a pail of warm water at the foot of the bed, and then she moved the infant onto the mother's stomach, snipped the umbilical cord and slapped the child hard on his backside.

The child screamed.

Mama Viche moved the child onto the bed next to Joan and proceeded to help the young mother exorcise the balance of the afterbirth. Joan emerged from the final stage of her labor pains to the bawling of the child and the voices of the neighbors teasing her husband.

"Well, it's a boy as you wanted," Mama Viche spoke above the blended ruckus.

"John wanted a boy, seemed important to him. I only wanted a healthy--"

"You have a decision to make, Joan."

"What's wrong, Mama? Is something wrong with him?" Joan grasped the screaming child, held him up to the light, and took in his entirety: a flawless face, mouth opened in a trembling scream, his watery eyes wobbled as she searched his expression.

"No. No. No. Don't be alarmed," said the Obeah woman.

Joan returned the infant to her chest, forced her right nipple into his mouth, flinched as his gums clamped onto her sore nipples. The child went silent. Outside, the assembled continued their joking and merriment.

"Your son came from behind the veil, Joan," Mama Viche said. "In all my years of helping you girls give birth, this is the first time I've seen..."

"You scared me. I thought something might be..."

"Well, nothing right now. But you know about all the fascinations with people born with a veil. The stories, the expectations."

"I see what you mean." The young mother clutched her infant.

"You have a decision to--"

"I understand, Mama, I understand."

The older woman leaned in, stroking the head of the infant. Soft as doubtful footsteps, the words left her mouth, "So what you want to do?"

"Let this be between us. Protect the veil. We can explain this to him when--"

"Wise decision, Joan, wise decision. I'll get John. He must be eager to set eyes on his firstborn." As she moved across the room to shout at

John, Mama Viche extended her left foot and nudged the pail of warm water with the veil under the bed.

In many ways, the birth of this child changed the trajectory of Jean Anglais. The boy would grow up with a lingering impression, like a forgotten dream, details once known and accepted became elusive.

* * *

His parents named him Ezekiel; gave him that biblical name because they knew it meant God toughens, and they derived pleasure from the inherent promise. Joan wrote his name in block letters and tacked it to the wall near the cardboard box they were using as a crib. Two weeks after the birth, Joan received a monetary gift from her godmother in England. She used the money to purchase a crib, wrote the alphabet on a section of the old cardboard box and fastened it to the wall next to his name. She had adopted the habit of speaking to her child, enjoyed the smiles on his little face and felt sure that he understood every word coming out of her mouth. Ezekiel surprised his parents. At the age of two he began attempting to speak complete sentences, showing frustration with them when they didn't understand, and then he started to recite the alphabet as his mother took him on walks. Three months later he began scribbling simple words. But he continued the chatter. His mother and father bristled with pride, invited their friends to hear the boy prattle his nonsensical narrative.

And for a time, life continued on its merry way as he gained access to familiar words. On his seventh birthday, the boy began to cry. Continued in a furry; he refused to eat, and would stop breathing for menacing minutes before gulping air through his nose and mouth, as if inhaling the world. In sleep, he would whimper and moan, scrape at his throat and mouth. Joan didn't want to seem insecure in her maternal skills with her first child. It took her a full week and the urging of friends before she took Ezekiel to Mama Viche.

* * *

The Obeah woman stared at the young mother. "What took you this long to bring him back to me? You do have to ask."

"I filled his brain with too much too soon, Mama. We all sat there laughing at his antics and all the time… I'm a bad mother, Mama, a bad mother. I should have taken better care__"

"It's nothing like that, Joan. The boy has been speaking for years, enough time for him to spit out all the nonsense you put in his head," Mama Viche smiled. "Leave him for a little while. You told me enough," she said. She tugged Ezekiel's palm out of Joan's clenched fingers. "I'll bring him home later."

Joan looked at Maureen sitting on the porch with her young daughter and then she glanced at the Obeah woman. "Okay, Mama. Okay," she said.

Mama Viche walked around to the back of the house with the little boy dressed in khaki short pants and a white jersey. They stopped near the rock that had rolled off the mountain.

"Why you making so much fuss?"

"Pain, Mama. Body aches, knees, stomach, and the vomiting."

"You don't look sick. Your mother said nothing about all that."

"Not me, Mama, other people all around here. I see it and feel it every time I close my eyes," Ezekiel said.

The old woman gazed at his face. "Wait here," she said and she went into the house through the backdoor. Mama Viche returned with a dry stem of black sage; struck a match and lit it. A small flame and smoke rose from the twig. She snuffed out the flame with a puff of her breath. The smoke drifted across Ezekiel's face.

He coughed.

"Take deep breaths," Mama Viche said. "Cough out what's hiding inside of you. Send it back."

The boy inhaled and coughed again. Mama Viche waved the smoldering twig under his nostrils. Ezekiel ran one hand over his face and moved his fingers across the bridge of his nose.

"What's hiding in me, Mama?" Ezekiel gazed at the Obeah woman. "I hear the voice whispering, the same voice all the time."

"Empty your mind," she said. "Take some nice images to bed with you tonight. Tomorrow that presence will be gone."

"Will it help you to prevent what I see coming?"

"No. But we will manage."

"Can you stop them from getting sick?"

"Ezekiel, the malady and wickedness you see coming on us must be coming from deep down," Mama Viche said. "I now have time to prepare."

"Every house, I see people bawling in pain. You are only one person, Mama. What if you get sick?"

"I know how to fight off this malady."

"I don't see my house in the dreams, Mama."

"Stay strong, boy, and no more tears. Come here; spit on this, help me to send that mourning spirit back to where it came from."

Ezekiel leaned toward the old woman, collected spittle in his mouth and spat at the smoldering bush. Mama Viche tossed the doused stem into a puddle of water near the rock that had rolled down the mountain. Mosquito larvae wiggled away from the disturbance. "Say nothing about today to anyone. We don't want people going crazy, flopping all over the place like chickens with their heads cut off. Leave this to me. Go back to being a child."

For a fraction of a second, Mama Viche considered telling Ezekiel about his veiled birth, but her last words had closed a door.

When dengue fever descended on Jean Anglais, the Obeah woman applied all of her skills, treated the rashes, treated the aches and pains, kept people hydrated and nourished by making them ingest copious amounts of ganja. The government sent men with large spray cans to exterminate the mosquitoes and destroy their breeding sights. Only three people died in the outbreak. Ezekiel's mother, Joan, was the last person to succumb to the ravages of the dengue fever. Six years after the outbreak, folks still spoke about the episode as if it were some kind of ancient plague. Some people started treating it as if it was just another story.

Mama Viche kept an eye on the boy as he grew into a docile youth. Only his connection to the boisterous albino, Malcolm Masanto, seemed to add zest to his life. She often speculated on the birth of her niece Alma and those boys, tried to ignore her nagging concerns about the children of Jean Anglais, and their prospects for the future.

* * *

A gust of wind plunged from the sky and engulfed Ezekiel as he walked up the new gravel road near Mama Viche's house. The gust coiled around, kicking up dirt and leaves. Small pebbles lashed at his bare arms and legs. He shut his eyes, shielded his face with his bag of schoolbooks and stumbled forward, disregarding all the vexations that had occupied his thoughts minutes before. The uproar lifted just as quickly as it came. Ezekiel heard it harassing the trees, compelling the branches to sway, the leaves to wail.

A hint of dust in the air tickled his nostrils, and the texture of the gravel road under the soles of his shoes compelled his stubbornness, back to his previous concerns about punishments, scolding and harassment from all sides. Even his dreams and suspicions seemed a hindrance. The boy stooped, picked up a rock and flung it at the rays of evening sunlight decanting through the foliage.

A maxim cited by one of his teachers and aimed at his friend Malcolm, came to mind: "You can't make sense out of nonsense, boy." Ezekiel had disagreed with the teacher without knowing why. Now as he walked up the road, the ambiguity of the words and how he had managed to arrive at a final conclusion about that idiom made him smile. It all began with a recurring dream. Deep groans emanated from a figure caught in a swirling vortex inside a vat of bubbling cane juice. A rising stench filled the air as the figure sunk into the hot liquid. In the dream, Ezekiel remembered thinking the end product would be thick, black molasses. He came awake thinking, what a stupid dream.

Two days later, Ezekiel happened on an incident that solidified his opinion. The boy had snuck up on his father and Mondu, the stuttering man, assuming they were just shooting the breeze about some fiasco that he might find interesting. Ezekiel started scratching the dirt with his toes, moving about under the plum tree with a stick in hand, sketching circles in the dirt, pretended to find pleasure in dead leaves and chicken shit. The boy ran his free hand over his closely cropped hair as he listened to the conversation between the two men. When he came to the realization that the discussion concerned the fate of Cosmus, the young villager condemned to life in prison, the hairs on his skin bristled. The discussion took on a stirring vitality as Mondu, the stutterer, claimed his turn to speak.

"White, white people they…they use their money and…and even their skin as a weapon, something…something to cut you. I…I should have warned Cosmus. They can, they can, steal your life from you like that." Mondu snapped his fingers. "They did it during slavery and… and…still doing it today. His…his mother is right to blame me for what happened."

"You can't carry that guilt alone, man. Other people must take their share," John said. "Those money people can buy lawyers and help judges to powder their wigs. Look at Duncan Elmo. The man is a Grenadian, black as coals, pure African, but look at him, acting like some…greedy fuckers. Money people... Play a fool around their belongings and they come at you like rabid dogs."

"Yeah…yeah…yeah, I…I know what you mean. Cosmus was only seven when I…when I started living with his mother. I…I see him as my own son. We have to…we have to get him out of Richmond Hill Prison. Life…life can be a long time."

"Stick to the plan. The opportunity will come," John said.

Ezekiel perked up at the hint of a scheme. He stood frozen in one spot waiting for the next words. His father caught the pause. "Boy, get lost. Think we don't see you? Mind your own business, moving around like some kind of loupgarou."

Mondu laughed.

Ezekiel wondered how the man could laugh and sing with that stutter. A rush of embarrassment struck Ezekiel. Hot blood rushed to his temples. He stumbled, and almost fell as he moved away from his father and Mondu. Images of a man with a suitcase walking down the road from Jean Anglais toward Belmont careened through his mind. The man was accompanied by three people, his father John, Mondu, and himself, all much older. He knew the fourth person with the suitcase had to be Cosmus. Ezekiel shook his head, and tried to recover from these fleeting impressions. He recalled his father talking to Mondu about epilepsy and complaining about the maladies plaguing both his sons. Ezekiel understood nothing about epilepsy, but he knew it had nothing to do with him.

He found it remarkable to have stumbled on the identity of the person from his recurring dreams about the figure in the boiling cane juice. Near the end of that school day, Ezekiel had tried to explain to Malcolm how the nonsense of his dreams had materialized into the prisoner called Cosmus. Malcolm couldn't recall the maxim thrown at him by the teacher. Ezekiel became frustrated with Malcolm, the intricacy of how he had managed to alter nonsense to sense, the explanation fell flat, like trying to elucidate a vivid dream and realizing that words alone can be inadequate.

Ezekiel had attempted to shift the conversation by reminding Malcolm about the hunting trip they had planned for later that night. Malcolm had burst into laughter, alerting the teacher, and resulting in Ezekiel walking home alone and the encounter with Mama Viche. The boy grappled with the notion that negatives can produce positives. The bacchanal of the last election reflected on him as a negative. Those men prowling up and down the road in trucks with loudspeakers, trying to change minds, and the arguments about how the government had sent workers from outside of Jean Anglais to disturb people's lives, all this left a negative impression on him. But as he challenged the contrary, Ezekiel wondered what it would take to become one of the men shouting through the loudspeakers, the men responsible for conquering mud and bringing water closer to homes through the standpipe. He aspired to be one of those men, people with the ability to turn negatives to positives.

He pressed on toward home, indulging in his mental sprees. Mama Viche, the Obeah woman, resting on her front porch, caught his attention. She sat there looking at him and smiling. The woman waved, and Ezekiel waved back, wondering if she had conjured that gust of wind for her amusement.

The boy knew she had watched as he wrestled the wind. Ezekiel wanted to make sense of this woman. There were so many stories about her: They say a ruffian and thief from Belmont came up the hill one night to commit mischief and brutality on the two women who lived with no man. According to the story, the Obeah woman confounded the thief by turning him into a crapo, a big frog that she kept tethered to a pole near a puddle in her backyard for several days. She released him eventually, and he reverted to being a man, but he retained all the warts and kept croaking. His people had to take him to the crazy house where he has remained to this day.

And then the man called Yaga, the one who inherited the radio from Swallow, a rude man who disrespected Mama Viche. One day Yaga was boasting to a group of men, when Mama Viche walked by, snatched his voice out of his throat and flung it far into the bush. The man couldn't speak for almost a week, and when his voice did return, he spoke with a lisp. Yaga sold his radio to a young fellow called Selwyn and moved out of Jean Anglais, claiming the Obeah woman had worked some kind of sorcery on him because of her resentment of the radio. No one has heard from Yaga in years.

Usually after school, Ezekiel would walk home in the company of Malcolm and others, but this evening he walked alone. The teacher had caught him trying to explain to Malcolm how he had made sense out of nonsense. The teacher invited Ezekiel to come forward and share with the class what amused Malcolm so much. When he remained seated, averting eye contact, the teacher sentenced him to the blackboard with chalk in hand. He stood there at the end of the day, writing the same sentence: "Sometimes it's the smallest decisions that can change your life forever." He languished there, scribbling those words over and over as his classmates exited the room.

Near the Obeah woman's house, a group of villagers labored on the construction of a new Christian Church. Their babble reached his ears before he saw them. What they had accomplished since earlier in the day surprised him. He stopped to take stock: shiny roof, the completion of all walls, and people moving about like ants. Ezekiel questioned the haste, marveled at the result of their work, and wondered how it would change Jean Anglais. Actually, he favored a shop for the village, instead of this church.

Two months before, the white preacher and the villagers had started with truckloads of sand, gravel, bags of cement, and several long steel rods. After displacing the dirt, they formed a concrete slab from the materials and started building. A wooden frame soon stood on the spot, complete with rafters waiting to be covered. Then all work came to a halt, and the Missionary Man left Grenada. But he came back two weeks later, and truckloads of lumber and roofing material started to appear. His supporters rushed to help him nail the materials to the frame for fear the bits and pieces would vanish into the night and rematerialize on other people's houses.

Ezekiel stood and scrutinized the people putting the finishing touches on the building out in the trees. They laughed and hammered nails, while others circled with buckets of paint. All black people, except for the man the Obeah woman had nicknamed the Missionary Man. The white man held his own bucket of paint and a brush, pointing here and there, dabbing at the exterior walls. As Ezekiel walked away, he wondered what his deceased mother would have thought about all this. He felt sure she would have favored the shop.

The boy approached his family's home near the path they called the Bottom Road. Two flowering plants, a hibiscus and a bougainvillea dominated the walk to the old wooden house, littering the grass with contrasting red petals. Ezekiel saw Tilly, his stepmother bend over, picking tomatoes and lettuce, placing the vegetables in a basket while she pulled weeds and mulched them at the base of the plants. His younger brother, Lloyd, stood nearby, gazing at his mother. Lloyd was almost five and could barely speak. At times, he would stand and stare into the distance, as if seeing things that others could not. Ezekiel loved his brother but found his difficulty with words confusing, his actions annoying.

Lloyd ran toward Ezekiel. The little boy wrapped his arms around his elder brother's legs and grunted some sounds. Ezekiel stumbled, and then caught his balance. He patiently steered Lloyd to one side.

"School got out over an hour ago. Where have you been?" Tilly stood and fixed Ezekiel with a firm stare.

"I got caught talking in class and had to write the same sentence on the blackboard, two hundred times. It took me forever. My fingers ached."

Tilly shook her head and smiled. "That will teach you," she said, bending over again, pulling the weeds, and tossing them.

Ezekiel turned away sheepishly, strolled into the house to shed his khaki pants and blue shirt. Tilly spoke to him as he came back outside, pulling an old T-shirt over his head and down to the waist of his dungaree shorts.

"How many times have I warned about respecting your teachers and paying attention in class?"

"Daddy never lent a hand building that church…how come?" Ezekiel asked.

Tilly turned to him and pointed her index finger at him. "You think you so blasted smart, changing the subject."

Ezekiel tried not to smile.

"Boy, you too damn bold-faced," Tilly said.

"I heard you say this many times: 'He who asks a question is a fool for a minute, and he who does not ask the question remains a fool forever.'"

Tilly cocked her head and favored Ezekiel with a smile. "Boy, what am I going to do with you? Must be some old spirit skulking behind those eyes," she said.

"Old spirit hiding behind my eyes," Ezekiel said and scoffed. "Mama Viche removed that thing years ago."

"What you talking about, how would you know? I hear the squabbles between you and Malcolm about who visits Cosmus in prison and the meaning of life in prison. You two are not as smart as you think you are. The punishment means exactly what it says." Tilly turned her back to Ezekiel and returned to pulling weeds.

Ezekiel spoke into the silence, using his words like a wedge. "How come people get so frightened when they're talking about Cosmus, and we--?"

"Go ask your father," Tilly snapped without looking up from her task.

"He won't tell me anything," Ezekiel said.

Tilly pointed her mud-stained fingers in the direction of the mountain. "Go harass your father, about Cosmus, the church, and whatever. Go."

Ezekiel stood staring at Tilly, wondering why the simple question made her so vex.

"Go ask your father. He's up there. I'll have food ready when you get back."

Ezekiel ran toward the Top Road, fearing Tilly might ask him to take Lloyd. His bare feet slapped at the dry dirt. Halfway up the road, he slowed down. If Lloyd came, the trip would take forever. Lloyd would want to chase every butterfly, put his nose to every flower. Ezekiel would often speculate on the outcome of a bee flying into his brother's nostril.

He felt his heart pounding in his chest as he swallowed and tasted the onset of thirst. The heat and exertion from the short sprint caused beads of sweat to pop out on his scalp. His eyes tingled as the perspiration trickled from his forehead. The boy ran both hands over his face and rubbed the sweat off on the front of his shirt. Sunlight reflected off the black and yellow wings of a monarch butterfly as it floated across his sight. Ezekiel thought of grabbing a stick and swatting the butterfly out of the air; instead, he watched it drift on a wind current, floated high above a cluster of black sage bushes, and vanished.

Ezekiel left the graveled road and took a dirt path leading to the Valley of Bones. He kicked at the dirt, recalling the story he had heard about the freak storm that had dropped from the sky two days before his birth. A depression on the edge of the path, cloaked in water-grass and other weeds brought matters into focus for him. An ancient mahogany tree once stood on that spot, the same tree from which the English had hung some of the slaves who had joined the revolt led by Jean Anglais. The colonists kept the young Frenchman for last, used him as a spectacle, and hung him with the other black ringleaders in the market square in Saint Georges, allowed the bodies to dangle until they could no longer tolerate the flies or the smells.

The story goes, on the day the storm brought down the old tree, people brought their saws, axes, and adzes, carved the old tree into chunks, and carried it away. They even dug up the root-ball and hauled it off. Only the depression in the earth remained. Ezekiel harbored an assortment of emotions about the dead slaves and the missing tree. Halfway up the hill to the place where his stepmother had sent him for explanations, he searched the distance for his father, John.

A faint noise from beyond the trail caught his attention. It came out of the thickets, hushed and muddled. Anyone else walking on the trail would have ignored it. It could have been an iguana crawling over dry leaves or a bird building a nest. The boy entertained notions of being a great hunter like his uncle Lester. Ezekiel decided to follow the noise. Searching for a clear route, he advanced on the disturbance.

He had heard tales of Mama Malady and Ladablais, but these creatures never came out in daylight, he told himself. People always said, if you keep quiet, there is nothing the bearer of diseases, Mama Malady, can do to you. Ezekiel had long ago surmised that the fable about Mama Malady was intended to keep children quiet at night. But Ladablais, that she-devil with one cow foot, something like that could never outrun me, he thought. The boy stepped carefully to a strategic point where he could peer through the bushes without revealing his presence.

At first, he thought the two people might be playing some kind of game, the way they were huddled in the clearing as if wrestling. He recalled scenes of animals mating: his father breeding the milk cow with the bull, the yowls of cats, roosters riding the backs of hens and dogs stuck to one another by their genitals.

Ezekiel had gathered more information from listening to other boys bragging about sex. The presentation before him looked incredible. Two people, half-naked, the man's pants pulled down exposing his ass, the woman's skirt pulled up to her navel, and the top half of her blouse pulled down from her breasts and bundled around her stomach. They appeared attached at the hips, moving up and down, thrusting at each other, amid moans, sighs, whimpers, looks of anguish and joy. Ezekiel became dazed by the angles of the woman: breasts the size of grapefruits, and legs firm, pressed up and enfolding the man, while the man grasped the woman as if she might try to escape.

Ezekiel absorbed the dealings with a baffled fascination. Moving closer still, he felt the front of his pants rising as the two people went rigid and collapsed onto each other. He thought they might be dead, but they moved and laughed in unison. In that instant, Ezekiel recognized them, Monica, the Missionary Man's servant and his father, John. They turned in his direction. He ducked down, tried to make himself invisible, felt excited and afraid at the same time. He pushed on the front of his pants and willed it to stay down. Closing his eyes, he crossed his legs and squeezed.

Ezekiel knew what he had witnessed, and he understood why it should be kept secret. Such a fantastic exhibition and the details could not be shared. He decided to reveal what he had witnessed to one person, his best friend Malcolm, the albino.

The boy sat in the bushes and watched as his father and Monica rearranged their clothes, picked the grass and twigs off of each other. He became aware of his own breathing the moment the two people rose from the ground. The air left his nostrils like a whistle. Ezekiel clasped his hands over his nose and mouth. John and Monica kissed briefly and separated. Ezekiel relaxed as the two people moved out of sight, told himself that he should not go to his father right away. Something revealing might remain on his face.

His heart pounded, his confusion felt like ants crawling on his skin. The screech of a bird scolding her young raised Ezekiel's ire. The repeated shrieking of the bird compelled him to search for the nest. He moved slowly out of hiding, his bare feet moving across a bed of dry leaves and downed twigs. The repeated fractures sounded like the clapping of hands. A green lizard with large bulging eyes scurried up the trunk of a tree. Ezekiel found the nesting place of the bird, in the high reaches of an old trumpet tree. A curtain of Caquelin vines, yellow and red, stretched down from the branches, striving to return to the earth, searching for a stranglehold. In a matter of time, the tree would be dead, suffocated by the pretty vines that had started in its high foliage from windblown spores. He marveled at the weird and wonderful ways of Mother-nature.

The bird sat high on a limb, near the nest, feeding its brood. Their featherless necks stuck out over the edge of the arrangement of weeds and sticks, their open mouths ready to accept the offering. Ezekiel searched for a rock. The one he found felt heavy, but he knew he could make it reach. An unbridled screech startled him. On a limb near the nest, there perched the bird looking down at him with menacing eyes. As he pulled his arm back to throw the stone, the bird launched, flying straight at his face. Ezekiel ducked, and scrambled away. He turned and watched as the bird circled through the trees, returning to the spot near the nest, still gawking. He pulled back this time and flung, the rock bounced off a branch below the nest, and Ezekiel began a searched for another.

A shrieked echoed through the trees again, as the bird went into a steep dive, pulled up before Ezekiel's face, wings slapped his cheeks. He dropped to the ground and covered his head. The bird circled away and came to rest on a branch on another tree, away from its nest, still wailing, as if crying for mercy, or calling for help. Ezekiel dropped the rock he had found. Damn bird, he thought, as he walked away. The bird went silent, and Ezekiel felt a definite relief.

The droning sound of cicadas resonated off the trunks of the leafless trees. A transparent shell, the abandoned skin of a snake rested on a bed of fallen leaves. Ezekiel looked around, searching for the owner of the skin. He thought of taking the skin but had heard tales of snakes returning, and upon not finding what they had left behind, the search for the thief would begin, with the help of its cousin bird, it would track the thief and sink its fangs into his heel. Ezekiel left the skin on the leaves under the trees and made his way back to the trail.

As he came out of the trees at a point above the valley, he searched for Monica, expecting to spot her in the distance. She was nowhere in sight. Only his father appeared in the distance. A strip of green stretched across the valley, caused by water trickling out of a pond nestled in the rocks below Ogoun's Point. His imagination began a slow crawl: What if a Jumbie or some other nightmare turn up, one of those lost souls that people often speak about, the ones concealed in the cane, those spirits of dead slaves, still in chains, buried in the ground, what if they rise up and haul me under? Ezekiel shivered at the thought and the coming night.

He made his way off the ridge and came up behind his father. The man was bent over, digging in the dirt with a stick, pulling sweet potatoes away from the vines, and tossing them into a crocus sack. What Ezekiel had witnessed between Monica and his father remained between them like a wall. His many questions about the church and other matters seemed strange and frivolous now.

"Boy, what you doing crawling up on me like a roach?"

"Daddy," Ezekiel said. "I have a question."

"What you want?" John continued to dig at the dirt with the stick, thrusting his fingers under the vines.

"I heard Mondu and Papa LaTouche talking about Cosmus, about visiting him at the prison."

"Boy, you should learn to mind your own business."

"I don't have any business, so I have to…" Ezekiel glanced at his father and searched for the precise words.

"The other day when I was talking to Mondu, I could see your ears sticking out," John said.

"I only wanted to get the drift of--" Ezekiel said.

"What did Mondu and Papa LaTouche say?"

"I can't remember. Mondu was stammering, and Papa LaTouche started telling a joke, laughing about a Dutch policeman and a whore he knew in Aruba."

"What do you know about whores?"

"Mondu wanted to bring one into the prison to…you know…with Cosmus."

"Oh! That's nothing. What do you remember about Cosmus? You were young when..."

"Not much. I remember him through my dreams," Ezekiel said.

"You remember him through your dreams?" John folded the mouth of the crocus sack, grabbed his machete and stood staring at his son.

"I remember a lot more, the white people with those kids who lived in the house before the Missionary Man. I wanted to play with them, see what kind of toys they had, but they acted kind of funny each time I tried to speak to them."

"Oh, really, that's how things…you remember lots." John smiled at his son. "You have a sharp mind."

"Why do people speak about Cosmus in such secret ways?" Ezekiel asked.

"They have their reasons," John said.

"I know they have their reasons, but what are they?"

John pulled back and gazed at the boy. Ezekiel decided not to push right away, but to change the focus, circle back like a hunter, and then move in later from another angle.

"You know, I remember Cosmus from words and dreams, but not much more. Since he's been gone, the children are gone, and the yellow house has sat empty for so long, nice big house with nobody living there, until the preacher came."

"How can you dream about a person you don't remember?" John asked.

"I don't know. It just happens, and sometimes I am not even asleep."

"So it's like memories. You have some strange substance floating around in that brain."

"Oh, I remember much more. How nice things used to be before."

"So, you don't think things are nice now?"

"Not since Mommy died, not since the break-bone fever. Seems like confusion all the time." Ezekiel looked at the ground and pushed at the dirt with his toes. "Why is Cosmus in jail? Looks as if everybody is hiding something."

"I'll tell you when the time is right. Let's go." John pointed at the sack of sweet potatoes. Ezekiel picked it up with one hand. John turned and walked off and the boy followed.

Just down the path, Ezekiel spotted Malcolm grazing his goats. The albino was all legs and arms attached to a skinny frame with the features of a black person-hair, nose, and lips, but his skin was chalky white. His pale eyes were squinting, as if looking into a glare. John walked near the albino and the goats without casting a glance.

Ezekiel knew his father and Malcolm's mother, Cora, quarreled often, about fruit trees that dangled over fence lines, about stray animals wandering about on the wrong land and eating grass, and about things so trivial it made the boy question the good sense of adults. The two boys stood silently for a moment, watching John's back as he moved out of earshot.

Ezekiel attempted to seize the moment to share what he had witnessed between his father and Monica. But Malcolm spoke first.

"The church tonight. Okay? They're christening the place; I don't want to miss it."

"We're going hunting, remember?" Ezekiel dropped the sack of potatoes on the ground. The goats wandered over and began chewing on the sack. "Hey, keep those beasts away."

Malcolm yanked on the rope.

"You know, Uncle Lester is coming down with his dogs. I told you in class," Ezekiel said.

Malcolm puckered his lips, as if tasting something sour. "Yeah, and you got caught talking. What was that about making sense out of nonsense? Ha ha ha!" Malcolm's laughter startled the goats.

"You are a mean bastard," Ezekiel said.

"What did I do?" Malcolm looked at Ezekiel and threw his palms wide open.

"You laughed at me for getting detention. And now you don't want to go hunting with Uncle Lester?"

"Let the hunting wait, man. We can do that anytime."

"But Uncle Lester is coming down tonight," Ezekiel said.

"That's your problem. I want to see who comes to the first service."

"What difference does it make who comes to the first service?" Ezekiel asked.

"After everybody helped to build the church, I want to see who shows up...see if Mama Viche and Alma__" Malcolm yield the discussion to Ezekiel.

"What're we going to tell Uncle Lester?"

"Nothing," Malcolm replied. "Bring him along. He can use some blessing, that crazy little...You heard about the stick-fight he had with your father when they were young? Can't imagine how a stumpy fellow like him could have fought your father to a draw. People said your mother married your father to prevent those two from killing each other. If that's why she married your father, what does that make you?" Malcolm started to laugh, but stopped as if embarrassed by his chain of thought.

"What're you talking about?" Ezekiel looked at Malcolm.

"Nothing, nothing at all, that's all. Let's bring him along."

The two boys fell silent for a moment as if calculating the previous exchange. Ezekiel broke the silence. "I saw something that'll make your head spin," he said.

"Seen what?"

"Two people going at it."

"Going at what?"

"You know with." Ezekiel gestured down the road toward where his father had disappeared. "Monica, the Missionary Man's housekeeper."

"Boy, you beating around the bush. What did you...?"

"I saw them fucking,"

A contortion appeared on Malcolm's face and grew. Ezekiel watched Malcolm's big head bouncing around on his meager shoulders as he laughed.

"Boy, you a tomfool or what? Everybody knows about them."

The two boys stood beside the road, considering each other. The mouths of the two goats shredding the grass, rip, rip, rip. Ezekiel appeared shocked.

"What're you talking about?"

"Everybody around Jean Anglais knows about Monica and your father. You know, his piece on the side."

Ezekiel looked at Malcolm. The notion that Malcolm now had full command of the conversation irritated him.

"Well, knowing about them and seeing what they were doing is a whole other story. The next time they meet, we can hide and watch," Ezekiel said.

"What're you talking about? I mean, how you going to know where they're meeting?"

"Follow her."

"You think she's blind, deaf, and stupid at the same time? She will spot us for sure."

"No, she won't. We can sneak into the bush after she leaves the Missionary Man's house. Make a circle, come back below the ridge near Ogoun's Point and we're right where I saw them."

"We can waste a lot of time."

"Leave it to me. I'm sure they meet at the same spot. Or we can go early, hide, and wait."

"Boy, you crazy as a bat," Malcolm said. He paused, smiling. "Let's try it." He pursed his lips and nodded.

"Yeah," Ezekiel said.

"Meet me later on the top road; we're going to the church, okay?" Malcolm pointed at Ezekiel, winked, and yanked on the ropes attached to the goats.

"I still don't know what we're going to tell Uncle Lester." Ezekiel picked up the bag of potatoes and walked off.

Malcolm shouted at his back. "What's the difference between a girlfriend and a wife?"

"I've no idea."

"Forty-five pounds," Malcolm shouted, laughing at his own joke.

"You make those mannish jokes all the time."

"Just listen, just listen. What's the difference between a boyfriend and a husband?"

"What, what? What the hell…"

"Forty-five minutes." Malcolm continued to laugh. Ezekiel shook his head and walked off.

* * *

John glanced at his wife out of the corner of one eye as she served the bowls filled with the smooth green mixture, callaloo, pig snout and dumplings. He wondered why she dished up none for herself. Could somebody have told her about Monica? A twinge of guilt tightened his gut. Tilly kissed him on the top of his head and announced her planned visit with her mother, Florence. John felt the tension slide out of his body.

Dinner with his two boys, Ezekiel and Lloyd, has always been a pleasant and rewarding experience for him. But that evening, he felt unrestrained malice, aroused by the singing voices coming from the recently constructed church. A few villagers had banded into a choir under the direction of the Missionary Man, Harry Hudson. They would attempt a hymn, quit in the middle, and then start again. This went on throughout the meal.

The man lamented the many regrets of his life. Chief amongst them was the court battle with his two younger brothers over his father's will. The old man had said, the land belonged to the family and would remain in the family. They should build their houses and share the place, allow grandchildren to grow together. Instead, his brothers had hired a lawyer to contest the will. In the end, the court agreed with the wishes of their father.

His brothers packed their bags, and with the money willed to them by their father, they left Grenada, as the old man had anticipated. One went to Trinidad; the other to Venezuela. They never wrote and were hardly ever mentioned around John's house. From time to time, he would get news of them, and would think of how they grew up, the memories of drinking soursop juice, sucking sugarcane, romping about and attempting to dodge raindrops. Those recollections stirred John's pangs of regret.

That old house, with an outside kitchen and the scrap of land it sat on became his obsession. At one time, the place was a cabin with a dirt floor, a structure built by an ancestor known as Beaubrin, one of the survivors of Fedon's Rebellion. Jacque, John's grandfather, inherited the place from Beaubrin, installed a wooden floor and added another room. Wattou, John's father, inherited the place from Jacque, and with the help of his three sons and neighbors he had dug into the ground and bolstered the foundation by placing concrete pillars under the cabin. John held scant memories of these men. He grew up with his father, but by the time John had grown to the point of reflection, Beaubrin and Jacque had transitioned out of memory and history, and into the region of myths.

John had also added his touches to the structure, coating it with a cream-colored stain, and painting the trim green around the windows, doors and up in the eaves. But the man remained dissatisfied with his contributions, so he shifted his focus to more land, the piece next door owned by his neighbors; Jack Masanto, and his wife Cora, the parents of the albino boy.

He lived off the land, and the soil became a crucial part of his existence. Even a good scrubbing with soap and water failed to dislodge the mud. Besides providing food, the dirt could be seen wedged under his fingernails, black against the pigment of his palms. It oozed in through the holes in his old rubber boots and settled in the cracks between his toes.

The man held a deep devotion to hard work, but his relationship with his family and the culture that sustained them, positioned him for conflicts. John spoke to no one about his demons, imagined or otherwise. The confusion that sometimes crept into his life had major impacts, which he regarded as bad luck. Be more careful next time he would tell himself. Any disparity between John and his neighbors would be shouted down. He used volume as a weapon and regarded the only radio in the village as competition because it brought news, which prevented him from being the final authority on everything.

The presence of his two sons prompted John to consider the promise he had made to his father: to keep the land in the family, to stay and keep the home fires burning. John's mouth was set hard, his forehead furrowed. A slight chill ushered in the nightfall, and he sensed rain. Rain he could abide. It allowed food to grow, tranquilized the heat, and carried a comfortable tone reminiscent of music. The voices wafting through from the inauguration of the new church annoyed him. He always felt a dislike for religious songs and hymns, but this one especially bothered him:

One ah dese morn it won't be long/ Meh soul be at res'/ One ah dese morn it won't be long/ Meh soul be at res'/ Be at res'--goin' be at res'/ Meh soul be at res'/ Be at res' till judgment day/ Meh soul be at res'...

Who the hell died? John and his sons sat on the kitchen stairs, listening to the singing. The faint whispers of crickets and tree frogs chimed from the undergrowth. In the distance, a drum greeted sundown and challenged the voices coming from the church. John felt a glow as Mano's drum swelled across the village. He told himself the next time he saw Mano, he would have to shake his hand and buy him a shot of strong-rum.

John knew his eldest son, Ezekiel, harbored conflicts of his own. He felt sorry for the boy and what he knew he had to endure. How would he handle matters when push comes to shove? John realized that sooner or later he would have to talk to Ezekiel, explain the details about this property, and about Lloyd with his condition. He wondered how much he should tell Ezekiel, if anything, about the spirits trapped in the cane fields and the similar fate of Jean Anglais. John kept his troubles confined, putting them off, and biding his time.

Nighttime fell into the sky, and John lit the kerosene torch. He sat with the boys, listening to the squabble between the voices and the drum, speculating on how he would handle matters if Tilly ever got wind of the goings on between him and Monica. Instead of yielding to his worries, John decided to seek shelter in an old yarn his father had told him.

He massaged an itch in his crotch from his encounter with Monica, and he asked a question: "What do you see on the ground, Ezekiel?" John observed the boy as he shifted his attention to the dry patch before them in the faint light of the bottle torch.

"Dirt, chicken shit, dry leaves, blades of grass, and our shadows," Ezekiel said.

The man smiled, nodded, and felt a certain pride. Ezekiel's response was roughly the same as he had given to his father. The drum peppered the night, and the next words from John's mouth took on a significant tone: "The leaves will blow away in the wind. The grass will pass away at the will of rain, the ground will absorb the chicken shit, but the shadow will remain, day and night. You recall ever seeing your shadow in a dream?" John tilted his head and looked at his sons. He expected no real response from Lloyd, but he continued before Ezekiel could respond. "When the body sleeps, the soul wanders. The shadow guards the cradle of the soul against demons and evil spirits. The shadow-man has two forms: the natural, produced by the sun and the moon, that's the one with the power and the others, produced by candles, bottle torches and lamps, is just young, and playful. If you ever glimpse your shadow in a dream, you better wakeup fast. Demons are closing in."

For the second time that night, John saw Ezekiel glancing toward the top road. He fell silent as the singing rose with more harmony. The voices struggled to swallow the sound of Mano's drum. John regarded himself as towering above other men. The need to maintain his family's survival and legacy took priority over all else. Getting the politicians to situate the standpipe near his gap on the top road, he considered that a victory, payment for influencing his neighbors to vote Labor. Now there would be a constant trickle of water running through his land where he could plant callaloo and dasheen.

The man held desires for things unnamed, personal fixations. He would look at other men drinking rum, taking part in Panorama and Carnival, laughing and playing all kinds of games, and he would wonder: how could they be so happy, what did they know or have? Above all, John considered himself a man of purpose, one who deserved respect, one whose children would someday make him proud. Not having a complete education bothered him. He would think of people with schooling and fancy jobs, and he saw himself as more than their equal. He knew stuff and could make the ground do things most of them couldn't even imagine.

John considered himself superior to the Missionary Man. Where did he come from? The whole village embraced him and rushed to help him build that church. They carried the boards, the sheets of shiny galvanized tin, and the nails, worked by bottle torches until well after dark, as if determined to meet some deadline. John took no part. He held the man under suspicion.

The preacher had lived in Jean Anglais for almost three years. Frequently, he could be seen walking the bottom or top road, bands of children at his heels, his arms and legs tanned. The tropical sun had damaged his skin, making it peel, causing scabs to form on his lips. He would stop at the roadside, lift one of the smaller children into the air, and at the same time his voice would boom out a refrain: "All things bright and wonderful, the Lord God made them all." Or he would say a quick prayer, and then the procession would continue.

Behind the cavalcade strolled Ezekiel and Malcolm.

John took exception to all of this. They looked like a bunch of dogs latching onto the backside of the Missionary Man, he would say. When he caught Ezekiel, for the third time that night, looking up toward the top road, he spoke sternly:

"You look as if you have some plans. Before you go anywhere, get those dishes washed, and continue to teach Lloyd how to towel off and put them away," John said.

"I want to go down to the church with Malcolm to see who shows up for the first service."

"When you get back, let me know who you see down there," John said. "But get your work done first."

* * *

Only half her teeth remained in her mouth, and Mama Viche felt the return of the rainy season through those holes in her gums. The weather produced aches in other parts of her body, but the throbbing in her jaw remained foremost. She flexed, as if to absorb the pain, and accepted the discomfort as one of the virtues of growing old. Her toothache became a distraction from worries about the condition of the village and her concerns about Ezekiel.

The presence of the fellow she had nicknamed the Missionary Man and the history of the house where he now lives: the construction of the place and the fate of the family who once lived there, all this sat in her stomach like rancid food. Poor Cosmus, she thought, not much could be done for him. What next? What should be done about that man interfering with everything? She thought of invoking Agwe or Legba; try to see what stood at the crossroads. Or should it be Kalfu, the spirit of the night, the one who carries darkness in a sack?

One thing at a time, she thought. Deal with these aches first. Boil the seeds of the Jumbie bead in water, boil them to softness, crush and steep the pulp overnight in fresh cow's milk, then strain and sweeten the liquid with molasses. Drink the tonic. She smiled. Sixty is not a bad age, she supposed, and no sugar in the blood yet. She ran her fingers over her head, across fat braids and brought her hands down to her lap, palms up, as if in preparation to accept a gift.

She sat immersed in her thoughts and the various jingles: neighbors making their way down to the church, fragments of conversation floating by on the breeze, her niece Alma was in the kitchen, the bangs and clatter of the spoons and bowls mingled with the bark of a dog. A woman's laughter suddenly burst into all of this, a sound so delightful, so pure, it forced Mama Viche to smile as she recalled some details of the woman's life.

Monah, the unbeliever, the woman who had lost her husband to that hurricane in Florida, still had the courage to laugh. After five years, she refused to believe the man could be among the dead and expected him to come walking up the road one day with a pocketful of American money from his cane-cutting job. She found joy in her daughter, Delores, and listening to the radio she kept hidden inside her house, the radio that Cosmus had brought to her and told her to keep smiling.

Nightfall spoke to Mama Viche in a language she respected. She knew things that only the land and age could teach: the persistent voices of the past, those who had gone before and had added their flesh and bones to the soil, the ones she could hear demanding their release from the bondage in the cane and the Valley of Bones. When she first came to Jean Anglais with her mother many years ago, the place felt strange. Sundown became her favorite time of day; the shrinking shadows and the union of those old voices left her with a sense of wonder.

She recalled the old place where she came from with her mother, the place where dewdrops slid off nutmeg and cocoa leaves, crashing to the ground like shiny, little eggs. Mama Viche and her mother came from a village called Birch Grove on the far side of a mountain known as Qua Qua, near a nutmeg plantation where the mud was red. That was the place where she first heard the whispers of the spirits and followed the bees and butterflies to the healing plants and vines. But then they moved down to Jean Anglais near Saint Georges and the spirits became louder. After her mother settled in and constructed a tiny altar, the voices became restrained. Her mother warned her about sensitive ground, and illustrated the nature of the land on which they stood. She saw the village as the palm of a hand, with the pad as Ogoun's Point, and the fingers pointing toward heaven as if chastising God.

The collection of houses on the slope of the mountain had hardly impressed the young girl she was then, because each village had its own shop and Jean Anglais had none. But soon she realized the inhabitants of the place held a fierce pride, would boldly tell you they are from Jean Anglais, not from the neighboring town called Belmont where people collected their mail. And if they favored you in any way, they would tell you about this place of mystery and the stories that could not be stolen. Outsiders who visited friends or family spoke of the fantastic tales that were told, but could not recall the specifics of them. Somehow they could not separate the stories from these people on the hillside. Former inhabitants seemed to lose their memories of the stories once they had left the community, and outsiders who tried to write them down found their pages blank the next day.

Mama Viche and her mother came to Jean Anglais to take care of Uncle Swap, who had gone blind and had lost a portion of one foot because of the sugar in his blood. The man had no children and needed the care of family, so he looked to his sister and her daughter, Sybil. They took a bus down from Birch Grove and moved into Uncle Swap's house, intending to care for him temporarily. They had no idea that eventually they would call this place home. Mama Viche recalled the stink of bandages, boiling water for cleaning the raw flesh, the poultice of aloe vera and other herbs placed on the wound that refused to heal. Back then people called her Sybil. She could not recall when she became Mama Viche.

The old woman came to look upon Jean Anglais and its population as a bunch of messy children, but in the midst of it all, the steadfast land under sun and rain, delivering food, keeping everything alive. At the heart of her recollections remained her one sore disappointment, Rita and her son, Cosmus, the boy sentenced to spend the rest of his life in Richmond Hill Prison. What a waste, she thought.

Cosmus was one of the many children Mama Viche had birthed in her time as a midwife, counselor, and healer. She wondered why Rita didn't come to her for advice when she saw her son straying toward danger. It would have been of no consequence anyhow, she thought, the road chosen for us by the ancestors could never be altered.

Mama Viche's reputation went far and wide, all over Grenada, and north to the outer islands, people made the journey, came looking for cures, and charms. Wondering why they couldn't have all that they craved, showing the unlit hollows of their appetites, but still hoping for grace or forgiveness, completely unaware that she held no sway over the will of the ancestors. But those close at hand, neighbors and so-called friends, seemed to be drifting away; most of the young women no longer came for help with contraception or childbirth. Cora Masanto appeared to have started something by having her son, Malcolm, at the general hospital in Saint Georges. Look how the child came out. Mama Viche knew she would not have allowed an albino child to live, especially an offspring from incest. Out of nowhere, Jack Masanto come about, married Cora and claimed Malcolm as his son after the death of Cora's father.

Most of the older people looked as if they were reconciled to their fate, because their children showed no respect, with tall grass covering graves, lighting no candles for memorials on All Saints Eve. Why do they ignore the dead? The young ones don't even eat Asham any more, calling it old-time food. But worst of all, they appeared to be neglecting the old stories, with everyone crowding around that radio, as if it were some sacred object. She wondered why Swallow, long dead and buried, refused to take that blasted thing back to the devil who gave it to him. Now, here comes this white man, this Missionary Man. Everything seems to be adrift.

Mama Viche listened to the voices pouring from the church and the boldness of Mano's drum. The Obeah woman decided to roam away from these ructions, not with her feet but with her mind. She had discovered this game when she was a girl. In the lonesome season long ago, before the birth of her sister, Maureen, she had found a way to stay attentive. Any place she had visited, she could return there with her brainpower as the vehicle. She loved those elusive journeys, and with age, she had gotten better at the pastime.

The distraction worked best if she had a destination in mind. At this moment she had no target. She leaned back in the wicker chair and closed her eyes, trying to absorb the untidy heap of smells and sounds. An interlude between the church and Mano challenged her determination, but Mano's drum came back first, and swallowed the silence. The voices slipped in like wrestlers trying to grab at wet skin. Mama Viche focused on the beat of the drum, drawing strength from the rhythm. She almost gave in, but she held fast to the primal beat, and the impulse converged on her. The woman considered her wrinkled body in the dress, and she cringed at what time had done to her. Her figure had sagged as her mind grew stronger. The provocation of the singing voices and the drum forced Mama Viche to go inward, to embrace old memories.

She saw herself on the path that led from her house to the road. To her left resided the Missionary Man who had shown up one day and started trespassing on other people's lands, wandering through the bush like the day spirit called a jumbie, and then had started building that church. Mama Viche decided to go right. She hinged her thoughts, firmed her imagination, and tried to make the crossing similar to the experience of walking on solid ground. She pictured Tilly cultivating her kitchen garden near the house. *Get your nose out of the clouds and smell the air down here*, she thought. *You might detect the scent of that young girl on your husband.*

The old woman considered giving John a warning, alerting him to the simmering water he was sitting in, how it could come to a boil before he knew it, how his selfish actions with that girl could affect his home and family. But she knew he would not listen. He would resent her interference, and when the piper come calling, he would in some way, try to lay the blame at her feet. He would say the Obeah woman did this, the Obeah woman did that.

Mama Viche formed images of Cora and Jack Masanto, those people in the little house on the side of the road, and Malcolm, the taboo child, with skin and eyes, cursed by the ancestors. She fled the memory of Cora and her albino son, as she lodged her full attention on the stories of the old Africans, Ogoun's Point, and her sister, Maureen. A path lined with black stones led to Mano's house, the house where her little sister, Maureen, had crawled into bed with the tormented drummer. His drums had so enticed her.

Mano's place held a bitterness that Mama Viche would rather forget. She summoned the memories of the night she had chased her sister out of Mano's bed and up the mountain, grasping dirt and pulling herself upward in desperation, as she tried to follow her sister, wondering what possessed Maureen. Mama Viche recalled looking back to see if Mano might be following them. When she saw no sign of him, she drew some conclusions. She and her sister reached Ogoun's Point and squared off in fear and uncertainty in the bright light of a full moon. The look on Maureen's face was something the old woman would never forget.

Mama Viche remembered Maureen sitting down on the rocks and telling her about the child she was carrying, Mano's child. The old woman remembered shouting at her sister, *"Look down that hill, Maureen! Look! That man isn't coming after you!"* Mama Viche had uttered those words to poison whatever existed between Maureen and Mano.

She wallowed in her recollections of the mountain and the many stories told to her, especially the one about the old African slaves who refused to eat salt, which made them almost weightless. They escaped to Ogoun's Point, spread their arms wide, and flew back to Africa. Not all of them made it. A man's wife had eaten salt and could not fly, so he placed her on his back. They fell out of the sky over Jean Anglais and after one final scream of devotion and love, they hit the ground and turned into a shrub called Jump Up and Kiss Me. People often said that at times they could still hear their final cry on the winds. There was also a fellow who loved the island so much that he tried to take some dirt in his pocket on the flight back to Africa. He fell out the sky and became a mound of twisted rocks. And they are more.

The old woman imagined herself off the mountain and down into other haunting memories in the place called the Valley of Bones. She saw the Arawak and the Carib, who once inhabited the high valley, and all those wandering spirits engaged in the eternal struggles, and all those Africans slaughtered and buried; even in death they remained, thinking they were human and belonged, had moral claims like any other human. Would the prophecy come to pass? Who would be the one to set those ancestors free from their earthly torment and lay claim to the land in the Valley of Bones for the people? Could it be the father, John, or the son, Ezekiel, the one born behind the veil? Or would this village die?

Mama Viche slid into that edgy place between dreams and conscious thoughts. All she had been told and retained came forth in a mixture of the past and the imagination. The place called Jean Anglais, cultivated with fruit trees of all kinds and cleaved out of the estate of a French cultivator, a man whose ancestors knew persecution, but who still held slaves. He had assumed he could call them by alternative names, treat them with civility, and all would be well.

His contradictions had led him to Julian Fedon and all that bloodshed in the slave revolt that sent him to the gallows with most of his friends. The retribution carried out by the British colonists gave the valley that name: the Valley of Bones. The land in Jean Anglais was divided among the salt eaters, those who had said "no" to the allure of the old African spirits, Shango, Shamunja, and Dambala.

The land in the Valley of Bones had been bestowed on a Judas, Elmo the Elder, a wicked Voodoo man who had drunk the brew made from the conjuring bean called Donkey Eyes. He saw the faces of all those who had taken part in Fedon's revolt, and betrayed them to the British Authorities. He was the great-grandfather of Duncan Elmo, the man who now possessed the land in the Valley of Bones.

Fedon escaped, and was never captured. The legends went far and wide across the generations. Fedon's mother, they say, was a powerful

Mambo, a priestess of the Voodoo tradition who came from Haiti. She was determined to protect her son from his own peculiarities. In those days, she lived on the Belvedere Estate in Gouyave. When Fedon was just thirteen, she took him, along with a speckled hen, into the deep woods. Under a silk cotton tree, she offered the hen as a sacrifice to the spirit who dwelled there, the Loa known as Brise, to the Haitians. She asked the Loa to give her son courage and the ability to take the form of animals. The Loa accepted her offering, and before her eyes Fedon transformed into a young, gray owl and flew away. She returned to Belvedere and found her son waiting on the front porch.

Mama Viche knew all these accounts and kept them banked in her heart with the intention to transfer them to her niece Alma. She knew why Jean Anglais appears on no map, why it resides only in wilting memories. Most of the land continued in the safekeeping of the ancestors of the African slaves, but with each generation, the mix grew. Some came, some went, and others depart abroad. The names changed as men married the girls in the families and brought new names and new blood. People with names like Masanto, LaTouche, Marecheau, Viche, Stewart, and Augustine. They continued to cling to the place, fighting, and loving with their hands and feet caked in the mud of their lives. All along the bushy paths, in the shade of mango, breadfruit, banana, soursop, and guava trees they endured, their lives wedded to the soil.

The aged wooden houses with galvanized tin roofs painted red, green, or yellow nestled in a lush embrace of vines and shrubs that came and went with the seasons. If for some reasons no rain came, the farmers always paid a visit to their Obeah woman. They always got the same response: "Cultivate with your sweat, your ancestors will see you, and your hard work will move them to tears. Their tears will be your rain." Mama Viche took account of those old remembrances, and they caused a faint smile to play around the corners of her lips.

A hand stroked her shoulders. A young voice brought the woman back from her excursion. "Tante, Tante."

"Alma, what you doing, girl? You finished with the dishes?"

"Finished a long time ago and ironed my school uniform."

The old woman rubbed one hand over her face and looked up at her niece standing with a kerosene lamp. She squinted at the glare.

"I just dozed off, you know. I was dreaming about your mother. What time is it?"

"It must be almost eight. How can you sleep through that racket? Listen to it. Let's go inside."

"Yes, you're right. Let's go inside, your father still trying to drown them out with his drum."

"Yes, I hear him," Alma said.

Mama Viche stood and lurched toward the door. Alma followed with the lamp. From the church, the voices singing the hymn grew clear and heartfelt in the night: The narrow road is heaven's road/ Believers I know/ with here and there some travelers/ Believers I know...

* * *

As he came up the path, Ezekiel saw the flicker of a flashlight, then his uncle and Malcolm, standing in the road with two dogs darting and sniffing.

"What took you so long?" Malcolm asked.

"Boy, you messed with everything," Ezekiel said. "What did he tell you, Uncle?"

"He told me you don't want to go hunting. Sinners all of you, little sinners," Lester laughed. "Go ahead, go listen to the white man calling you sinners. Don't take it to heart, though. Only two things in this world I'll call sinful. Murder and covetousness covers everything," Lester said.

The beam from his flashlight collided with the weak rays draining from the nearby houses. Lester switched off the flashlight. His two hunting dogs sniffed here and there, darting in and out of the gutter, into the nearby trees. Fireflies winked in the foliage; crickets and tree frogs chimed as if signaling rain. Mano's drum and the singing from the church hung over the collection of houses on the slope.

"There must be other sins," Malcolm said. "How about bearing false witness?"

"No one bears false witness for nothing," Lester said. "There's always something to gain, unless they are crazy."

"Must be what happened to Cosmus, covetousness or false witness," said Ezekiel.

"What you talking about?" Malcolm said. "You must be dreaming about that vat of molasses again? People can't turn into sugar or rum."

"Listen to how you're making this sound," Ezekiel said.

"You two, cackling like old hens," Lester said. "What kind of visions you seeing?" He turned to Ezekiel and waited. "You some sort of fortune-teller?"

"I never said anything about fortune. I should have said nothing to you," he pointed at Malcolm.

"He thinks he can see the future." Malcolm looked at Ezekiel and smiled.

"I'm never telling you anything from now on."

"Well, if you ever see a horse winning a race at Queen's Park let me know," Lester said.

"Tell me about Cosmus, and I'll let you know if I see a horse winning a race."

"You making a deal with me?" Lester looked at his nephew, then smiled and shook his head. "It was a wicked thing they did to him. At least they didn't hang him."

"Who did he kill?" Ezekiel asked.

"Not now. This one is like a loupgarou, blood sucker draining your blood. I need my energy to run with those dogs tonight."

"He didn't kill--" Malcolm halted, as if searching for the precise words. "If he had, they would have hanged him a long time ago, right, an eye for an eye, right?"

"You two don't understand the least--" Lester said, glancing at his two dogs darting about as if seeking a scent.

"You dressed as if you expect rain," Malcolm said.

"Always be prepared," Lester said. "That way you never get caught by surprise." Lester ran one hand across Ezekiel's head. "I'll tell you about Cosmus, what he got involved in…when we have more time. It takes more than a few words to spell out."

"Look at those dogs, look at them. They know, they can smell the rain," Malcolm said.

"You sure you don't want to come along? A little rain won't hurt you. You two won't melt."

Ezekiel looked at the dogs and back to his uncle. "He's dying to go down there and listen to the Missionary Man. I can't persuade him." Ezekiel looked at Malcolm.

"I have a feeling I'll catch a couple big ones tonight. You two will have to come with me soon. You know I'm leaving for Trinidad soon. Move out," Lester shouted at the dogs and took a couple steps away from the boys.

"Uncle, watch out for those angry spirits roaming the Valley of Bones," Ezekiel cautioned.

Lester stopped and looked at Ezekiel. "Who told you those spirits was angry?"

"Well, we ignore them; we act as if they only left their bones," Ezekiel said.

"I heard about those spirits when I was a little boy. At first, it was just a story about a child born to save his village and his ancestors. But eventually, it changed form, and I came to believe I was that child who would save Jean Anglais and rescue those spirits trapped in the Valley of Bones. I told no one about my belief. I suspected all of us thought we might be the one to save the village and rescue the ancestors. But all of that changed after they came to me one night with no anger, just sadness."

"You saw them? They came to you? Ezekiel and Malcolm asked in unison.

"Yeah," Lester said. "One night, the dogs treed a manicou in the mango tree near the cane. The animal crawled way out on a small limb and sat snarling in the beam of my flashlight and looking down at the dogs, as if ready to leap out of the tree and take on both of them. I climbed up and began shaking the branch. The manicou dove into the cane, and the dogs dashed after it. By the time I came down from the tree, the dogs were backing out of the cane with their tails tucked between their legs. They continued to whimper as they came toward me. I could hear the rattle of chains and thought a cow must be loose in the cane. Then I heard some miserable moans, didn't sound like any cow, and some figures in rags emerged from the cane chained together, and stood looking at me. I ran like hell, and the dogs kept barking behind me. I didn't want those spirits to follow me home. So, I went straight to Mama Viche's house, knocked on her door, got her out of bed, and told her what I saw that night. She told me I should learn to feed the spirits, and she gave me a list: a pint of rum, a pint of whiskey, and some pipe tobacco, then she promised to do the rest. Never saw those spirits again, and I lost the belief that I could be the one to save Jean Anglais and rescue the ancestors from the Valley of Bones."

"Feed the spirits with booze and tobacco?" Ezekiel asked.

"Those spirits must like to fete," Malcolm said.

The two boys cackled a dry mirth that came more from their noses than their mouths.

"You find this amusing, huh? Go ask Mama Viche…She told me one more thing: 'The person destined to release those poor souls from the cane would have no idea about his calling, so stop thinking it could be you.' I felt a great burden lift from my shoulders when she said those words." Lester turned and walked away.

The boys remained standing in the weak light on the road, as if they might change their minds and follow Lester. But Ezekiel and Malcolm started toward the church.

The singing voices grew louder as they approached.

The narrow road is heaven's road/ Believers I know/With here and there a traveler/ Believers I know/The big road is hell's road/ Believers I know/ Thousands walk together there/ Believers I know...

The two boys stood at the back of the congregation, near the door. It seemed like everybody had come: Checklea and Geneva with their five children, Rita's father, Papa LaTouche, Mondu, Duncan Elmo and his family from down near Belmont, Tante Monah with her daughter Delores, and her sister Olga, and many others had filled the sanctuary. Ezekiel smiled and nudged Malcolm when he saw Monica sitting down front. The congregation was singing songs that Ezekiel had never heard, and he wondered where they had found the words. Reverend Harry

Hudson walked to the back of the church and, with a smile he greeted the two boys, and asked them to take a seat.

Harry Hudson, The Missionary Man, walked back through the crowd, nodding and talking as he made his way toward the front. Voices faded as he took his place at the podium. Beads of perspiration streamed off the man's head, down his neck, and into the collar of his shirt. He looked out on the many faces, pounded his fist on the podium, bit his lips, and brandished one finger. "Repent you, sinners! Believe in the power of the almighty God!" His voice bellowed into the small room. Ezekiel expected the preacher to sermonize about the deities of Obeah. Everyone claimed that topic made his blood boil.

He stood behind the little podium, a tall, hook-nosed man, dressed in khaki pants and a short-sleeved white shirt. The harsh glare of the kerosene lantern made Ezekiel squint. The preacher's tongue licked his lips now and again in a kind of reptilian way. Ezekiel wondered if this one service would count toward his entrance into heaven, and what Malcolm might be thinking or hoping to achieve by listening to the admonitions of the missionary Man.

"I always hear the question, 'what must I do to be saved, Reverend Harry?'" The preacher scrunched up his face and shook his head several times. "In every household where we have held our services, I kept hearing the same question. 'How can I be born again, Reverend Harry?' The very same question was asked centuries ago. Nicodemus, a leader amongst the ruling Scribes and Pharisees in the time of Jesus, had a similar query when he heard Jesus say, 'except a man be born again, he cannot enter the kingdom of heaven.' 'How can a man be born again when he is grown? Can he enter his mother's womb, and be born a second time?' the man asked. Jesus responded, 'that which is born of the flesh is flesh, and that which is born of the spirit is spirit.'" The Preacher lifted his index finger into the air again and shook it. "The Bible is clear on this. You must experience a spiritual rebirth. Acknowledge your sins. For all have sinned and fall short of the glory of God: Romans Three-Twenty-Three. You must see yourselves for what you are, sinners!" And he threw out both his palms in a wide gesture as if to cuddle the congregation. "Sin is wrong, sin is tragic and vile. It blights your lives, refuses to let you grow in Christ. To be saved you must repent of your sins. Repent then and turn to God, so that your sins may be washed away: Acts Three-Nineteen.

"You can't say . . . well, I'll do better tomorrow." The crowd chuckled. "This will not do," he continued. "You know, all of you have promised to do better. All of you know you have done wrong, and must repent. You must turn from sin. You must change your minds, change your hearts. Then and only then will you be able to change your actions and face God, abundantly pardoned and free of the degradation and destruction of sin."

The preacher gasped a lungful of air and Ezekiel heard him exhale as the next words left his mouth.

"You must believe in Christ, children. For God so loved the world that he gave his only begotten son. That whoever believeth in him shall not perish but have everlasting life: John Three - Sixteen. Believe in the work Christ did on the cross. He died for you, so that you may be forgiven, and enter the kingdom of Heaven."

A ripple went through the crowd as many voices in unison said "Amen!" and started singing softly: "When the roll is called up yonder/ when the roll is called up yonder/ when the roll is called up yonder I'll be there." The singing blended with the rest of Harry Hudson's sermon, as if orchestrated.

"You must believe He has risen from the dead and sits at the right hand of His Father in Heaven, children. Believe in the Lord Jesus, and you will be saved from the fires of Hell. Believe in the Lord Jesus and you will be in Heaven, feasting on milk and honey. Which of you will dedicate your life to Christ tonight? Come forward."

Malcolm's first movement amused Ezekiel. Silly joker, he thought. But Malcolm continued, moving toward the front of the church. Ezekiel almost shouted and grabbed at him. Three other people fell in behind Malcolm, among them, the notorious Checklea, a man who beats his wife, screams at his children and have a girlfriend down on Lagoon Road. They all moved forward to the Missionary Man.

"And a youth shall lead the way." They all went down on their knees near the preacher. The Missionary Man smiled. He placed a hand on

Malcolm's head, and then he began pleading with God, as he moved from convert to convert. Ezekiel stood watching, astonished at his friend and wondering what sins Malcolm could have committed, murder, covetousness. Too young for that, his uncle's sentiments ricocheted. He thought of original sin, as he had learned in the Book of Catechism, and wondered why any of these people could be burdened with the sins of two white people living in a botanical garden.

Ezekiel kept looking at the small group that had moved to the front of the church and listening to the prayers for the soul of Malcolm, and the others. How come the preacher kept referring to all those grown people as children? The service ebbed into more pleas to God as Malcolm and the others returned to their seats. A smattering of songs filled an awkward void as the Missionary Man moved to the door and people rose, beginning to move out. Ezekiel and Malcolm followed, walking in silence to get out of earshot of the preacher.

"Malcolm, what the hell did you do?"

"Nothing, just wanted to know what it feels like to be born again." Malcolm laughed, and they continued to move, lingering behind the other villagers making their way home.

"You feel anything when he placed his hand on your head?"

"Yeah—it felt sweaty."

"You mean you didn't feel less burdened or anything, with your sins lifted?"

"Well, I didn't have a lot of sins. Easy job, but imagine a fellow like Checklea, beating his wife, beating his children and his girlfriend. He must feel as light as a feather right now."

Ezekiel chuckled as he tried to visualize the burden of sins. All he saw was a donkey hauling a load of sugarcane.

* * *

Tilly crawled into the bed beside her husband John as many agitations churned the recesses of her brain. The earlier conversation with her mother had revived certain issues. Ezekiel had returned from the church, giving his father a detailed accounting of what he saw, including the people who went forward to be born again. Now the boy had retired to the mattress he shared with his brother Lloyd on the other side of the partition, which split the house in two. The woman went about her nightly routine: combed and braided her hair, rubbed scented coconut oil into her skin. She hummed and gazed at her reflection in the mirror, and then she blew out the kerosene lamp. John had stopped grumbled about the clamor from the church, and Tilly tried to accept the harmonies of the night, as she rejected Mano's drum. He had continued to pummel the goatskin long after the service had ended.

At times, after drinking his rum, Mano would beat that drum for hours. Darn him, she thought, I wish it would rain and drown him out. She thought of Alma, Mama Viche's niece, Maureen's daughter, asleep in her bed in the house down the road. Tilly cherished those times when the girl would come to visit. She saw this puzzling girl, with braids and crooked teeth, as the daughter she would never have. The girl would show up, help peel the yams or potatoes for dinner, laugh and talk with Ezekiel, play with Lloyd, read books to him, books she borrowed from the lower standards at her school. But before it was time to eat, the girl would find a pleasant excuse to leave. Tilly always wondered what Mama Viche may have said to the girl about eating food cooked by her.

When the first drops struck the tin roof, Tilly felt amused that such a whim could come to pass. But the rain failed to lull her to sleep. She knew it wouldn't last long, just one of those dry-season showers that came and went in short minutes. It should be enough to quiet Mano, she thought.

The large drops pelted out some hasty beats on the roof, a downpour punctuated by gusts of wind, generating pockets of silence that would be quickly devoured by heavier rain. Tilly could hear Ezekiel and Lloyd, rustling beyond the partition. She flinched, slightly, when John's hand slid up across her back and down to her stomach. She thought he had fallen asleep.

She quieted her surprise with one deep breath. Tilly cherished the feel of his hand through the fabric, but then comparison took over. She wondered if she would always compare the only two men she had known: Jake, her late husband, and John, this man in the bed next to her. She reached for his hand, brought it up to her lips, and kissed his fingers. Tilly felt the rough calloused joints of John's hand as he moved it away from her mouth and back to her stomach. Not like Jake's, she thought. That ganja smoking, music playing, country boy from Willis had hands as smooth as a baby's backside. He was Mama Viche's godson. Tilly smiled at these mixtures of memories.

Their lips met in the dark, the kiss long and obliging. The rain swept across the house as she tasted his mouth, and inhaled the smell of cocoa tea on his breath. She snuggled into his arms, centering on the raw feel of his palm. How fingers so rough could evoke such yearning, made Tilly wonder what she had ever found so appealing about Jake. Would memories of him always skulk around like a stray dog? It had been over five years. That darn fool had to go and get himself killed in America.

She tried to banish comparison from her thoughts, but it kept sneaking back. Jake had always stroked her with words when they made love: *you taste like fresh passion fruit, sweet, tangy and lively, baby.* He would laugh that stupid laughter. *You remind me of fresh dew on cut grass. You are the timbres in my minor chords. Girl, you make me want you like a thirsty man near water.*

But John, on the other hand, would just grunt, breathe and sigh as if doing a task, serious business, the way he reached into her. The difference confounded her. And yet, every time she made a direct comparison, John won. She loved Jake's sweet words. They made her feel precious. But John's attention to detail and his serious approach to her body added a dimension to love making that Tilly had never experienced with Jake. Poor Jake. Tilly knew if she hadn't left him, she too would be dead. That assessment gave her little comfort.

Tilly buried her face in John's chest, smeared kisses over his bare brackish skin, and took deep breaths. His smell came to her nose hot, and gratifying, making her moist. She pulled back from the rush of passion and drew in a gulp of rain-laden-air.

All distractions faded as she searched, with her hand, and found his mouth again. She fell into the taste, smells and feelings, her breasts crushed against his chest. She abandoned all considerations. When he pulled her nightgown up around her waist, she moaned softly into his mouth. All her senses came together on a single need. Everything else became secondary, and the need expressed itself in sounds that she could not control. She knew the noise came from her, but also from outside of her, as if her skin resonated.

"Tilly, you alright?" Ezekiel's voice broke into the moment. She heard a moan of resignation and felt John roll away. The rain had ceased. She wondered what the boy may have seen or heard.

"I'm fine. Your father and I were just playing and talking about--about when he's going to buy us a radio."

"Our own radio?" Ezekiel said.

"What you talking about, Tilly," John turned in her direction and propped his body on his elbows.

"It just came out of my mouth," she said.

"Well, you better put it back in. I'm not spending money on a radio when I can listen to one for free," John said.

"So you want to go up there to Monah's house all the time to listen to her radio."

"I'm not going up there all the time. Everybody just sits outside and listen to the thing until she's ready to go to sleep or the radio-station shuts off."

"All of you sitting near the woman's house. Remember when everyone treated her like a leper? Calling her crazy because she refused to accept--?"

"Jesus Christ. The government told her. Hurricane killed the man in Florida," John said. "But she still--"

Ezekiel cleared his throat and shuffled his feet.

"Go back to bed, Ezekiel," Tilly said.

"Lloyd's kicking me."

"You two!" Tilly shouted.

She fumbled under the sheet, pulled her nightgown into place and swung her legs out of the tangle of the sheets. Her bare feet hit the wooden floor like a slap. She shoved the boy away.

"You are too old for this, Ezekiel. Stop faking that foolishness. Go back to bed."

"Are we really going to get a radio?"

"We'll see. Get in there. And Lloyd, stop kicking."

She steered the boy toward the mattress and placed the sheet snugly around both boys. Tilly lingered beyond the partition for a moment, trying to regain her composure. Ezekiel sleeps so restively, she thought, making sounds as if talking to someone or something. She recalled the time she stood gazing at him as he slept and his eyes popped open. The boy then took a deep breath and continued to sleep with his eyes wide open. What does he witness in his dreams?

Everything slept, except Tilly. Anxiety held her on the edge. John was curled up against the wall. She slid under the sheet, felt the moisture on his skin, thought of insisting on a continuation of the ride to where they were headed before Ezekiel's interference.

She closed her eyes, and rumination took her down a familiar road. In the middle of her path stood a woman, an abundance of braids decked her head. Tilly remembered Joan, John's first wife, that way. Without opening her eyes, she shifted her position on the bed, and she ran one hand over her face. John's breathing sounded like the croak of a frog. Tilly knew the moment she tried to sleep the specter of the dead woman would start a quarrel inside her head.

When Tilly moved into John Augustine's house, she could feel and smell Joan everywhere. She held certain qualms about the dead woman, and in spite of her efforts, she could not get rid of those misgivings. Tilly resented how people spoke about the woman, saying things like: Joan had music in her veins. She loved to sing as she worked. She could outwork a dozen men.

The worst of the pests was Lester Cox, Ezekiel's uncle, Joan's brother, a fretful man who carried his emotions on his sleeves like smeared snot. He drove Tilly crazy. *"John killed my sister, you know. And he's still acting like a show-off. Look at the clothes he wears, a blasted braggart, that's what I see. He should have taken her to the hospital. Instead, he listened to that Obeah woman and fed her herbs. You take good care of my nephew, Tilly. You hear me? That boy is special. He needs a good mother."*

All these things drove Tilly to the brink of despair. She knew there was no love lost between John and Lester. Even as boys they fought over everything, marbles, girls, but bad-mouthing John to her? She simply dismissed Lester as a babbling idiot.

Tilly was John's senior by four years. She stood nose to nose with him, tall, thin, and unbent. She hated her height and her looks. With a long solitary face and a voice that projected, she could be heard across a room if she just whispered. And she knew this. She learned speaking with a soft voice made people listen more intently. Her one regret, how little this worked on John. She wore reading glasses, used them like an exclamation mark; took them off and replaced them at chosen moments, attempting to obscure telling eyes, affecting an air of sophistication. She loved to untangle her surroundings. Situations with the complexity of night bothered her. Nothing she did followed customary conventions. All her neighbors loved and despised her, at different times, for different reasons. Tilly was the bonus child of Henry and Florence. With three elder brothers, she had to learn to fight to survive. Her mother showered her with affection, soothing any bumps she may have received due to rough handling by her siblings.

She was a more experienced and educated woman than Joan; had been a teacher, and traveled abroad for a time. Eventually, she returned to Grenada and the safety of her parents' home. She told her mother she had grown tired of traveling on buses, living in hotels and competing with a saxophone and ganja for the affections of a man. Jake's death left Tilly with many unresolved issues.

John started making advances toward Tilly soon after Joan's death but she would have nothing to do with him. About a year later, to everyone's surprise, Tilly married John. She based her decision to marry him on one incident. It happened on Pandy Beach, in the shallows, near the rocks. She could still feel his hands on her feet, massaging and washing them tenderly in the seawater. When he brought his lips down to her instep, she felt it in her stomach, below her navel, a kind of minor orgasm.

Most of the people who knew Tilly Stewart conceded, grudgingly, that she might be the woman to tame John. In a short time, Tilly infused her essence into the house, seeking to move Joan's memory to its proper place. She lit a small bundle of the herb called Black Sage, allowed the smoke to drift all over the house, and then she burned a stick of jasmine incense. If this house had to be her home, she had decided, some other parts of her early life had to be present in the landscape.

Tilly went to her mother's garden and dug up the offshoots from two of her favorite plants, hibiscus and bougainvilleas. She took the young plants out of the ground, taking special care to protect the roots and she planted them, just before the rains came, along both sides of the path leading to the house from the bottom road. It didn't take long. The young plants grew quickly. In just a few weeks they took to the soil, sprouting new buds, looking sturdy, and on the rise.

The blood-red hibiscus flowers popped out and were cradled by green leaves. Long stamens, with little yellow knobs of pollen, protruded out of the petal cups. Carpels rested tenderly on the end of the stamens. The bougainvilleas exhibited a temperate red, with white stamens and pistils that complemented the array. From a distance, the white insides of the bougainvilleas looked like a swarm of tiny white butterflies in a field of crimson. The arrangement pleased Tilly.

She became pregnant with Lloyd, and continued to tend her kitchen garden of tomatoes, lettuce, cabbage, big-thyme, and sage. Tilly also raised chickens and collected the eggs, which she sold to neighbors. John worked the land in the Valley of Bones and tended his cows. Life appeared good. When the child came, she accepted it with joy and settled into motherhood. But her joy came to a halt when she noticed Lloyd's lack of mental development. She planned for what she saw coming. My son would not be left behind, she told herself. I will teach him to read, write and do his arithmetic. I'll drum it into him if necessary. Tilly reclined on the bed, paying scant attention to what surrounded her, but the soft panting of her family couldn't be ignored. The entire house appeared to have a life of its own that existed inside the darkness. As she slid off into sleep, she wondered if she would dream.

* * *

God damned the night and all its minions, Ezekiel thought. He recalled being out in the bush with his uncle Lester when the bulb in the flashlight went out, the thickness of the dark as Lester fumbled to replace the bulb and the slight touch he felt on his back just before the flashlight sprung back to life. The boy waited for the noise between his father and Tilly to resume. *Remain calm and listen, no getting out of bed,* he told himself. Ezekiel flopped over to face his younger brother. Lloyd slept and snored softly, his warm breath struck Ezekiel's face, ripe and disgusting, like rotten mangoes. Ezekiel turned away. He couldn't shed the thought of a radio in the house.

The boy refocused his attention on the night. He could hear the darkness. Fowls cackled and moved about in the trees, trying to get away from something, probably a Manicou, big chicken thief, rat looking marsupial. He knew the manicou would either eat a few mangoes or grab a young pullet and drag it into the bushes. *One of these nights it'll be me, you and one of Uncle Lester's dogs*, Ezekiel thought.

But he feared the night, outside, alone__ not simply the darkness, but the creatures that dwell in the muck: La Diablesse, Mama Malady, and the dreaded Loupgarou. He visualized the Loupgarou moving across the night sky as a blaze of fire; sitting down near the resting place of humans or animals, crawling on them and sucking their blood. Ezekiel understood his fear of the night prevented him from going after the chicken thief alone. He planned to seek Malcolm's help without divulging his fixation on things that dwelled in shadows.

Ezekiel drifted slowly toward sleep, still contemplating the men who turn into Loupgaroux and suck blood. He pictured a man standing naked at a secret place in the Valley of Bones and peeling his skin. This skin must be hidden well so no one can find it. If found, and sprinkled with salt, the Loupgarou can reclaim his skin but would suffer an excruciating death.

He remembered the buckets of sand and the mirror inside the front door of people's homes. A Loupgarou must enter through the main entrance and leave the same way. If it glimpses its reflection in the mirror, it must remain and count every grain of sand in the bucket before sunrise. If it fails, it would be trapped counting the grains of sand. Avoid eye contact with the Loupgarou. If you look it in the eyes, it's gone, escaped. If you want the Loupgarou dead, strike it three times with a broomstick. It will run away, but within a week, somebody would come down with a mysterious illness.

Ezekiel recalled the rumor about Malcolm's grandfather, Cora's father. They claimed he was a Loupgarou who got caught.

When sleep did come, the boy found himself in a quandary. He could not distinguish dream from premonition. Ezekiel stood in a doorway, looking into a room that he recognized as the mind of Cosmus LaTouche. At first, Cosmus sat alone, looking at rain drops hitting dry dirt and leaving tiny indentations. And then Cosmus stood relaxed with his back against a wall, as he spoke to Jack Masanto about a razor blade and a Bible. When Ezekiel looked askance, he saw Jack Masanto, hanging by his neck, eyes bugged out big and red as if bleeding. Ezekiel felt cold from the sweat breaking out on his skin. The boy shivered between the sheets, struggling with a scream that refused to leave his throat.

The next morning, Ezekiel floundered in a sea of concerns as he ate the fried breadfruit and coco-tea that Tilly had prepared for breakfast. He wondered if he should tell Malcolm about his dream. Ezekiel decided to say nothing. He met Malcolm and the other boys where the road forked, and they walked into Saint Georges for the school day, everyone all jovial in the early sun, except Ezekiel. He felt weighed down. School was uneventful, except for a little teasing directed at Malcolm for going to the front of the church and allowing the Missionary Man to pray on his head.

Ezekiel returned from school in a mood fueled by his vision about Jack and Cosmus. He asked Tilly if she had ever seen a Loupgarou. And without waiting for an answer, he switched the conversation to the radio his father planned to buy. Ezekiel saw Tilly cringing. She attempted to brush the puzzlement aside by gazing intently at Ezekiel. He thought of pestering her for details about Cosmus but decided against that course of action. The boy planned to wait for another time when he could corner Tilly, force her to give him relief from his obsession. He asked Tilly's permission to go play, and he found Malcolm waiting on the top road. They took off toward the Valley of Bones to conceal themselves near John and Monica's love nest.

* * *

Cosmus LaTouche sat in the prison yard at Richmond Hill thinking about the children of Jean Anglais. One image among the many was playing tricks on him. Unlike the various memories he had brought into the prison locked inside his head, and the scraps delivered to him by visitors, one impression of a boy held significance. He wanted to understand why this boy he knew from the village kept popping up on the periphery of his dreams, but the moment he turned to look dead on, the face would vanish. Cosmus recalled Ezekiel, the son of John Augustine, as a bashful child. While other children ran amok, he would sit to one side surveying the tomfoolery with the albino. Cosmus recalled the day Ezekiel and the albino began teaching a little girl called Delores to play marbles.

A patchy beard had sprouted on Cosmus' face in the years spent behind bars. He calculated his compunctions to keep his brain enthused. Cosmus was staring at the rows of barbed wire stretched across the top of the brick wall, wondering about the necessity. How could any of the prisoners get to the top of that wall? A radio from one of the guard towers boomed a calypso by the Mighty Sparrow. Cosmus stood smiling about an old recollection of another radio, the one brought to Jean Anglais countless years ago. Swallow, the original owner, was a good friend of Yaga, the man who had gotten into the conflict with Mama Viche. When Swallow died, Yaga claimed his friend had told him he could have the radio as long as he never removed it from Jean Anglais. Yaga kept his promise to Swallow, and shared the radio with the other villagers, until the disagreement with the Obeah woman and he had decided to flee Jean Anglais. To uphold his promise, he settled on an exchange with a fellow called Selwyn.

Selwyn's father was a man who worked with wood. Before he left for England, he had made a quarto out of a single piece of Mahogany from the old tree, hollowed it out and carved a neck. The instrument was crude in appearance but produced a beautiful sound. Selwyn could play a few cords, but could not tune the instrument. Yaga could play and tune the quarto. So they made the exchange. Cosmus sat smiling about how he had managed to snatch the radio from Selwyn with the help of three peculiar children, the albino, the girl Delores, and Ezekiel.

Selwyn had received papers to immigrate to England, and he planned to sell his radio, use the proceeds as pocket money for the journey. No one had enough cash to purchase the radio on their own, so they pooled their cash and still they didn't have enough. The idea of the radio not being in the village became worrisome, something the villagers just couldn't abide: no more cricket matches, no more football or top-ten calypso broadcasts, felt like the end of the world to them. They offered Selwyn the money they had gathered, reminded him of the promise, but he refused. When Cosmus came up with the plan to pit Selwyn, one of the best marble strikers in the village against Delores, they all thought Cosmus was crazy. Selwyn couldn't resist the opportunity. He utilized the cliché taking candy from a baby.

Delores was the only child of Tante Monah, the woman who still grieved for her husband. Everyone thought of the little girl as wild and boyish. She gravitated toward the two other misfits, Ezekiel and Malcolm. Cosmus decided to prey on Selwyn's pride, and his greed, pitting him against a little girl. If he refused, he would become a laughingstock. The situation turned into a chance for Selwyn to keep his radio, sell it to someone else down in Belmont, and still receive the money the villagers had offered. First he had to win.

Cosmus had noticed Delores, with tutoring from Ezekiel, and Malcolm, hitting marbles consistently from twelve feet. He placed one marble twelve feet away, gave the participants thirteen chances. The person with the most hits won. The little girl had an unusual style. She sat on the ground with her legs stretched forward, instead of on her knees, the way most people pitched marbles. Selwyn made the fatal mistake of agreeing to employ her posture without a trial.

At the end of the contest and to the disappointment of Ezekiel and the other boys, Cosmus and Delores took the radio to her mother's house. No decision had been made as to who would be the keeper of the radio, so Cosmus choose the little girl. Tante Monah took the radio from Cosmus and no one saw it from that point on, except Tante Monah and Delores. People walking by heard the radio, and could request one or the other of the two stations it received. At times they would pass a hat around to collect donations for a new battery. Everyone who wanted to listen to programs sat or stood outside in her yard. Cosmus suspected the radio might still be sitting in her house, transmitting music, sports, and death notices to those assembled outside.

Cosmus had ways of reorganizing his memories, playing with reality to calm his nerves, chewing on them, stretching them like bubble gum to create scenarios fitting his needs. He never recounted his fabrications to anyone, kept them deep inside for fear they might lose their viscosity.

For instance, on the day they transported him from the courthouse, shackled with chains and padlocks, to the fortress on the hill, he recalled a man sitting in a room with one table and one chair. The man sat in the chair. "You will have no visitors for your first thirty days," he recalled the man saying. "That's your orientation period. You will be alone for that time, allow you to cool down and think about your new life, and then you will be allowed to enter the general population. No fights, no backtalk to the guards, and we'll get along real fine. Life in this place will be what you make of it. Your education could be of help to you, but on the other hand, it could be a hindrance."

The man paused, sat up straight in the chair and looked directly at Cosmus. "You may think: I'm already in prison for life, what can they do to me? Serious mistake to follow that line of reasoning," the man said. "We have ways of making your life in here a living hell. Do you understand me?" Cosmus looked at the man's face, set hard as a rock. He nodded, and his stomach grumbled. They took away his clothes, gave him jeans and the gray shirt that all prisoners wore, and then they locked him in a narrow cell in the bowels of the fortress.

Constance Carlyle, the reason for Cosmus' predicament, flooded his dreams. In the hole where he was kept alone, she came to him nightly, dressed in the garbs of memories and feelings inconsolable. When he slept, those images would consume him. He would bolt straight up on the cot in the cell, eyes wide open, ready to dive into the ocean and rescue her. He could do nothing. She was dead, and he remained at the mercy of men with no compassion.

Cosmus came out of solitary confinement a changed man. Thirty days took on another meaning. He looked at the other men locked up with him at Richmond Hill and sensed they had lost some of their humanity. That perspective became his saving grace because he saw himself in roughly the same way. Although barely a man, he had decided to take on the responsibility pushed on him, to honor the memory of Constance and pay the price. He knew he had done nothing except love her. So he accepted what they threw at him: the trial, the rehashing of everything that had transpired from so many angles, the judge with his powdered wig sitting there, the lawyers and the police spouting their opinions. He looked into the eyes of the people he had known under different circumstances, especially his old schoolmaster, Vernon Stewart, Tilly's father. Cosmus searched for some reassurances. The looks on their faces tore at his heart.

His love for Constance and his mother, his regard for the people of Jean Anglais and the burning ambition that made him one of the top students at Grenada Boys Secondary School, all of it, trumped by the accusations he saw on the faces of those congregated in the courtroom. *Who are you? Who do you think you are? Ignorant, country boy, you thought you were somehow special?*

Those recollections had flogged him like a bull pistle. With only the ability to work, eat, shit and piss, Cosmus retreated into himself, searched his past, and his present, played imaginary games, reached out for context and shades of meaning, compared his decisions and came to some startling conclusions. He realized how much he enjoyed looking deep into the eyes of other people. In this place, no one did that. It could be taken for something else.

Cosmus had tried to keep his distance from the other inmates when he came out of isolation. His mother, Rita, came to visit and brought food, spoke about life on the outside as if she had returned from a vacation. He listened, hid his feelings, and wondered if she understood any of this. He cataloged the other prisoners: uneducated country boys, town-boys who considered themselves smart and found out otherwise, desperate old men with rage smeared all over their faces. Cosmus wondered how often God entertained prayer from this place.

For the first few days, they left Cosmus alone. But then an old prisoner with holes in his gums and rotten stubs of teeth started: "You will be helping me shovel pig shit before too long, School Boy," the man spoke to amuse the other prisoners. "I'll be right here to comfort you when you get scared. Your mother won't always be around, School Boy."

"Stop calling me fucking School Boy, old man." Cosmus snatched his plate of rice and peas, brought to him by his mother, and retreated to another table.

"Look everybody, School Boy, running away, hiding in the corner. No balls," the man said. The room erupted with laughter.

A young prisoner with a pronounced limp moved to the other table with Cosmus, as if through some kind of solidarity. "I don't need any shit," Cosmus said. "I don't need any friends. Stay the fuck away from me."

"Gimpy," the young prisoner extended his hand. Cosmus looked at his fingers without touching them. "Just like my first few months here," the fellow said, pitching his voice low and retrieving his hand.

"What did a cripple like you do to land in this place?" Cosmus waited for Gimpy's reaction.

"None of your fucking business."

"Don't get all riled, I was only trying to ..."

"Well don't." Gimpy looked at Cosmus. "Can't ask that kind of--what you expect, the truth; a confessions?"

"Who gives a shit? Only trying to make conversation," Cosmus said.

"Be quiet and listen. Show no fear. That's how they chose their victims. And pay no attention to that old fool. They call him Maga. He'll pretend to be your friend and then turn on you like a vicious dog."

Cosmus and gimpy were shoveling mounds of food into their mouths as the other prisoners conversed and laughed.

"You see that one in the corner?" Gimpy said. Cosmus attempted to look. "Don't look at him. I don't want him to know we're talking about him. That's Butcher Rat. The warden is his godfather. The Rat can get you anything you need from outside, even a woman, for a price of course," Gimpy smiled. "You're smart. You'll get the hang of things."

Cosmus realized that loneliness could be the coin of this realm, and he already had enough. Desperation and hopelessness held a unique smell, he realized. He found Gimpy engaging, and out of a cynical need, he decided to accept Gimpy's association.

He wished his mother would stop making the trip and bringing stuff. Doing his time alone seemed less complicated. But when she told him she would come whenever she was allowed, and she had moved into a house just outside the prison walls, it moved him to tears. Cosmus decided he had to endure, and not just live, but thrive. Since he couldn't move with his body, he would move with his mind, he would live for his mother, and for the memory of Constance.

"Those books your mother brings all the time, you read and keep them to yourself?" Gimpy asked Cosmus as they walked around the yard one evening.

"Yeah, what's wrong with--?"

"Like masturbation, sharing nothing with others."

"What the hell does that--?"

"You know what I mean. Wait until you're in here for awhile."

"I don't know what you're talking about."

"Ideas," Gimpy said, "thoughts, opinions. I know how to read some, but writing has always been a problem for me, putting words together on paper and having them make sense."

Those words unlocked the prison gates for Cosmus. He found the way to be useful to the population at Richmond Hill Prison. Cosmus became a model prisoner, gained the respect of guards and inmates, taught some to read and write, showed a few how to write official letters to lawyers and judges.

Still, worries and difficulty sleeping would drag him to places barely conceivable. Most nights he would sit in his cell with his memories and the news brought to him from outside. The attempts to keep him connected to the world became all blurred and hazy. Cosmus existed in a space where past and present became mixed. The whole world seemed to be moving along without him. All of it felt like a movie, and the moment he closed his eyes, the movie would start rolling, and the voice telling the story would be his voice.

He would sit in the dark cell, listening to the snores, farts and groans of the other prisoners, and he would chase details in circles, over and over, trying to rectify the known with the unknown. How did he end up caged like a beast? In the space between sleep and wakefulness, but not quite dreams, Cosmus would play a mental game set in a maze of sugarcane. There he would search for a blade to cut through the cane and hack down a secret door, allow himself inside where all the details from his past languished in thick, black syrup. There he would attempt to rearrange the essentials, put them in concert. The fantasy always ended with him yearning for the taste of rum.

As Cosmus recalled the memories of Jean Anglais, the house, and the white family who came to live there, he found himself smiling about all the tricky details kneading his mind. Everyone in Jean Anglais knew about the house. Years ago, a group of men showed up and hired a few laborers from the village to dig a foundation. They dug up some human bones and thought the house-spot may have been an old graveyard. And that was that. They gradually constructed the concrete house and painted it yellow with red trim. During the final stage of construction, an incident occurred, involving a man called Bravo.

Papa LaTouche came to visit Cosmus at the end of his first month in prison. They sat in the visiting area, a kind of big chicken coop, with one guard looking on. The old man appeared tired and dejected. His disheveled clothes and the way he kept looking at his worn-out shoes almost moved Cosmus to tears. The old man spoke, shaking his head, never looking directly at Cosmus. "I let you down, my boy," he had said.

"What are you talking about, Grandpa?"

"I went to see Mama Viche when people started talking about your girl's parents looking to hire a servant. I asked her about the bones and Bravo falling from the roof. She told me she saw nothing wrong. 'People will talk, Augustus. I heard Bravo drank a lot of strong rum the night before and didn't drink enough water the next morning. Hot sun and no water, makes you real giddy. Obvious bad luck, but I don't know about those old bones.' So I told your mother, no problem working for the white family. No curse on the house. Then people started coming to me when they noticed you with the girl."

In the tradition of the people of Jean Anglais, Cosmus consumed those pieces from his grandfather and renovated his own narrative about what had transpired in Jean Anglais, leading to the present state of his existence. This is how he saw the whole thing: for years, the old bones, and Bravo breaking his neck remained the only memories that the people of Jean Anglais kept in mind about the house until Constance and her family moved in, and he and his mother started working for them.

The front of the yellow house sat near a paved road that ran up from Grand Anse. The back of the house was positioned across a field of grass, and a stand of mahoe and briah trees. Those trees shielded the brick house from the cluster of wooden houses perched on the hillside. A dirt path ran up from the town called Belmont, and forked behind the house, forming two paths through the village, one at the top and one at the bottom, the Top and Bottom Roads.

The Carlyle family consisted of Ronald, the general manager of George F. Huggins__ his wife, Margaret, a doctor at the General Hospital in Saint Georges and three children: two small ones__ a boy and a girl__ and Constance, their older sister. Memories of them kept Cosmus awake at night and interfered with his conscience. Images of Constance especially played havoc on him, the way she brought him sorrel and other drinks as he worked, shirtless, in the sun, joining him in the work as he pruned the roses, the pink hibiscus, and fuchsias. Constance and Cosmus were the same age. They would often converse and make jokes about their peers, how the posturing and apparent lack of concern for others irritated them. He would spray her with the garden hose, and she would run and laugh. The folks from Jean Anglais, walking by on the path, would peek through the trees, study the two young people and shake their heads. This could only lead to trouble, they surmised.

Some of the villagers spoke to Papa LaTouche about their observations. The old man went to the house that his daughter, Rita shared with her only child, Cosmus and her man, Mondu. Her husband had long ago departed when the doctor told him that Rita couldn't have any more children. The old man spoke to his daughter, and she promised to speak to her son about his forwardness with Constance.

The rumors started circulating, about seeing Cosmus and Constance swimming way out in the deep water off Pandy Beach, racing and laughing, holding hands, and strolling on the sand. They seemed ignorant of the effect their behavior could be having while everybody else knew there would be hell to pay. Before long, Rita and Cosmus got dismissed from their jobs, and Cosmus was warned to stay away from the house and Constance. A white policeman called Dennis Didderot was dispatched to reinforce the warning to Cosmus and his mother.

Cosmus had to withdraw from the secondary school. His mother no longer had the money to pay his fees. He took a job as a busboy at a hotel on the beach at Grand Anse working for pocket change. Some of the villagers became upset at what they saw as an injustice done to Rita and her son. Talk of burning the house to the ground ran rampant, after all, Rita was a village girl, and no one treated people from Jean Anglais like trash. Cosmus recalled his pride at the way the people of Jean Anglais had embraced his mother.

One day Cosmus and Constance disappeared. A huge manhunt started all over Grenada with police working overtime, and a sizeable reward offered. The Carlyles declared that Cosmus had kidnapped their daughter, but everyone around Jean Anglais and Belmont, including his mother, knew the truth.

Mondu, the former fisherman, now a farmer, told Cosmus of an old turtle fisherman's shack, set back in the trees on the leeward side of Glover Island. He also spoke of a supply of fresh water from cisterns near the place where the whalers, in the old days, butchered their catch. "Don't forget to boil the water," he warned Cosmus. And Constance secretly amassed some supplies, food, fresh water, paper and pencils, and some books, Robinson Crusoe, Don Quixote, in Spanish, for Cosmus to read to her, and the play Romeo and Juliet, for her own reading. They borrowed Mondu's boat, rowed out to the island, moved into the shelter, and then hauled the boat out of the water and hid it in the trees.

Cosmus anticipated this adventure would last two or three days. He expected Constance to grow tired of living in the wild, and he would have to row her back to the mainland. She would return to her parents; he might have to disappear for a time, but he didn't care, it was a small price to pay. Spending time alone with Constance was worth any penalty. The shack was only big enough for sleeping and getting out of any severe weather. So they spent most of their time outside, exploring and making trips to the old whaling station, marveling at the mounds of bleached bones dissolving in the sun. Two or three days turned into a week, and then into two weeks. They were still there, playing in the ocean, obsessed with the intoxication of sex, on a blanket, on the wooden floor, skin discerning skin, and sleeping folded tightly into each other, invigorated by the momentary satisfaction and the freedoms. The sound of his name in her mouth became an intoxicant.

At night, Cosmus found himself enthralled by the delicate, seductive harmonies, the wind whistling through the trees, the waves rolling in and crashing on the sand, and Constance breathing tenderly against his chest. He realized this situation could not last. One day, he looked into her seawater eyes, hair bleached blond, back, stomach, and legs bronzed by the sun. In spite of their intimacy and the seclusion of the island, she still wore a bathing suit. Seeing her wild and free, he hatched a plan he thought could keep them together forever.

"Constance, we can't stay out here much longer," he said.

"Why not? I know our food and water is running low, but we can get more. You have friends at that hotel where you worked, right? We can dive and fish. We don't have to go back. Not now, not ever."

"Constance, the turtles will be migrating soon, and people will start coming out here, digging in the sand for eggs, and before long, they will find the boat."

Cosmus saw tears glistening in her eyes. He put his arms around her.

"What are we going to do?" she said. "I don't want to go back home and face my parents. Everyone would look at me as if I've done some terrible thing. My parents will send me back to England to live with my aunt." She crushed the warm sand with her toes and turned away.

"Mondu has friends," Cosmus said. "Arrangements can be made. The moon will be full in a few days. No problem getting a vessel to sail close. Swim out to it and be gone, Trinidad, Venezuela, anywhere. I speak some Spanish, remember."

She laughed and threw her hands in the air. "That sounds good. You are so smart." She wiped her tears, brought her arms down around his neck and kissed him intensely, as if sealing a deal.

"You stay here. I'll row in tonight," Cosmus said. "I'll talk to Mondu, and get some more food and clothes. I have money hidden in the house. Trinidad is less than a hundred miles that way." He pointed southeast and smiled at the delight he saw in her eyes.

Cosmus knew coming ashore on Grand Anse beach would be the safest route. The spirit of adventure energized him as he rowed back to the mainland in the dark; using the lighthouse off Point Saline for guidance, he hugged the beaches with names like Magazine, Dr. Grooms, Morne Rouge and up into Grand Anse. It took him almost two hours, rowing against the tide. Hauling the boat out of the water, Cosmus made his way off the beach, and up to the main road through Grand Anse. He didn't make it far. Near the Faledge, the police spotted him crossing the road, and after a brief chase, they arrested him.

These memories stirred bitterness in Cosmus. He kept reshuffling the details and wondering, searching for the justification in what had come to pass, recalling how the police had kept him awake all night and halfway through the next day, asking all kind of questions. Different officers taking turns, asking the same questions about Constance, "Is she still alive, where did you hide the body?" They kept hitting his face to keep him awake. It got so bad he would have agreed that the sky was pink, just for the pleasure of closing his eyes for five seconds.

Cosmus ran those moments through his mind many times looking for something to undo. He kept speculating on what may have happened to Constance, and what she may have done the morning he failed to return. She must have guessed what happened. By the time the police made it out to Glover Island, she was gone. They found a note from Constance to Cosmus, telling him how much she loved him and saying nothing will ever keep them apart. She said she would be swimming to the mainland and would do whatever she could, to make her parents understand.

The note never appeared in evidence at his trial.

Constance's mother, Doctor Carlyle, brought the sheet of paper to him at Richmond Hill Prison, minutes after his grandfather had left. The officials allowed them use of the small room where Cosmus had received his introduction to prison life. They knew that he posed no threat to the female doctor. Cosmus stood with his back against the wall, and the woman stood in the center of the room with the piece of paper in her hand. He looked at her fingers as she handed him the note, read it, looked up at the woman and clenched his jaws, curbing himself from speaking about Constance and the note. He knew that the piece of paper could go a long way toward his release from prison.

"Her father wanted to tear that up and burn it, didn't want it around. I couldn't let him. Hatred is a terrible thing, Cosmus. It does little to the person being hated."

Cosmus leaned off the wall, took two steps toward the woman, the note fixed between his fingers. "Doctor Carlyle, I know how you and your family must feel about me. I accept your scorn, that's how I survive in here. Although you know the truth, someone decided that her life was worth more than mine."

The woman looked at him, shook her head and what could have been a smile darted across her face. "This is way too--for you this is all over, but everyone in my family must live with their memories."

"Doctor Carlyle, I too have memories. I get the double dose. We were not children. I still love her, and this note," he waved the piece of paper at the woman, "Did you bring it here to torture me? Why didn't you take it to the judge or to my lawyer?"

"I hope one day, through some miracle, you will have a family. Then you will understand the loyalty and the dedication. Ronald did all his deals with the police, the judge, and the lawyers to have you locked up. I can't go against…"

"Then why are you here?" Cosmus looked at the woman. It would be so easy to grab her, and twist her neck like a chicken's. Instead, he smiled and saw Constance in her features.

"Wish I knew. I've a feeling if I had given this piece of paper to the Courts or lawyers it would have caused a huge rift in my family or may have even caused your death. Lots of people conspired to put you here. One day someone will take a second look at your case. I'm not sure what I'm doing here. I once had a lovely family, but now…" she sighed, "now Ronald's animosity toward you seeps into everything. If I had allowed him to destroy her last message on this earth, it would be like eradicating a final portion of her."

The woman lowered her head and Cosmus realized tears might be coming. "Doctor Carlyle, this is no place for something like this," He extended the note to her, and she took it back. "That note is a dangerous thing to many people. The colonial community, lawyers, judges, they took your husband's money to make an example of me. I guess I'll never understand why. Some things are beyond discernment. You keep her note. I'll keep her here." Cosmus patted the left side of his chest. The woman looked at him, her eyes red and wet. She then, looked away.

"I came here to assure myself that you are still alive. Yeah, that's why I came." She chuckled. "To look at you, make sure they didn't kill you."

"I'm still alive, Doctor Carlyle and plan to be for a long time."

"Good. Live, Cosmus. Live long." The woman turned, knocked on the door, a guard came and let her out.

Cosmus wished he could get a bucket of water, wash his face and hands, and be rid of all this, but his memories and his imagination lingered like the scent of the perfume the doctor had left behind.

All roads led back to Constance. From her note, Cosmus had made some presumptions: when he didn't return, she must have tried to swim back. Halfway to the mainland, Constance must have realized she couldn't make it. She turned back to Glover Island, but perhaps cramps set in, her calves stiffened, and she sank to the bottom like a stone. Every time he thought of her, in her last moment, he imagined her calling his name, and her final words floating to the surface in bubbles. Cosmus had remained thankful that they never allowed him to see her body. The fisherman who found her claimed he almost burst into tears at seeing that it was a human, not a mermaid tangled up in the lines of his fish-trap.

John Augustine's visits to Richmond Hill became a source of pleasure for Cosmus. He would look at this man he had known all his life, and he recognized something in the way he sat and spoke as if attempting to convey a message. His gawky legs stretched away from the chair, his robust face almost smiling. John's expressions and conversations articulated hope.

"Everybody in Jean Anglais wanted to help you real bad," John said. "They appointed me spokesman and I went into town to speak to Cummings. He's our new district representative. The man took me into a big office with pictures on the walls: the Queen, the Premier, and the Governor. He showed me to a soft chair, and he remained standing, speaking a bunch of shit, whining at me like a dog." Cosmus and John laughed out loud. "I heard his words, but-- 'You see, John, we appreciate your efforts in getting your people up there in Jean Anglais, to vote for the Labor Party in the last election.' Cummings began rubbing his hands together. 'But Grenada is divided into pieces. The police, judges and lawyers, that's only one piece, the big piece. And then there's us, the politicians. We can't interfere with the judges and the police, not in any important ways. The last of these are the people with money. They influence everything, and the girl, what's her name, Constance, she belonged to the people with money. So you see where that leaves us? We can march and demonstrate, but that wouldn't do any good.' I returned to Jean Anglais with that miserable news, and we all thought you were a goner."

They both smiled, and Cosmus heard a fly buzzing around the enclosure. He saw the fly resting on the wall behind John, rubbing its tail and then it took off straight up and through the wire mesh above.

"I'm amazed at the magic in this world," Cosmus said.

"What keeps you so at ease in this place?" John asked.

"Everything, everybody especially my mother," Cosmus said. "She came to see me right after I was released from my thirty days of isolation. It was so good to hear a friendly voice and see a pleasant face. I just sat there, listened to her and gazing at her face. She looked happy and sad at the same time. I had no idea those two emotions could mix, but people always say the same thing about oil and water. She told me what she did and my heart almost exploded in my chest.

She went to the home of those white people to plead for my life. She waited at the front gate, at the entrance away from Jean Anglais, near the gap where Ronald Carlyle had to pass with his car. She told me she saw his wife looking at her through the curtains on the kitchen window. She said she wanted the girl's mother to see the conversation, but not hear it. I had no idea my mother could be so cunning. She told me she didn't want to disturb the mother's grief. Ronald Carlyle stopped, got out of the car to open the gate."

'What are you doing here, Rita?'

"She spoke about the encounter with a bit of glee in her voice as if she was telling one of those Jean Anglais stories." 'He moved toward the gate, as I spoke to his back,' she said. 'Mr. Ronny, you know Cosmus is a good boy. He would never do anything to harm Constance.'

'Rita, his recklessness has damaged my family. My wife is in there crying her eyes out, my younger ones are wondering what happened to their sister.'

'Mr. Ronny, you know what will happen to him. Help me save his life. You know he's a good boy. I'll work for nothing. I'll do anything you want.'

'This is in the hands of the law, Rita. There's nothing I can do. Please don't come here anymore.'

"He got into his car,' my mother told me, 'drove it into the yard, got out, and just stood there. I imagined him looking at me with my head down as I walked away."

"Your mother is a clever one," John said. "But most women are."

"We'll never know what transpired between the man and his wife, but my mother's plan worked," Cosmus said to John. "They found me guilty of kidnapping and causing her death, which could have sent me straight to the gallows, but I think Ronald Carlyle interceded with the judge, and they concluded allowing me to live with my memories of Constance would be a greater punishment than death. So they sentenced me to life plus one day." Cosmus smiled. "I heard soon after the trial, the Carlyle family packed up and left."

John sat nodding at Cosmus and pursing his lips like a man contemplating. "We kept an eye on your mother, wondering what would become of her. Your grandfather took this to heart also, as if he held some blame. Your mother and Mondu got into a terrible fight one day, right in front of everybody. 'How would he know about that hut out there on the island? And they had your boat. People think they stole it, but I know you gave it to them, you romantic fool. I love you, Mondu, so I'll come home when you figure out how to get my son out of prison.' And she calmly strolled from the house with two bags. Mondu stood looking at her like a wet dog," John said.

Cosmus shook his head and shrugged. "How is that eldest boy of yours? Certain things about him I'll never forget."

"Ezekiel is fine," John said. "He reminds me of you, face always in a book."

Cosmus smiled and took a few steps around the enclosure.

"Your mother moved out of her house and left Mondu. He cooks for himself and washes his own clothes." John stared at Cosmus. "I hear she still cooks for you and washes your clothes? You are the cleanest prisoner in here. That job in the laundry room at that hotel on Grand Anse Beach must be hard on her. People are saying she also seemed to be imprisoned." John pitched his voice low and leaned toward Cosmus. "You know, Mondu took her words to heart."

"What is that stutter going to do, stage a jailbreak?" Cosmus whispered and smiled.

"Where there's a will there's a way," John said as he pulled his legs in and stood up. "You take care, Cosmus."

Cosmus watched John as he signaled the guard. The guard walked slowly toward the big chicken coop, placed a key in the lock and let John out.

Part 11

Ezekiel began managing his engagements with his father, and this alerted John to trouble. The man contemplated various strategies to deal with the behavior of his eldest son. The boy had begun to grow a little fuzz over his top lip. John wondered if that bit of hair could be steering the boy toward rebelliousness. John felt irritated at the way Ezekiel would glance, avoiding direct eye contact, and answering his questions with only a few words. He knew he had to knock down Ezekiel's attitude in one way or another. The man wondered if taking his son to visit Cosmus would change his behavior, bring him back to earth. Ultimately, John decided against scaring his son.

The next time John visited Cosmus, he conveyed news of the goings on around Jean Anglais, as if unaware that Rita, on her frequent visits, and Mondu on his visits, hadn't already brought all the lusciousness to Cosmus. Instead, John spoke as if to entertain, like telling a tale from the village and allowing Cosmus to interject, therefore creating a flow. "A white man named Harry Hudson, some kind of preacher moved into the house," John said.

"No one can tell me where the Carlyles went." Cosmus spoke, rubbing his palms. They sat on a bench in the visiting area, guards paying meager attention to their conversation.

"I've no idea," John said. "Those white people don't tell me their business."

"I thought you might have heard something."

"The preacher hired a girl called Monica, from Golf Course, to take care of the place. She's a good looker, boy," John smiled.

"Monica? You mean Sydney and Clarisse's daughter? She was still a little girl when I…"

John glanced at Cosmus, felt a twinge of guilt for bringing up the hint of sex, and the inkling of boasting about life on the outside. "You should see that preacher, roaming all over Jean Anglais, talking to people about God, holding prayer meetings under a tent in the field behind the house. They say he plans to build a church soon. Mama Viche nicknamed him the Missionary Man."

"Just like her to give him a pet name." Cosmus spoke, stood up, took a few steps and placed his back against the wall. He looked at the prison issued sneakers with no laces on his feet and ran one hand over his beard. John got the impression that the boy he once knew was turning into a man in the prison.

"The guards think I'm going crazy," Cosmus said.

"Well, are you?" John asked.

Cosmus smiled and looked at John. "Who knows? I'm having some weird dreams, and the guards are acting strange, giving me space as if my mental state might be catching. Allows me all kinds of extra time in the fresh air, and all the visitors, they don't treat me like the other prisoners."

"That's good. They might be aware of the details of your crime."

"My crime, hard to think of my actions as criminal," Cosmus said.

The older man realized that all the years behind bars had endowed Cosmus with some outstanding coping skills. And now this conversation only added urgency to the plan he and Mondu were waiting for the opportunity to execute.

"You're right, nothing wrong with what you did," John said.

"So why am I here?"

"Let me give you the goings-on before I have to go," John said. "After the Carlyle family moved out, the house sat empty for a long time, and then Harry Hudson moved in. We held our breaths, waiting for the other shoe to drop. Harry Hudson moving amongst us seemed like a Ladablais moving about in daylight." They both laughed.

"Anything to transpire would start with him, I suppose," Cosmus said.

"But nothing happened, and slowly, we slid back to our old routines, always ending the day sitting near Monah's house, listening to the old radio and commenting on the music and the news." John continued. "We took the Missionary Man for granted. The recollections of you and Constance seemed to be fading."

"What happened to those people who knew stories about Africa, and from the cane fields? Such short memories these days," Cosmus said.

"You can say that again," John said. "One day we heard a ruckus, and as if to make amends for some unknown offense, a big, ugly bulldozer, belching fumes and black smoke, appeared at the gap near Belmont, dropped a blade, began pushing the dirt, knocking down trees in the way; widening the path up the hill to our houses."

"Holy Ghost," Cosmus said. "Tell me more, I thought the world would wait for me, for the day when I get out of here, to start rotating again," he chuckled.

"The rumor had been in the air for years. None of us thought it would come down to earth. Men followed the bulldozer with tripods, levels, and strings, lots of twine, seemed like a show at first. No one in

Jean Anglais thanked me. I was the one who encouraged them to vote Labor in the election."

"I remember you always talking politics, speaking about what those big wheels might do for us one day," Cosmus said. "You have great foresight, John."

"You should see the village. Everything changed, that bulldozer, the fellow driving it, and those laborers, amazing what they did to the place. You know the top and the bottom roads through Jean Anglais could barely hold a car, not it's this wide," John extended his hands and Cosmus smiled. "With some trees gone and the dirt rearranged, truckloads of gravel from River Road came next. It didn't take long to bury the dirt under gravel. We all knew we had won twice. We no longer had to walk those muddy paths to get home in the rainy season, and the men from Jean Anglais who got to work on the road made money that would circulate between us for years. And did anyone tell you, we now have a standpipe on the top road above my house? But I have no idea what to make of this Missionary Man." John rose, shook hands with Cosmus and left the prison.

Everyone in Jean Anglais volunteered to help the Missionary Man build the church except six people: John, his wife Tilly, and their two boys, Ezekiel and Lloyd, also the Obeah woman, Mama Viche, with her niece Alma. Cosmus digested all this from the confines of Richmond Hill Prison, as he distilled and reassembled alternate version of things that could have been.

* * *

Ezekiel and Malcolm had always played a game with the incident of their births. Each year, they would be the same age and then Malcolm would have a birthday, spring forward and be older than Ezekiel. The boys dabbled in two distractions that flowed into each other, helping at the little church, and keeping an eye on Monica. Each time John and Monica met, Ezekiel and Malcolm concealed themselves nearby. They shared hidden glances and private smiles each time they saw Monica cleaning or cooking for the Missionary Man. Ezekiel carried some guilt and confusion about the activities of his father. He wished something would flash in his mind; reveal the closing phase of his dilemma.

Eventually, Malcolm grew tired of the escapade. He preferred to spend his time at Harry Hudson's house, reading the Bible, and books by Charles Dickens and Oscar Wilde. Many books packed the shelves of the Missionary Man's house. Malcolm zeroed in on the books with the word confessions in their title: Especially Jean Jacques Rousseau and Saint Augustine. He found their ideas eloquent. When he discovered the Meditations by Marcus Aurelias, he skipped around and found the admonitions that appealed to him. The words struck him as unadorned and to the point. He memorized some favorites, and would frequently quote them to friends as if they were his own thoughts and words.

Ezekiel usually helped with the chores around the church, and would read some of the books from the Missionary Man's shelves: Prisoner in the Iron Mask, Count of Monte Cristo, and The Black Tulip. He also read Kidnapped, Treasure Island and the Strange Case of Doctor Jekyll and Mr. Hyde. The adventurers intrigued him.

Once, Ezekiel attempted to discuss with Malcolm why he had decided to become a Christian. The conversation strayed, and Malcolm steered it into a converse about the absolute power of God, and why God will always forgive sins, if only we would ask. *Ask and ye shall be forgiven.*

Ezekiel resisted conversion, yet he continued to read the Bible with Malcolm. They would sit in the church for hours, reading aloud to each other, about the crazy girl called Salome, who danced with her seven veils for the head of a man, about the betrayal of a strong man by his girlfriend, and foolish kings who went against the word of God. Ezekiel especially enjoyed reading about the other Ezekiel__ the prophet, about the divine throne above four living creatures, and the wheels of fire next to the cherubim with many faces. The boy enjoyed these fantastic tales about the voice of the Almighty, and the voice of many waters. Ezekiel would look at the sky at night and imagine the chariots of fire he had read about in the Second Book of Kings. Malcolm became intoxicated by the prophet Joel, son of Pethuel, and the vision of Pentecost with the tongues of fire. He started preaching to the other children and carrying a Bible, the preacher had given him for Christmas.

The albino boy would pontificate on biblical quotes to his school mates. *"I will pour out my spirit on all flesh. Your sons and your daughters shall prophesy, your old men shall dream dreams, and your young men shall see visions. Even on the male and female slaves, in those days, I will pour out my spirit."*

Hecklers who dared to laugh at Malcolm would be met with stern admonitions. "Some are chosen," he would say. "Those will meet Him in the sky come Judgment Day. Blasphemers are doomed. I already have my visions. Where are your visions? I see all of you in Hellfire." Malcolm's stern recitals caused his detractors to wonder.

In time, the children of Jean Anglais grew tired of Malcolm's constant scolding. But then, he discovered the Book of Revelation and started preaching about the Mark of the Beast, the Great Whore of Babylon and Life in the Last Days. His friends had almost busted their guts with laughter. Adults began approaching the Missionary Man about the antics of the boy. Harry Hudson promised to speak to Malcolm and tutor him in the proper ways to sermonize the Gospels.

Ezekiel, on the other hand, wallowed in uncertainty about his loyalty to Tilly and his interest in his father's actions. The boy could not resist following his father and Monica, watching them plunge up and down, and twirling on the ground between the trees. He had grown daring, would crawl closer with each encounter. Ezekiel figured Malcolm must be thinking of all those human actions as sinful. Malcolm was a man of God now, so all things human became sinful. The sudden change, the way Malcolm walked and talked, the way he would use words like, God, Christ and Power;" All this appeared peculiar to Ezekiel.

The day of this occurrence, Ezekiel had been working beside the Missionary Man, washing the pews, sweeping the grass and dirt carried into the church on people's feet. Malcolm had left earlier to tend to his goats, promising to return. Ezekiel understood why his friend hated these chores. Soap irritated his skin. But Ezekiel didn't care, there was nothing to do except play marbles or cricket. His father had warned him about spending so much time down there at that church. Tilly had intervened on his behalf.

"Church never hurts anyone," she had said.

They stood in the church near some chairs stacked in a corner, buckets, and rags in hand. The work finished. It had taken less than an hour. Cleanliness is next to godliness, the Missionary man would often say.

"Come on up to the house and have a glass of lime squash," the Missionary Man said as they walked out of the church. "Monica must be gone by now. She always prepares a big jug of that stuff, and she fills it with sugar," he laughed.

The preacher spoke in a steady outpouring as they walked toward the house. Crickets leaped here and there, chirping as they scurried in the dry grass. Harry Hudson was speaking about power and men and God. Ezekiel thought the man sounded like Malcolm, or did Malcolm sound like the Missionary Man, Ezekiel wondered. Is it possible that one day Malcolm would suddenly stop speaking like everyone else in Jean Anglais and adopt an English accent similar to the Missionary Man's?

At the house, they stood in the kitchen. The preacher kept talking about the power of God and men, as he held the cubes of ice between his fingers, dropping them into the glasses, and pouring the liquid onto the ice. The Missionary Man shifted the focus of the conversation to the power men share with each other. Ezekiel felt confused, had no idea what the preacher meant. He stood looking at the sweaty face of the Missionary Man and a plain question slipped off his tongue. "What kind of power do men share with each other?"

"Come in here, let me show you." Harry Hudson turned, rested his glass on the edge of the kitchen counter and moved down the hallway toward the bedroom. "Bring your drink," he said.

Although Ezekiel had been in the kitchen and living room many times before in the company of Malcolm, he felt uneasy leaving those areas. But he followed the Missionary Man down the hall and into the bedroom. Harry Hudson reached under the bed, pulled out an old steamer trunk, threw open the lid, and reached inside. The stench of camphor filled the air. Harry Hudson dug into the trunk, and retrieved two glossy magazines. He closed the trunk, sat down on the lid, and opened the magazine.

"Come take a look, Ezekiel."

The magazine was filled with pictures, naked male bodies in various poses, men with men, young boys naked with men, erect penises. Ezekiel took the magazine when Harry Hudson handed it to him. He felt trapped, the magazine in one hand and the glass of lime squash in the other. An uncomfortable excitement mesmerized him. He brought the glass up to his mouth and emptied the content in one gulp. The glass almost slipped from his fingers, but he regained his composure and decided to be rid of the glass. He rested the glass on a small table near the bed and flipped a few pages of the magazine. The Missionary Man dropped to his knees, reached out with one hand and grasped Ezekiel's crotch. The boy trembled and dropped the magazine.

"This is your power," Harry Hudson said, looking into Ezekiel's eyes. The man squeezed, and then he began massaging the boy's genitals. "Men share this power," the preacher said. "Women would like to take this from you. Suck you dry."

Ezekiel felt dazed, his body stiffened, his heart pounded in his chest. The only clear thought that came to him said; "run". The boy tried to step back, but the preacher held firm and began reaching out with his other hand.

"Would you like to know how kings get their power?"

Ezekiel looked at the preacher's hand. It hovered, not quite pulling him into an embrace. The back of his hand resembled plucked chicken skin with tiny brown moles. Ezekiel recognized the trick the moment he looked at the preacher's mouth. His pink tongue and yellow crooked teeth looked miserable. As the preacher spoke, droplets of spittle pelted Ezekiel's face. The whiff of the camphor blended with the foul smell of Harry Hudson's breath. Ezekiel recalled the time he had stood near the bed where his grandfather had died, before anyone had the opportunity to clean his final excretion out of his pajamas.

His head throbbed, his mouth felt dry. Ezekiel thought he might vomit. Harry Hudson's voice sounded like a reverberation from some deep place. A sudden jolt of heat struck Ezekiel and he pulled himself erect, eyes open wide. A waking vision claimed his senses. Everything appeared bloody, and the Missionary Man lay curled up on his side, outside in the trees. The leaves around him sprinkled with red drops. Ezekiel shuddered, unable to move or understand.

"This is your power, power to rule, the power to go beyond gold, silver, and other precious things, to enter a new dimension. You could build your power, enough to rule your entire family and this village... let me show you the way." The Missionary Man's voice roused Ezekiel from the momentary trance.

The preacher's breathing came out short, as if he had run up a big hill. He tugged on Ezekiel's pants, getting them down to his knees. But as he reached for the band on Ezekiel's underwear, the boy grabbed at his pants, dragging them back up around his waist. Marbles jangled in his pocket, as he pulled away from Harry Hudson. Ezekiel dashed across the kitchen, and his hand bumped the glass Harry Hudson had left on the edge of the counter. It shattered on the floor. The boy ran out of the house as if fleeing a demon. He looked back once as he ran across the field toward the church and the road. Ezekiel saw Malcolm ambling up the path.

"What you running from, a dog chasing you?" Malcolm laughed.

"I'll kick a dog in the face. Let's go," Ezekiel said.

"I need to talk to Reverend Harry," Malcolm said. "I have a question about Lot and his wife. You remember Sodom and Gomorrah. His wife hardly did anything, but God turned her into a pillar of salt."

"Talk to him another time. Let's go," Ezekiel spoke and glanced over his shoulder.

"Go where?"

"Punky and Raymond always want to start a cricket match. Let's go see."

"I just saw Punky, Raymond, and Delores playing marbles, everyone else watching, they don't want to play cricket. What's wrong with you?"

"Me! Reverend Harry is the one acting kind of..." Ezekiel said.

"What you mean by that?"

"The man tried to grab my thing."

"What thing? What... You are lying on the man. Liar," Malcolm glared at Ezekiel.

"Lying for what?" he asked.

The Missionary Man came out of the house, walking toward them, taking long strides as if he would break into a run.

"Let's go." Ezekiel tugged on Malcolm.

"Boy, you acting like some kind of Tom Fool. I've to talk to Reverend Harry."

"I told you, you're on your own," Ezekiel said.

Malcolm shrugged at Ezekiel, started walking toward the house, and the Missionary Man. Ezekiel stood for a moment, watching Malcolm and Harry Hudson as they narrowed the distance. Ezekiel moved out of view near the back of the church. From the trees, he peeked through a clump of Japonne bushes. He had a clear view of the Missionary Man and Malcolm. No words but he saw their actions. The Missionary Man patted Malcolm on the back, glanced in Ezekiel's direction and they walked toward the house. Ezekiel left his hiding place, moved through the undergrowth and the mulch of dead leaves and brambles.

He moved toward the top road, at the sound of the radio and other babble. Hands in his pocket, he felt the smoothness of the marbles as he rolled them in his palm. Malcolm was speaking the truth. The game was in full swing near Tante Monah's yard. Music blared from the radio. The whole gang moved about, Punky, Raymond, Marsden, Kenneth, and Eamon. They shouted at Ezekiel to join them. He came close and stood watching the action. Delores seemed to be beating everyone, and had most of the marbles. Every toss of the taw, she knocked a mib out of the circle, and she would dance around, laughing and taunting the boys. *No need to get into that,* Ezekiel thought.

A group of younger girls screeched, as they skipped a rope. Nearby, Checklea and Papa LaTouche sat playing Wari. Mondu and two other men looked on, their elbows on their thighs and palms supporting their chins. Ezekiel perused these people and the dry season dirt of Jean Anglais. The incident with the Missionary man had left him weary. His need to get up and go seemed to vanish. Ezekiel thought of a person carrying a load and others piling more weight on as he went by. He saw himself in precisely that way. The abrupt sadness surprised him, he wondered about all the joy in the world. Ezekiel recalled the conversation between his father and Mondu about how money changed people into beasts. He realized that money may not be the only thing to have that effect on people.

He left the marbles in his pocket and he headed home. The boy found his father sharpening a machete and decided to help by pouring the water on the stone. He wanted answers to questions that he was reluctant to ask. John stood over the grindstone, his jaws clamped tight as he sharpened the blade and listened to his son. The boy poured the water onto the stone from a tin cup as he turned the wheel. The sound of the machete on the sandstone made his teeth throb. The boy spoke in fragments as the blade made its characteristic swish against the stone. Ezekiel watched his father and skirted the subject of the Missionary Man and the power that men share. He wanted to stop talking because the skin on his father's face grew tighter with each word. At first, John seemed annoyed, but then he moved away from the stone, stood holding the blade at his side, and looking into his son's eyes. John's lips had become as stiff as a board.

"He's a Buller-man, boy. What some people call a homosexual. He wants to turn you into his woman. Don't tell anyone about this. You hear me? You will repeat this to no one. And stay away from that man and that church."

Ezekiel wondered why adults were loading him with secrets: Mama Viche just before the Break Bone fever, his father right now, and he was sure the Missionary Man expected him to keep that episode a secret, and worst of all, the secret he kept about his father and Monica. He recalled his father saying: "If you feel confused or unsure about anything, talk to me about it, come to me." But as he spoke to his father, he saw something on his father's face that frightened him more than the Missionary Man's groping. John left Ezekiel standing in the yard, took the sharpened machete, and headed next door to the home of Jack and Cora Masanto.

* * *

The idea of going to the house of Jack and Cora Masanto, those people with whom he had been feuding for so long, left a rancid taste on his tongue. John held grudges against Jack and Cora, each of them for a different reason, Jack for not taking part in the strike against Duncan and the other owners of the cane-fields, Cora for being a woman with a big mouth. But he refused to keep this assault by the Missionary Man to himself. He knew pretty much everyone in Jean Anglais referred to Jack Masanto as the blood sucking Loupgarou, but never to his face. John considered the Loupgarou allegation as nonsense. He thought of his feud with Cora and Jack as a thing of substance, a prelude to snatching their piece of land.

The man walked under the branches of the plum tree which had become the pretext of their disputes. The tree grew on the other side of a barbed wire fence, on the piece of land owned by Jack and Cora, but most of the branches on the tree hang over the property line, over John's land, and John claimed most of those plums.

He would pick them, sell them, and give them away to his friends. Cora resented this; they quarreled regularly. They never once brought the boys into their squabbles. Ezekiel and Malcolm remained friends while the parents feuded. John held the secret hope that one day Jack and Cora might move away, to Tivolli where Jack came from and had family, or down to Belmont, where Cora's people owned land.

John approached the house and although he saw movement, he still shouted, "anybody home?"

Cora Masanto answered him with a barrage. "What the hell you want? Spiteful braggart, think you still a young boy? Acting like some--" They were quarreling before John had the opportunity to deliver his suspicions. As always, Cora's husband, Jack, came between them. In a hushed tone, John tried to put into plain words what he had learned about preacher and the boys.

"What we going to do?" Jack asked. "Your son is also--"

"What you mean by We? I'll handle him my way." And John walked away with a lump of coal burning in his gut. *If there remained anything to be known about the Missionary Man, Mama Viche would have the facts,* John thought.

He didn't quite believe in Obeah but he respected the wisdom of the old woman, had seen her counsel at work in the affairs of many of his neighbors. John and Mama Viche shared a clandestine attachment. Everyone in Jean Anglais feared the old woman. John considered himself too cunning to fear an old woman. She spoke to him before he spotted her sitting on a chair near the house.

"I'm not surprised to see you, John. The spirits told me you would come down here this evening."

"The spirits, Mama, or all the noise you heard coming from up the road?"

"The spirits strive in many ways, boy, and their essence is always strong with me right after a full moon."

"What spirits you talking about, Mama? And it's only first quarter."

"I'm talking about the spirits of our ancestors, the deities of Obeah, your mother, your father, grandparents, all the way back to Africa. Of course, you don't believe in… So what you doing here talking about first quarter?"

John smiled and yielded to her vigor. "What you know about the Missionary Man?" Their eyes locked.

The Obeah woman's face looked blank. John searched for reassurance, expecting Mama Viche to say something to soothe his rage. Instead, her words touched him like a gentle, playful pat on his head.

"Troubles ahead, John. I see you carrying that cutlass in your hand. Don't go doing any foolishness. Your visit to Cora and Jack didn't turn out so well, huh, heard the quarrel. Almost everyone around here vex with Jack, calling him a Loupgarou. Jack is an ordinary man. He stayed working in the cane because he needed the money to keep food on his table, and he's afraid of Cora."

"He's no mountain of a man, but still, why would he be afraid of a woman?"

The old woman wrinkled her brows, tilted her head away from John, but remained focused on him out of the corner of one eye.

"Men are afraid of women for many reasons. Don't forget those twin girls from River Road. I see all kinds of changes ahead, all those new motor cars, government building bigger roads, thieving people's land. The spirits showed me blood. Blood will be shed." Mama Viche paused for a moment and looked directly at John. "So tell me, you and Mondu are thick as thieves these days. What are you two planning?"

The question struck John as strange coming from an Obeah woman. He wondered why she avoided talking about the Missionary Man. John didn't tell the old woman what he knew, nor did he answer the question about his conniving with Mondu. There was no need to tell her anything since she knew everything and could talk to spirits. He would often tease the old woman by not sharing information. John left Mama Viche's house with nothing resolved. He looked at the church and the house across the field and thought of going over, laying a few licks on the man, running him out of Jean Anglais. The machete felt heavy in his hand.

He remembered another cutlass feeling this heavy. Some years ago, in the middle of a long dry season, after a disagreement with Duncan Elmo, the man called the mongoose, the man who owned the land in the Valley of Bones, John swore to never take a swing with a blade against a man, never again. He started practicing with a briah pole for self-defense. The situation with the Missionary Man caused him to question this decision.

John and Duncan Elmo found themselves in conflict over the same woman, the true cause of the clash. The rent on the piece of ground in the Valley of Bones turned into an excuse. Joan, the woman who became Ezekiel's mother, wanted to be with John, and Duncan hated the idea. He already had a wife and a child, couldn't do much about that. So he came after John about the rent on the piece of land. No one in Jean Anglais had any money. Nothing grew that year, and everything was expensive as hell in the shops. A pound of salt fish was almost one dollar.

They quarreled for a while, calling names, cursing, mother this, and mother that. Duncan kept pushing John with one hand and sizing him up with his machete half-raised as if about to chop. Suddenly, John broke and dashed for his blade.

The two men came at each other and sparks flew. John's blade touched Duncan, and his shirt flopped open across his chest. It took a long time for Duncan's wound to bleed. The shirt slowly turned red and wet, as the blood flowed down his chest. They grabbed arms, tumbled to the ground, rolled over and over in the dust, with the blades flying. They pushed off and came to their feet, eyes wide and glaring, cutlass raised. John was bleeding also, cut across the back and bruised down one side of his face. Both covered in dirt, blood, and sweat. They looked a fierce mess.

They sliced their blades through the air, going for a killing blow to the neck. But steel met steel, and two pieces of metal fell to the ground. The two men looked at the handles left in their palms and they understood how close they came to ending each others lives. Right there they made a deal for John, or any of the other villagers, to pay the rent on their sections of ground in any way they could. That incident became the starting point of John's influence in Jean Anglais. Everyone wanted to know how he had persuaded the Mongoose to agree to that new arrangement.

John took a deep breath as if sucking those old memories out of the air. For the first time since listening to his son divulge his experience with the Missionary Man, he felt in control of his emotions. He gripped the handle of the machete and swiped at some low hanging branches on the side of the road.

* * *

John was one of Mama Viche's favorite people. The old woman held a conflicting affection for the man. His attitude toward life left her with a sense of compassion and disbelief, his denial of all things unseen for example. Is there anything this man considers sacred? It amazed her that a man could see himself in one way while others saw him in another. Mama Viche saw John as the natural leader in Jean Anglais, and she knew everyone thought of him as such, even the Missionary Man. Although, Duncan Elmo, the mongoose acted as if he controlled the villagers with his field of cane, his nice house, his car and the money he sometimes paid to them. She wished she could counsel John more deeply about all those matters, but other troubles occupied her thoughts.

Alma was growing fast. Those bumps on her chest were pushing against her clothes more and more and she now had hips. Boys were paying more attention to her, and she seemed to be watching them too, especially Ezekiel. Time to progress with her domestic training, John's business would have to wait.

Since John's departure, Mama Viche had barely shifted her weight. The wicker chair had slowed the circulation to the lower part of her body. The chair felt hard against her backside when she shifted and resettled her weight. A slight ache shot down her legs.

The sound of children playing haunted Mama Viche as she looked down through her fruit trees. At times like these, she could see Vernon, Tilly's father, the man she had fallen in love with many years ago. The Obeah woman remembered walking with him one evening. He seemed tense, held her tightly around her waist, oblivious to any inquisitive eyes. When he asked her to be his wife, she almost burst into tears. But when he gave her the rules by which they would live, her joy vanished.

"Within a year, I'll be a headmaster, Sybil. I'll be in control of my own school. I can't have my wife running around with all those Obeah people. It just won't look good," he said. The rest of his words made things even worst, sounded like hollow inquiries: "You will give it up? Be my wife? Make me the happiest man in the world? We'll make a great team." His voice, the feel of his hand, she almost lied to him.

But the religion remained too much a part of her. Her mother had trained her since the time of her puberty to be a Mambo, one of the few who could raise and feed the Loa, charge the spirit of the ancestors to do her bidding. She had to let Vernon go. Sometimes she would watch him from a distance; saw his wife, Florence, and the family they raised. And after all those years, the memories still caused a dull ache.

Now Mama Viche and Vernon Stewart were two of the reigning elders of Jean Anglais, each on their own side of this spiritual and intellectual divide. None of Vernon's children knew what transpired between them so long ago. They no longer spoke to each other and the people who knew of their past love affair were either dead or chose to remain silent.

When Alma came out of the house and sat down in the chair next to her aunt, the old woman smiled and began speaking slowly, formally, in the language of school. Her dialect had completely disappeared. She placed one hand in her pocket as if she meant to retrieve something, but her hand remained hidden in the cloth.

"I need to tell you a few things," she said. "I was more of a mother to your mother than a sister. Your grandmother died the year I turned twenty. Your mother was only thirteen."

"Tante, you don't need to--"

"Yes, I need to."

The girl looked at her aunt. "People talk and I listen well," Alma said.

"So listen now. She was my little sister, and I loved her so much, tried to raise, and protect her. I can't figure out how she got away from me. When Maureen told me she was pregnant with you, I almost killed her. She had no husband. Your father, Mano, nice enough, but he was no mate for Maureen. Pure Grenadian, contented to plant a garden and raise a couple cows, but your mother had read all those books. She knew a great big world awaited her."

Mama Viche glanced at Alma, saw a mixture of doubt and panic rushing across her face, and then the girl smiled.

"People would say things, pretend that they knew you did something to him," Alma said.

"I did nothing to him. We spoke one day, your father was sober, which he seldom was, and he told me there was nothing he could do with a little girl, I should take care of you and I would have no problems from him interfering. I thought someone else may have put a Zoogoo on him, but I looked and saw nothing. Your father is a tortured soul, been that way since the break bone fever took his parents."

"All those years, all that pain and then my mother left him and went to Trinidad," Alma shook her head as if condemning.

"Your mother promised me she would send for you as soon as she got settled. She wrote often, informing me of her progress and all the fun she was having. She sent money and boxes of food and clothes. I wrote back letters of encouragement, but deep down I wanted to say, settle down and quit gallivanting, girl."

An owl hooted from a tree behind the house, a soft wind rustled the leaves and the faint echo of children's voices embraced the occasion.

"I have no idea whatsoever about all those years," Alma said.

"If you listen you will understand."

"Okay, okay, Tante."

"After your mother had been in Trinidad for nine months, I began to wonder if she would ever come back for you. Then her letter came. She had booked passage to Venezuela, where she said work was plentiful and money better. I wrote back telling her how much you missed her, she should come home for a while, and this may not be a good time to go to Venezuela, right after the soldiers overthrew that writer fellow."

"What writer fellow?"

"Romulo Gallego. A Spaniard I met on the wharf in Saint Georges told me about him and I threw it in to scare her. I received one more letter. That was the last time I heard from her."

The noise of the children playing gained force. Alma fidgeted when Mama Viche brought her hand out of her pocket. The old woman held a wrinkled envelope. "This is the last letter your mother wrote me."

She handed the envelope to the girl. Alma took it from her aunt and tugged at the single sheet of yellowing paper. Mama Viche knew the girl had found and read all of the letters a long time ago. Yet, she used this occasion as a prelude to what she really wanted to say. Alma slowly unfolded the sheet of paper and looked at the words.

> Trinidad
> February, 1, 19...
> Dear Sybil,
>
> I know you're right about me coming home, but if I could just spend six months in Venezuela, I would probably be in a better position to take Alma with me. The oil companies have lots of Americans living there, so it shouldn't be much of a problem finding a job doing

something for one of them. I booked passage on a boat run by an East Indian fellow called Singh. He takes people to Venezuela every week. The price is high. His agent said it's because he has to pay off his contacts in the government. I know it's dangerous, but it is so adventurous, and I could make some real money. We leave Thursday, the fifteenth of this month. You should hear from me soon after I get there. Kiss Alma for me, and tell her it won't be long before we are together. Love to both of you. I would like to write more but I'm off to work and the bus should be here any minute.

Your sister,
Maureen

Alma read the letter silently and tears came to her eyes. Just the moment the old woman had waited for. Alma swiped both her palms across her face as if using the letter to wipe her tears.

"Alma?" the old woman said. The girl looked up.

"Tante, can I keep this?" She held up the letter.

"Yes. It's yours."

Alma looked at the letter again, then at the ground. Mama Viche felt like taking the girl in her arms but decided against. Such contact would only diminish the importance of what she wanted to convey.

"I knew it was a bad idea when your mother decided to go to Trinidad," the old woman said. "But she had to get out of here. She was no longer getting along with Mano." Mama Viche paused for a moment. "It was my fault. I should have stayed out of their business. When I didn't hear from her, I knew I had to go find her.

"I booked passage on a cargo vessel for Port of Spain. John's brother, Carl, met me on the wharf. We searched around and found the vessel run by Singh. The government of Trinidad had impounded it. They said Singh was some sort of pirate. They found the body of a dead woman at his house. My heart sank. We rushed to the mortuary to see if it was Maureen. I can still see the face of the dead woman. I praised

God it was not your mother. It made me ashamed and sad because my good fortune was another person's bad luck. Three days later, Singh began to confess. Most of the people who booked passages on his boat to Venezuela never made it there. He robbed and murdered most of them. Some he threw overboard, others he left in the swamp of the Orinoco River to be eaten by varmints. I had to know what happened to your mother. Carl and I went to the jail to see this Boysie Singh, a man with dark brown skin and a very big nose. He couldn't even remember Maureen when I showed him her picture.

"I came home after a month, with the hope she might still be alive, and would write, went to the post office every day. After about six months, I stopped going, lost all hope. It was you and me from then on."

Mama Viche cleared her throat, reached out and squeezed Alma's hand.

"Tante, I want to know more, I want to hear more but it's all so sad."

"I swore to protect you at all cost and that's what I'm going to do. You and your friend Delores, I heard you talking about sex."

Alma sat up strait and looked at her aunt. The old woman continued.

"Don't let her lead you astray. As you grow older, I realize I can't protect you all the time. I'm too old. I see how the boys look at you and how you look back, especially at Ezekiel. Remember, to most boys and men, it's just a conquest and some pleasure. But as a young woman, it's another story. There might be some pleasure in it for you, but it doesn't end there. It's time you learn the many ways of protecting your womanhood. It's important that you pay attention to what I'm about to teach you."

Mama Viche searched Alma's face, trying to discern how she might be taking what was being said. She read understanding and belief on Alma's face, and continued to speak to the girl in a blunt tone.

"Everything comes from the earth. There's power in the earth, a power you will learn to use and share. The spirits of Obeah come from the plants, and the trees, the spirits of natural life. The oldest of these are Mabouya. Mabouya came with the Caribs, even Dambala knows that Mabouya came here first and deserves respect. I've already shown you some of the plants, herbs and berries, told you of their uses, things like Plumbago, Caapi, kudjuruk, Petit Mayoc, and Cat's Blood. What would you use if a woman comes to you with a child in her belly that she wants to throw away?"

"Plumbago, Tante," the girl responded.

"If she wants a child but the man is unwilling?"

"Kudjuruk steeped in rum."

"A man comes to you complaining about his bad luck?"

"Bathe in Caapi, once a day for seven days."

"A person comes to you complaining about their rheumatism?"

"Essence Fragile, Petit Mayoc, Caca Poule, boiled as a tea."

"A woman comes to see you. She wants to be with a man, but is afraid her belly might get big?"

"Bathe with Cochineal, and then brew a tea from sea water and Cochineal. Drink it daily."

"You learning, can you spot those plants? You know where to find them?"

"I go by the shape of the leaves, the color of the flowers, just like you showed me. And sometimes bees and butterflies would lead me to them."

The old woman nodded in agreement. "You already know the chants. There will be a time when I will not be here. You will have to take my place. This is not a thing to be taken lightly. You always charge a little something. People never have any respect for things they get for free. Let me tell you something else. Always listen, and listen well. When people talk, fasten your ears to the words. But most importantly listen for what they don't say."

The old woman looked at the girl sitting with the letter in one hand. She recognized a touch of reluctance, and wondered if the girl might be paying lip service. What does she really think of all this? Will she use any of it? Or will she just forget and allow it to go to waste? The old woman decided to try and solidify things, punctuate all of it with a measure of harsh reality.

"What I'm about to say to you is for you alone. You can't repeat it to anyone. This is not gossip. It's a trust. If the trust is ever broken, you will lose. It will come back on you hard. There's no forgiveness. All you do, you do with women and children in mind. They will come to you for childbirth or family matters. Not many men will come to you. And when they do come, they come for personal reasons."

The old woman drew her index finger across the air as if to underline her warning.

"A young girl came to me some years back. She was just about your age, with tears in her eyes. Her belly was big. She told me she couldn't have the child. Her mother was dead. Her father was beating her, and sleeping with her. She couldn't have a child by her own father. She hated him, planned to pour a pot of boiling water on him one night as he slept. I told her there are other ways and the police couldn't be involved because she would go to jail.

"I gave her a jar of Plumbago and told her how to use it to throw away the child. Then I told her where to find Oleander, put it in his food. It didn't take long. He died within a month."

The old woman saw accusation on her niece's face.

"You joking right, did you help her to poison him?" A little silence hung between them. "That's murder, Tante."

"No girl. Where there's no law for the protection of the innocent, the law of nature takes over. I only gave her some advice. If a man goes to the store and buys a cutlass, then kills another man with it, the clerk who sold him the cutlass is not responsible. Her father was a beast, a cruel beast. He got what he deserved. People around here still say he was a Loupgarou who got trapped. Cora didn't even thank me. To this day, every time we pass each other, she looks at the ground. She never spoke to me after. After she married Jack, she got even worst. She acted ungrateful, as if I had done some terrible thing to her. Shame is such a powerful creature."

For the second time during the conversation, Mama Viche saw doubt on Alma's face. She wondered if telling the girl about Cora was a bad idea. The old woman had only intended to speak to Alma about her mother, Maureen, but now that she had gone this far.

"Alma, Cora used the Oleander on her father, and we buried him, but she never used the Plumbago. Malcolm is what, about fourteen years old? I get this strange feeling every time I look at his chalky face. I'm divided that she didn't listen to me entirely."

"Tante, Malcolm is a nice boy. None of this was his fault."

"The boy carries the burden inside. In the old times, no one would have allowed him to live."

"Because of his complexion?" Alma drew back on the chair and looked at her aunt.

"No Alma, because of his parentage."

"How's that his fault? I should go see my father, see what sort of memories…see what breed I am."

"You upset about nothing, you not an albino. Leave your father alone. One day he will come to you."

For just a moment the old woman wondered if she should warn her niece about Ezekiel and his hidden gift. She decided to leave that alone, allow it to take its natural course.

* * *

The next day Mano saw his estranged daughter walking up the gap to his house, glancing over her shoulder, acting the same way her mother did all those years ago. He thought of slipping out of the backdoor and hiding in the bush, wondered why he didn't make time for the haircut that Checklea had offered; thought of his filthy clothes and how he must smell. Alma knocked on the door and rushed in the moment he opened it. Mano decided to be calm and gentle with Alma, unlike the way he had handled her mother Maureen. The girl stood there glaring at him the way her mother often did.

"Have a seat," Mano said, pulling the only chair in the kitchen next to his daughter. He looked at the table with a half-used can of coffee, a half bottle of rum and a tin cup. "You need something to drink? I have a bottle of sorrel in the ice box." He opened the box without waiting for an answer, filled a clean cup with the red liquid and handed it to her. Alma took a sip as she sat down in the chair facing her father. Mano moved about the room rearranging things, first the can of coffee, the rum, and then a can of condensed milk. He placed them on a shelf in the corner and turned to face Alma.

"Papa, I need you to speak to me. We can't ignore each other forever," she said. "You are my father and I hardly know you." "I know, I know. You look so much like your mother."

"We need to have a conversation, Papa."

"I may not be as educated as you children nowadays, but I still know about a conversation. We can't have a conversation until you understand. Or else we might just end up in a quarrel."

"Why didn't you go looking for her?"

"You see what I mean?" Mano threw open his palms. "I did. I worked my way to Trinidad on a cargo vessel owned by some friends of Mondu." Mano searched his daughter's face for a reaction.

"The Gulf of Paria, Trinidad, Venezuela, and that crazy murdering, son of a bitch, will always be a part of my regrets." Mano kept looking at Alma. "I found Boysie Singh's boat moored to a dock near a hospital where the Trinidadians treated leprosy. I've no idea why I wanted to see the boat. Felt like burning the thing. At the police station, I told them Maureen was my wife, ask them to lend me a cutlass and give me a few minutes with Singh. The policeman laughed, said many people would like to have a whack at him. Go home, man, go back to Grenada," he said. "She's gone."

"That's it, that's it? You gave up too easy," Alma said.

Mano looked at his daughter, felt the sting of her words, but decided a quarrel with her would do no good. After all the years of them just walking past each other and nodding, he decided to never go back there.

"Finding someone in Trinidad is nothing like walking around Saint Georges or even Grenada and asking people if they saw somebody. The place is big with lots of angry people. Don't think of me as a coward. I had no idea where to start."

"Tell me about her, when she was young. Tante told me some things but I need to see her through your eyes. The way she danced to your drums, the way you both..."

Mano saw his daughter trying to smile.

"Let me tell you." Mano gestured with both palms, brushed his fingers through a shaft of sunlight coming through a hole in the boards of the kitchen. "From the beginning Alma, she was so beautiful. In order to see your mother through my eyes, you first have to see me back then, not this . . ." He slapped his palm to his chest. "The doctors used the words dengue hemorrhagic. Everyone else called it break bone fever. Your grandparents' death became the first heartbreak of my life, and I started drinking rum to bury my sorrow."

Alma glanced around the dingy room, at the flies caught in the cobwebs way up in the corners and the shafts of light with floating dust. She looked as if words would burst out of her mouth.

"Please don't say anything, Alma, just listen to me for a moment. I need to get this off my chest."

Mano moved away from his daughter and stood across the room near the ice box with his head down.

"When your mother came into my life, I thought things might be moving in a pleasant direction. I slowed down on the rum drinking and began taking better care of this house, the land and the two cows my father had left me. But your aunt's objections to our relationship soured things. We started quarreling about the slightest things, and when Maureen became pregnant and started making demands, I lost my temper. In a drunken rage, I told Maureen her pregnancy could have been caused by any man in the village, how was I to know."

Mano looked up and grabbed his skull with both hands, squeezing hard as if to press something out. He released his head, glanced at his daughter sitting in the chair with the cup of sorrel, and he wondered if he hadn't gotten drunk that day many things may have turned out different.

"She never spoke to me after I insulted her. I tried to apologize, offered to marry her; she would have none of it. She gave birth to you, and soon after she moved to Trinidad. I experienced my second heartbreak as I tried to create my own luck, show her that I was worth her while. I sold my two cows and began getting my papers in order to follow her. I thought that if we stayed gone from this village and her sister, things might be easier. One day your aunt came to me with bad news. Maureen had gone missing in Trinidad and she feared the worst."

The last words left Mano's mouth like a whisper. He felt an impulse to take the girl in his arms, but he remained across the room and watched her struggling to hold back tears.

"A few days after I got back from Trinidad, I climbed to the top of Ogoun's Point early one morning, sat there looking east, trying to figure out why fate might be dealing me these wicked blows. The sun rose, slowly out of the sea, casting a yellow light across the houses, the trees, and the vegetation. I looked at the sunrise, and I buried my face in my palms. Tears poured out of me. I thought of the old Africans who had jumped off this mountain and flew back to Africa, wondered what it would feel like to do the same."

Alma looked up at her father. He wondered if he may have said too much about this vulnerable stage in his life. But he found the courage to continue.

"In the next instant, I raised my head out of my palms, stood and looked up at the early light. I knew your mother would not want me to wallow in despair. She was the one who told me, after the death of my parents, that life must be lived. That life must go on in the name of the departed if their time on earth was to have any meaning. She was so wise," he smiled. "Out of nowhere, an idea came to me. Money can be made from harvesting some of these trees and turning them into charcoal. I could use the money to travel, possibly find out what happened to her. But more than two hands would be needed to execute my plan.

"I approached Checklea and Mondu with my idea. We began cutting down trees, dragging them to the flats where we had dug some pits. Before long, we were manufacturing and selling hundreds of bags of charcoal to people all over Grenada, and sharing the money. John joined us by cutting grass to cover the pits and helping with the tin drums of rainwater for dousing the coal. Everyone made money."

Mano shrugged his shoulders and Alma looked at him as if she might say something.

"Before long, the side of the mountain facing Jean Anglais became treeless, and rainwater began washing the dirt off the side of the hill, exposing those big boulders. One rainy season, several of them rolled off the mountain, missed all the houses and came to rest down on the flats. The government sent men to look into the situation and it was determined that by cutting down the trees, the mountainside had become destabilized. No more cutting down trees on Crown Land, no more denuding the mountainside. But we continued anyhow."

"You guys were bold, not listening." Alma said.

"It was all about the money. Anyhow, a big row developed, about the safety of people's homes. All the blame fell on me, although John and the others had reaped the benefits of my idea. I said nothing and gave my self up to the police after hiding for awhile. The lawyer I hired took all my money just to tell me I was in big trouble. No one came to my defense. I was sentenced to one year in prison. When I came back home, there was talk of moving the business to another patch of woods further from the slopes, but too much guilt lingered between us."

"This is all so sad, Papa. I've many questions, but I need to go. Tante might get suspicious and start asking all kinds of questions. I don't want to start lying to her."

"So what are we going to do the next time we meet on the road?"

"Let's leave things as they are. Don't worry. I'll come by every chance I get."

"Your mother often said those exact words to me."

Alma stood, took two steps and threw her arms around her father's neck. Mano felt the strength of her grip pressing on him and the beating of her heart. It had been a long time since another human had hugged him. As she eased out of the embrace and started moving toward the door, he felt hopeful. A multitude of questions confronted his feelings. Why now after so long? What kind of a man disregards his only child? He saw the visit from his daughter as an opportunity for change. Mano glanced at the bottle of rum sitting on the edge of the shelf.

* * *

The idea that he knew he was a man and all the other men around Jean Anglais chose to ignore that fact made Ezekiel angry. He came home from school to a group of them in work clothes with forks and cutlasses at the ready under the plum tree in his parent's yard. They continued a steady rant about the virtues of the West Indian Federation, about T.A. Marryshow, Eric Williams, and Alexander Bustamante, some of the lead architects of the new scheme of Caribbean authority. The men spoke as if they knew all the ins and outs of inter-island politics. He knew once they got tired of talking politics, the topics of discussion would switch the state of affairs in Jean Anglais, about Jack, Cosmus and other bits. Ezekiel wanted to hear more about all that boiled in their guts. He knew the talk would run wild the moment they started drinking rum. Only one man would remain silent, Mondu the stutterer. The other men often teased him about tripping over his tongue and chewing on his words for too long.

John came out of the house carrying a paper sack, handed it to Mondu, and looked at Ezekiel as he tried to slink toward the front door of the house with his bag of books clutched in his armpit. "Christ boy! You broke the handle on that blasted bag again?" John shouted. Ezekiel stopped and looked at his father. The other men ignored the altercation between father and son. The broken strap dangled at Ezekiel's side like a dead snake. A tussle with Malcolm had broken the strap. Now he would have to find a way to duck out of this fix if he wanted to join the men. They would be headed to the Valley of Bones to tend a piece of land that his father would cultivate with corn and pigeon peas.

"Daddy, can I come, can I? Tilly will repair the handle for me," Ezekiel pleaded with his father.

Small beads of perspiration trickled down his forehead. Khaki shorts and blue shirt, standard school uniform, the garments stuck to his skin. Ezekiel beamed with anticipation. "Go ask Tilly. She might have work for you to do," John said.

Ezekiel sought Tilly's permission and noticed how quickly she agreed, even decided to mend the strap on the bag. The boy changed out of his school clothes, dashed out of the house, and caught up with the men a short distance up the road. Mondu, John's closest friend, handed Ezekiel the paper bag with the bottle of rum. The boy smiled at this task when Mondu handed him the paper bag and the container of water. He accepted this responsibility with pride.

"You in charge of that now, pass it around now and then, but not too often. We can't fork the land if we drunk," John said.

"What you talking about? I forked a piece of ground once when only the fork held me up," Checklea said.

"Is that the time you put the fork through your foot?" John asked.

"Is that; is that before or after Marchal?" Mondu teased.

The men broke into laughter, Checklea grumbled.

At the plot of land, two other men were already there, working the soil near the Julie mango tree. They all exchanged pleasantries and began the assault on the land. The boy sat under the mango tree with the bottle of rum and the water. His mixed feelings about this place they called the Valley of Bones always made his mind wonder. He loved this place in the sunshine, but the accounts about the fate of ancestors murdered, and buried in this soil, the blood connection stupefied him. Some people even claimed that they had heard the rattle of chains as they left this place after sunset. Ezekiel wondered what it would take to release these spirits and make them go to a place of tranquility, away from this Valley of Bones.

Ezekiel visualized his father and Monica, on the grass, in the bushes, a short distance from where he sat. These adults, he thought. He watched the men poking at the soil with their tools and he coupled all that to what men do with women. Turn them under, plant that seeds, watch it grow in their belly. The boy doodled in the dirt with a stick as he watched the men performing this ritual with the land.

His considerations on this place and the men before him felt like a rubber band. The valley looked as though a giant carrying a big bag of food came at lunch time and needed a place to eat. So he swept everything aside with one motion of his hand; place looked like a big plate decorated with clumps of greens. On two thirds of the valley, Duncan Elmo and his partners cultivated sugar cane. On what remained, farmers from Jean Anglais cultivated plots of corn, pigeon peas, sweet potatoes, pumpkins, and eddoes. These same men harvested the sugarcane for Duncan Elmo, the mongoose.

They lived in balance with the money from the cane to supplement their harvest from the soil. The plots were separated by black-sage bushes and mango trees that towered above cow pens that produced the manure for nourishing the crops. Now and then, a cow would get loose and ravage the gardens. But most of what survived the misgivings of storms, rats, and strays, went to feed the families of these men; some produce also reached the market where they were sold for cash.

The sun lost its brilliance, taking on an orange glow in the early evening. It hung there like a ball on a string. Ezekiel took to his duty with a passion, passing the bottle around with a shot glass and a larger milk jug of water. The musky scent of fresh soil mixing with the sugary aroma of the strong rum tickled his nostrils. He felt disappointed because no conversations about Jack, the Missionary Man or Cosmus came up. The next time he passed the bottle around, Checklea asked, "Why don't you have one?"

Ezekiel glanced at his father, saw no reaction, and heard no objection.

"Don't worry about him," Checklea continued. "Have one. It's good for worms."

Ezekiel poured a little rum into the shot glass and threw the liquid into his mouth. The rum oozed across his tongue, collided with his tonsils and cascaded down his throat, burning all the way into his gut. He shuddered, went back under the mango tree, and sat listening to the men telling jokes about the anatomy of women. Ezekiel understood the meaning of the jokes, but acted as if he didn't.

A flock of starlings flew over, squawking as they flew to their nesting place after a day of raiding the fields. Ezekiel thought of Cosmus and wondered if he saw the world in the same way as other men. What does he think of women, does he feel jealous of birds, and do sunsets make him sad?

A small voice inside Ezekiel's head began teasing: "Have another. Go ahead, have another." This time, he hid behind the mango tree and had a big one. His tongue went numb, as the rum lingered in his mouth. He swallowed, and the burn flowed through his body all the way to the tip of his toes. The warmth turned into an inner chill that strived to escape through his pores.

Ezekiel offered another shots to the men, hid behind the mango tree, and threw down a shot the way he saw the men do. This time, the rum went down smoothly, with a sweet aftertaste. He put the cork back into the bottle and sat down facing the men. They seemed far away, and then close, moving slowly, as they plunged their forks into the soil. The men appeared to split and he closed his eyes. Everything spun like a merry-go-round. He opened his eyes and the sun exploded. The colors filled the evening sky: shades of yellowish red, chunks of bluish yellow and large patches of deep flaming red, swirling into black strips surrounded by ribbons of blue meandering across the sky. He struggled to control this sight, and then he realized he couldn't hear, but then he heard something that sounded like thunder.

"Ezekiel, what the hell is wrong with you? Pass the bottle." John's voice jolted him.

Ezekiel stood and took a step; his feet felt yards too long and pounds too heavy. The boy surprised himself with the control he mustered to make the rounds. On his way back across the turned-up dirt, he stumbled and fell, almost smashing the bottle against a rock. The fresh warm soil felt good. Ezekiel remained there for a moment before rising to his feet. No paid attention to him. The boy hid behind the tree and took another shot. This one tasted like sugar. Ezekiel sat with his back against the rough bark of the mango tree. The evening's vigor still danced across his eyeballs. The boy shut his eyes and slid into darkness.

A vague combination of events brought him back, sounded far away, calling his name, but feet moving nearby. "Ezekiel, Ezekiel. He's drunk as a fish," a voice said and indistinct laughter clouted his ears.

"Leave him. I'm not going to carry him," another voice said.

Ezekiel ventured toward semi-consciousness as his stomach lurched and bile touched the back of his throat. He swallowed and kept it down. Tears ran down his cheeks. "Don't leave me," he begged. He stood, staggered and fell. The boy remained on the ground and surrendered to the darkness again. It could have been an hour, a minute, or seconds, Ezekiel had no idea. The sound came out of the bushes, moving toward him. Rough hands lifted him, onto sweat-soaked shoulders and carried him away like a bundle of cane.

As Checklea carried Ezekiel into the house, the boy could hear Tilly's voice. "What happened to him?"

"He drank some of the rum," John said.

"What's wrong with you? You allowed the boy to drink rum? Jesus John."

Ezekiel could hear Checklea escaping from Tilly's anger as the door slammed.

"No one allowed him to do anything."

"You might as well give him a cutlass and throw him into the cane already."

"I was cutting cane and drinking rum at his age. He'll be fine. He'll sleep it off."

Ezekiel tried to sleep, but the room refused to remain still. He thought if he could place one appendage on the floor the motion would stop. Reaching out, he placed a palm on the floor and the room came to an abrupt halt. But immediately Ezekiel's situation changed to a place with men groaning, cussing and coughing with the occasional burst of laughter. Although he had never been to this place, he recognized it, the prison at Richmond Hill. Cosmus LaTouche and Jack Masanto stood in a narrow concrete space discussing something about a Bible and a razor blade. The revelation ended and he assented to a dead sleep.

The next day, it rained hard, preventing Ezekiel and Lloyd from going to school. The smell of food made him queasy. A mixture of amusement and contempt remained on Tilly's face. Ezekiel hid from her gaze. A little after midday, the rain diminished; Ezekiel lay curled in a corner of his bed, listening to John and Tilly discussing the virtues of pleasure and pain, how they informed us that we are still alive. He folded his arms across his stomach the moment he heard Checklea and Tilly moving across the room to open the door.

"Geneva asked me to bring home a head of cabbage. She gave me some money," Checklea spoke, as he came into the house.

"Don't worry about the money," Tilly said.

"John," Checklea said, "We did some serious work yesterday. This Maroon habit is a powerful thing."

"I know what you mean. That ground is soaking up the rain right now. I'll sow the seeds tomorrow."

"For sure, for sure," Checklea said. "Let me know if you need help. It might be a little muddy, but what the hell."

"Ezekiel is in there," Tilly said. "That's why you came, isn't it?"

Ezekiel took in the conversation. He anticipated Checklea's head appearing around the partition. Rolling into a ball, he turned his face to the wall.

"What you hiding from? The next time you get drunk out there, I'm going to leave you," Checklea said. "You vomited all over me on the way home last night."

Ezekiel turned again and faced Checklea. The man stood there, next to the partition, a bemused grin on his face.

"You told me to have one," Ezekiel said.

"I didn't tell you to get drunk. A man must know his limits."

John's voice came from the other room. "At your age, that rum is going to stunt your growth, mark my words, midget for sure."

"He's already a midget, got his height from his mother," Checklea said as he moved back into the adjoining.

Tilly laughed, and Ezekiel's younger brother Lloyd laughed with her as if he understood.

"Take two heads, and say hello to Geneva," Tilly said.

Ezekiel rested in the bed and he recalled the story of Checklea before and after Marchal. His father had told him about Checklea and the people of Jean Anglais coming to his defense. John had no qualms about telling his eldest son stories about the people and the village. Ezekiel contemplated the particulars of the old Checklea and this nice quiet man, had digested all the details and came to a conclusion: the old Checklea wouldn't have carried him home last night, and come here this morning to see about him, laugh at him, and cheer him up with humor?

The old Checklea, a rough, rum drinking womanizer who would get drunk, stay out all night, beat his wife and ill-treat his children with little cause. Checklea's reign of terror ended one night, near Marchal's rum-shop and dry goods. Checklea had the habit of singing when he got drunk. He especially favored the Nat King Cole's song, "*Stay as Sweet as You Are*" off-key, baritone that sounded like the yowl of a dog. Ezekiel remembered his father using those exact words.

One night, after drinking and visiting his girlfriend down in the Mang, Checklea came up through Belmont after midnight. Everybody already asleep, Marchal's shop closed. The shopkeeper must have been aggravated by Checklea for disturbing his sleep. The man fired a single bullet, which struck Checklea in the head. He claimed he caught Checklea breaking into his shop. No one believed him. Checklea was a brute, but no thief.

The grown men of Jean Anglais took up their cutlass to avenge their friend. The boys picked up rocks and scattered into the bush, down through the shortcut. The women led the way to Marchal's shop. Checklea's wife and children joined the mob. The young boys of Jean Anglais arrived first and began pelting the shop with rocks, breaking windows and running into the bush. Marchal began firing his gun into the air. The police came and surrounded the shop. When the men and women of Jean Anglais arrived the police had already taken Marchal into protective custody. No charges for vandalizing the shop were lodged.

A doctor removed the bullet from Checklea's skull, and they nursed him back to health, but his personality changed: He became calm, no loud quarrels came from his house anymore, and his wife and children seemed happier. Most people from Jean Anglais stopped going to Marchal's shop. And to this day, Marchal will never turn his back on anyone from Jean Anglais. If he noticed a person from Jean Anglais walking down the same side of the road as him, he would cross to the other side. Some people suggested Checklea's wife, Geneva, should have thanked Marchal. Ezckiel recalled his father telling the story and a question came to him that he should not have voiced. "If the people of Jean Anglais have such might, why are they allowing Cosmus to rot in prison?"

His father's face had scrunched up with anger, and he shouted at Ezekiel. "You stay out of that. Mind your own business, you hear me?"

Ezekiel rested in the bed, thinking about the many circumstances that force people and places to transform.

* * *

Harry Hudson came to see John Augustine around noon one Sunday. He had visited the home of John and Tilly only on rare occasions. Tilly saw him coming, called John and pointed. She instructed Lloyd and Ezekiel to go into the house and don't come out, then she stood in the yard with both hands on her hips. John went past Tilly with his machete in hand, and met the Missionary Man halfway.

The preacher looked tired, as if he hadn't slept in days. His bare feet on the ground made him look crazy. The gray pants and short-sleeved white shirt he wore made him appear sallow.

"What you want here, man?" John looked into Harry Hudson's eyes.

"No one came to church today, stood in an empty church and preached to the walls. So I came to see you. You are the big-one, the boss around here."

They stood glaring at each other, waiting.

"I've nothing to say to you. You interfere with people's children, molesting boys. Get off my land before I've to…" John raised his machete, took two steps toward the preacher.

The Missionary Man shifted his weight from one foot to the other. He inhaled, and exhaled, and then he grunted and gulped as if choking back tears.

"John, you think you know all about it. You strut around here like the cock of the walk. Everybody trust and admire you. I don't know what for. But I think you are the only one who can appreciate my demons, because you know them, know them well."

John looked at the Missionary Man. "What the hell you talking about? Demons my ass, what, what…"

"They ride you too." The Missionary Man smiled. "The minions of Satan: La Diablesse, Loupgaroux, Mama Malady, all the deities of Obeah, nothing, nothing compares to the evil that pursue you and me.

We can't hide, we can't lock the doors. Our demons are in here." Harry Hudson slammed his closed fist against his chest.

The man is rum soaked, John thought. What the hell is he talking about? Foolish shit. John fixed his stare into the pupils of the Missionary Man as the slice of truth in what the man was saying soaked in. He doubled up his left fist and moved closer to Harry Hudson, the machete clutched and ready in his other hand. This fool is not drunk, John thought, just a lunatic. What the hell is he doing in my yard talking shit? If he mentions one word about Monica, I'll cut his head off and smash his ugly face flat.

"You want to chop me up, huh?" Harry Hudson asked. "Go ahead, John. Two strikes of the blade and it'll be all over. Cut me down. You know we are one and the same. Only the grace of God can help us out of the snare of Satan. Pray, John, learn to pray."

"What the hell for, to an old white man with a long white beard? Old white men think they own the whole fucking world. You people turned God into a slave master. Look at you, blaming your nastiness on the devil. Even the devil isn't safe."

The two men stood, glaring at each other, and then the Missionary Man began shaking his head. He made a move toward John as if he would continue to speak. John gripped the handle of the machete and with his other hand he pointed down the gap. "Go, start running, man, before I loose my temper." John turned his back on the man.

"You running, John? You can run but you can't hide," the Missionary Man said and started walking away.

"Crazy ass white man, get away from here, move," John shouted. He noticed Tilly staring at the Missionary Man with confusion on her face, and he had no idea what to make of it.

"What did he mean by all that?" she asked.

"I'm not in his head. I don't know... What you want me to do?" John yelled at Tilly. "Be nice to him? Invite him in for food? I told you what he is, what he tried to do to Ezekiel."

"There's something else going on here besides__ He was speaking to you as if..." Tilly hesitated and wiped one hand over her face. "The idea of that man talking about God. He belongs in the deepest part of hell."

John shuddered at Tilly's words and spat out a mouthful of profanities to cover his discomfort. The accusations of the Missionary Man burdened him. What's going on in his blasted head? Why here? Why me? John walked past Tilly, went up the path to the top road, wondering if Mondu had any rum. Cora Masanto sat on her front porch listening, a sly sneer crept across her face. John swiped his cutlass at the plum tree, hacking off a branch, laden with fruits. Rumors of the row between John and the Missionary Man would now spread all over Jean Anglais.

* * *

Ezekiel woke that morning with crickets in stomach. His thoughts centered on John and Monica. Since they had abruptly stopped meeting almost a year ago, he had developed new strategies to satisfy his obsession. He began lurking in certain spots near the road where people would stop to gossip. Not quite the same as gawking at John and Monica, but it still held an intriguing quality. On his way to find Malcolm, Ezekiel spotted Alma and Delores, walking toward the water pipe with buckets in hand. He found a spot in the trees just off the road and waited. Alma placed the bucket on the concrete slab, turned the knob and the water dribbled into the bucket, low pressure in the dry season.

"Ezekiel is kind of cute and smart," Alma said, speaking above the noise of the water falling into the bucket.

"Yeah, I guess so. He's all right, but he's too shy, and always loafing with that Malcolm," Delores said. "Did you know they taught me how to play marbles?"

"He could make a good husband," Alma said. "With a little training, how to do dishes, wash clothes and cook," they both giggled.

"None of those boys can give me what I need," Delores said. "But you don't know anything about that, do you? Your Tante keeps you locked up like some kind of Rapunzel."

"Hey, no one keeps me locked up. I know what I want and I'll have it. But I need a husband first."

"Husband, what for? Man stinking up the place, beating you when he drinks rum or gets vex. Who needs…?" Delores grabbed Alma's overflowing bucket from under the spigot and replaced it with her bucket.

"Girl, I don't know about you. You always have to win? If you let those boys win now and then, they might be kind to you." Alma said.

"Let them win? Why should I? They are after one thing. I don't need them to be nice to them."

"Girl, you full of spite, where did you get that from?"

Delores smiled at Alma as the water clattered into her bucket. "Take Ezekiel for instance," Delores said. "If he isn't some kind of fairy, I can have him just like that," she snapped her fingers.

"Girl, you sound nasty, and leave Ezekiel out of this," Alma said.

"Me, nasty? Nah, just natural." The girls looked at each other and laughed. "I'm joking about Ezekiel." Delores said. They both picked up the buckets. "I know you have a yen for him." The two girls moved away from the standpipe, out of Ezekiel's hearing.

He found Malcolm and couldn't wait to relate what he'd overheard. Malcolm laughed and shook his head as Ezekiel spoke about what the girls had said, and then Malcolm started:

"If a cucumber is bitter, throw it away," Malcolm said. *"There are briars in the road, turn aside from them. This is enough. Do not add, and why were such things made in the first place?"*

"I'm trying to tell you about the girls and all you can do is spout stuff by a dead Roman."

"Why you keep calling him the dead Roman? His name is Marcus Aurelius. You understand his words?"

"Well, sort of. At least he is speaking about things we know, cucumber and briar. We have both of those here in Jean Anglais."

"One of these days you might eavesdrop on something you don't want to hear."

"There's nothing I don't want to hear or know," Ezekiel said.

"Easy to say." Malcolm pointed one finger at Ezekiel. "You'll see. Just keep it up."

It didn't take Ezekiel long to appreciate Malcolm's warning. First, a centipede crawled up his shorts and bit him. The moment the swelling went down, he went right back to his tricks. He would crawl under houses and lay still, listening to women, as they patched their husbands' old pants or shirt, talking about sexual capers. Who's responsible for raising a child that isn't his, who got a six for a nine? The boy immersed himself in the hidden sex lives of the adults. Even the sting of red ants and chiggers in the dirt under the houses didn't hold him back. Malcolm took no part in this voyeurism.

One night, after listening to the radio, the other villagers had retired to their houses. Ezekiel found himself behind Tante Monah's house with his eyes pressed up against a crack in the wall. Inside, Tante Monah and Delores were waltzing to some soft music oozing from the radio, both of them naked to the waist. As he drifted into the thrill, a rough hand grabbed him from behind and pushed. Ezekiel fell to the ground. Without looking back, he scrambled to his feet and ran.

When he tried to tell Malcolm what had happened behind Tante Monah's house, Malcolm looked at him and laughed: night runs till day catches it," he said.

"What you mean by that?"

"No sin goes unpunished." Malcolm threw his palms wide open. *"So what is left worth living for?"* he continued. *"This alone: Goodness in action, speech that cannot deceive, and a disposition glad of whatever comes."*

Ezekiel thought of Malcolm's recitation and none of it held any meaning for him.

That same day, Ezekiel heard Cora, Malcolm's mother, shouting and howling like a dog. Her whipping on Malcolm could be heard from way up the road. Ezekiel wondered if a mistake had been made and Malcolm was paying the price for what had happened behind Tante Monah's house.

As Ezekiel walked with his father to the Valley of Bones the next morning, the cool, delicate drizzle signaled the onset of the rainy season. He marveled at the change of seasons, the way things went from brown to green, and yellow and blue and back to brown. He knew, if it rained long enough, he would not have to carry water for a few days. On the other hand, the rain would soak through his straw hat, drenching his clothes, making him shiver to the bones.

The boy carried a milk bucket in one hand, and a crocus sack in the other. He would use the sack to carry home the ripe mangoes which fell out of the trees onto the cow pen at this time of the year. Some of the fruits would be caked in fresh cow shit, but a good washing would make them clean again. No one would know.

Ezekiel walked beside his father, annoyed at his bad luck of the last few days. It's Saturday, why does it have to rain? Any school day would be fine. Here is this rain, messing up a day meant for playing.

"This rain would do the corn we planted last week some good," John said to his son as if he could read his thoughts.

"The garden needs it, Daddy," Ezekiel agreed.

John grunted and nodded. They walked on up the mountainside in the slight drizzle. The wind held the rain like a shy lover, releasing only small droplets. At any moment, a deluge could fall, but they continued toward their destination, undaunted.

Ezekiel wondered if Tilly had already spoken to his father. Tante Monah had told Tilly about his lurking under her bedroom window. The woman had come down the path from the top road, taking long determined strides, wearing that customary apron across the front of her dress. He wished he could strike her dumb or dead. Monah spurned Ezekiel and the women spoke in a quiet tone. When they were through, and Tante Monah was halfway back to the top road, Tilly came at Ezekiel. "You are a little Macco, a Peeping Tom, huh?" She slapped his face hard. Ezekiel recalled the sting of her palm.

First the Missionary Man, and then getting caught ogling Tante Monah and Delores, things seems to be piling up, he thought, and on top of that, the sudden disappearance of Tante Monah's radio. The air seemed to blow around him in an unusual way, and people seemed a little peculiar, with all the rumors floating around the village about what may have happened to the radio, and people no longer going to the Missionary Man's church. Ezekiel thought of the whole situation in Jean Anglais as one big knot.

He returned from Mabimbay carrying the pail of milk and the sack of mangoes. His father had remained to cut grass for the cows. It was around eight o'clock and everybody should have been awake and stirring, but Ezekiel saw no one on the road. It was as if everyone in Jean Anglais picked up and left or decided to sleep late. He reached the house and stood for a moment wondering: Where did Tilly and Lloyd go? And then he heard voices from somewhere down the road. He placed the milk on a shelf, dumped the sack of mangoes in a corner and followed the voices.

A group of people stood near the church. Ezekiel saw Malcolm first. Malcolm came rushing toward Ezekiel. His face looked like a paper mask, his eyes red as burning coal. He moved as if about to leap out of his skin.

"His neck, Ezekiel, his neck, someone cut it bad. Somebody killed Reverend Harry. Somebody killed him."

"Malcolm, you like playing stupid tricks. Stop that. What's wrong with you?"

Malcolm looked as if on the brink of laughter or tears. Ezekiel pushed past his friend and moved to the edge of the trees on the side of the road. The body lay curled up in the clearing. Ezekiel saw the shoes first, then the rest of the body with no head. It was exactly like the waking vision he had seen. He closed his eyes and turned away. He felt trapped in a liquid dream, thought of swimming to wake up, but realized he was already awake. As he opened his eyes, he saw Malcolm standing beside him, moving his head from left to right as if to deny the obvious.

Ezekiel began searching the crowd for Tilly. He found her holding Lloyd's hand. She looked small as if she stood further than the few steps away. When he blinked, she came back into focus, and their eyes met. Ezekiel knew what she was thinking. A dazed expression distorted her features. It was all there, on her face like a misplaced morsel of food. Ezekiel started walking toward Tilly. When he looked into her eyes, it bolstered his belief that his father had decapitated the Missionary Man.

* * *

The day they found the body of the Missionary Man, Inspector Dennis Didderot came to Jean Anglais with three other officers in a wagon, POLICE stenciled in white on each side. His eyes were like burnished steel, reflecting the impression of greedy. The inspector came from a family of colonials who had lived on Grenada for many generations. They were once members of the Gerondists, contemporaries of the Jacobins during the French Revolution, escaping persecution, seeking fortune, spreading misery. His family was one of the few of French ancestry to remain on the island of Grenada through many upheavals. They had not run off to Trinidad like so many others, not even after Fedon's Rebellion and the mistrust of everything French.

That was the kind of history taught by Tilly's father, Vernon Stewart, the ex-headmaster of the primary school in Saint Georges. He called his lectures maintaining a perspective on white Grenadians. The old man was perhaps the only person who knew that the village was named after the maternal great, great grandfather of Dennis Didderot.

The Policeman made his way through the crowd surrounding the body. People stood in the morning sun gazing at the corpse of the Missionary Man. Preacher's neck completely severed. Many blows with a dull blade, the inspector thought. A marionette with cut strings, head separated, skewed to one side in a puddle of blood, eyes wide open, mouth ajar, as if in some final protest. Flies hummed and circled. He processed the body and then he noticed the rest of the scene: the corpse rested in a circle of sprinkled herbs. Bugger-man, scuffed in the dirt with a stick, using the preacher's blood as ink

After checking the balance of the surroundings for evidence, Inspector Didderot gave the order to remove the body and he continued his investigation at the dead man's church and house. He spent half the morning between the two places, searching through trunks, drawers, and closets. The policeman found the pornographic magazines. First, he questioned the preacher's housekeeper, Monica, John's former girlfriend. Monica imparted the bare essentials. The inspector concluded the preacher's death had nothing to do with robbery. He was left with a curious feeling: the house, the fellow called Cosmus up in Richmond Hill, the drowned girl, and now this preacher fellow. Knowing the history of the place and his family connection, the inspector struggled to link these random events, as if the land could be responsible. Around noon, he walked down the road to the house of the Obeah woman, Mama Viche. They spoke outside, at the foot of her stairs, standing face to face.

"Duncan Elmo told me you are the person with your finger on the pulse of this village," he said to the woman.

"Duncan Elmo? He's not a part of this village. They cut his cane, he pays them precious little and then he takes that back as rent on his land. You know what we call him? The mongoose, he sneaks in now and then to grab a pullet, and he's gone."

"Certain things about this murder point to Obeah," the Inspector said.

"You born and raised here, young Didderot. You know this island and her people. They should be training you to be an administrator rather than the chief of police. The Missionary Man got killed and the finger points at Obeah. Why would the worshipers of Dambala want to kill that pitiful soul, especially with a cutlass?"

The Inspector smiled at the woman. She looked at him like a snake ready to swallow a young frog.

"There is nothing I can tell you about the herb," she continued. "I'll say this. If anyone in Obeah wanted the Missionary Man dead, they wouldn't have to use a cutlass. A few crushed seeds of Jumbie Beads in a glass of ginger beer or sorrel would have done the trick."

"I understand what you are saying, Sybil. But tell me, how did you know I wanted to discuss the herb found around his body?"

Mama Viche's face softened as if she would smile. "The bush has eyes and ears, young Didderot, and sometimes even mouths. He who talks about his secrets on the side of the road should first search the bushes. If you must walk on the back of a snake, move from the tail to the head."

Despite his awareness of accountability toward the village, Inspector Didderot knew that the deed was performed by human hands and finding the person or persons responsible for the murder of Harry Hudson would be no easy task. Inquiries would be answered in ways similar to Mama Viche's and Monica's: adages, parables, proverbs, and analogies, all designed to conceal.

As he conducted the investigation, and a profile of the dead man emerged, Inspector Didderot realized he felt no sympathy for the man. Harry Hudson's Will bequeathing his property to Malcolm Masanto seemed unusual. The inspector decided to keep the issue of the Will quiet for the moment. He knew whoever killed the preacher had a definite reason. It disheartened him that he may have to arrest one of these villagers for the murder of this nasty man.

He made a stop at the home of Jack and Cora Masanto, Malcolm's parents. Cora Masanto was a stout woman who always carried a cruel look on her face. Her nose stuck out below darting, little eyes. She corrected her husband in a shrill voice that leaped through her missing front teeth. Twice during the interview, she reprimanded Jack on his conduct in the presence of the inspector, as if speaking to a child. Jack, a short thin man, with a smiling face, seemed to shrug it all off. Malcolm sat watching.

Cora offered to make tea. The policeman declined.

He asked all sorts of questions and made notes of the answers, place emphasis on how Malcolm sat there, stiff as a board, answering questions in monosyllables. Jack Masanto chatted and laughed all through the interview, like a simple man with nothing to hide. When the inspector decided to move on to John and Tilly Augustine's, Jack walked him to the door.

Dennis Didderot asked all of the same questions of John and Tilly. Ezekiel seemed nervous but said nothing about Harry Hudson. The Inspector gauged the situation and came to his conclusions. All the information, when pulled together and unified with his hunches, pointed to one person, and it had nothing to do with the will.

* * *

John saw this situation with the Missionary Man as the perfect time to make his move on the piece of land owned by Jack and Cora. He planned to be rid of Jack and Cora, and own their piece of land, and he would use the policeman to do it. He recognized the risks, but he told himself, in this world, everything worthwhile carries some risks.

The man returned early from his morning routine in the Valley of Bones. He told Tilly he had to go into town on some business at the bank. John changed out of his work clothes, put on a pair of gray slacks, a pair of black loafers and a cream-colored short-sleeved shirt. Thoughts of wearing a tie came to mind but he decided against looking too proper. Out of the house and down the road to the bus stop, he moved with haste.

John came to the spot where the church stood. Although he had no belief in God, he couldn't help but wonder if all of this was godsend, to help him attain his dream of adding to his piece of land. He told himself that, when opportunities present themselves, one should take full advantage.

The man moved through the shadows of breadfruit trees, and coconut palms, glanced at the wilted strip of guinea grass lining the path up to Duncan Elmo's house. John shook his head and smiled at the animosity that once existed between him and Duncan. In some ways, John admired the man. In others, he detested him. "Duncan the braggart" people would call him behind his back, Duncan the mongoose, because of what he inherited and how he handled his inheritance. Many stories existed about how Duncan's ancestors managed to get hold of the land in the Valley of Bones. Some of the stories told of betrayals and how his people had used Obeah in an evil way.

John's scheme about Jack and Cora's piece of land felt unnerving, but he rehearsed it in broad terms to quiet his thoughts: catch the bus into Saint Georges, speak to Inspector Didderot, don't look or sound too sociable. The man had no ideas about specifics, but he understood the gist of what should be said. Apprehension drove him forward.

A half empty bus came to a stop in front of him. The conductor, a short man with a round smiling face, greeted John as he stepped onto the bus and handed over the fare.

Four other passengers rode the bus into town. John walked down the aisle between the rows of seats. A brown wad of spittle and mucus in the center of the aisle disgusted him. He stepped over the globule and flopped into a seat across from a woman dozing with a fly on her nose. The woman wore a loose-fitting dress. A plain straw hat rested on a thick head of braids. John glanced at her hands folded over a white plastic purse in her lap, hard-working hands with cuticles puffy and raw. He recognized her and thought of saying nothing. Reluctance and memories tugged at him.

"Hey, Rita."

The woman moved, opened her eyes, and the fly darted off her nose. "John, how you doing?"

"I'm doing fine. How's Cosmus?"

"As good as can be expected. I see him most days. He has some freedoms. Most of the prisoners up there can't read or write. He's teaching them, putting some of his own thoughts on paper and starting a small library." Rita pulled back in the seat and looked at John. "Why am I telling you all this? You see him often enough."

"Yeah. I'll try to visit him next month. Hold tight Rita, things will change. Lots of people believe what happened to him was unjust, some of them in high places, big-shots. I bring up his name every time I get the chance."

"Thank you, John. That will make him feel... knowing a man like you is on his side."

They went silent, as if there was nothing left to say. John felt the noise of grinding metal in his jaw and in his joints as the driver jammed the bus into gear. The bus lurched forward. John shifted his weight and settled into the seat.

The voices of the few passengers blended with the creaks and groans of the metal-and-wood beast of burden. It sped past palms, mangoes, and Ugli fruit trees swaying in the warm breeze as it knifed out of the countryside toward Paddock. At Tanteen, near the Botanical Garden, the bus came to a stop. Rita stood and tapped John on one shoulder as she moved to get off. John acknowledged the gestures by responding with a slight wave.

He looked at the men working on the new electric and telephone wires. The poles stood straight in the bright sunshine, as if marching toward Belmont. Progress, they called all this. They troubled him, those men in spiked boots, climbing the wooden poles as if they were some special breed, ascending to shake the hand of God.

The bus entered the Carenage, past iron ships and wooden vessels delivering cargo. Some stevedores unloading a shipment of cement looked like ghosts, caked in the fine gray dust. Motor wheezed as the driver shifted gears through the tight turns through the horseshoe harbor, past the treasury, the library and through the dark of Sendal Tunnel, onto the Esplanade.

John hopped off the bus, and walked slowly up Halifax Street, past the Syrian stores filled with cheap merchandise, past the old red brick structures with tile roofs, mixed in with the newer wooden frame houses covered with galvanized tin, painted bright reds, pasture greens, and yellows. At the top of the hill, near Barclay's Bank and Palmer School, where the policeman directed traffic, John turned right and headed up Church Street to the police station.

He now had his plan formulated, knew what he would say and how he would say it. Small beads of perspiration broke out under his shirt, crawling down his skin like ants. When he came into the station, he saw the Inspector far across the room, away from the counter that separated the waiting area from the rest of the station. The Inspector appeared happy to see John and ushered him into a small room. They sat down at a desk across from each other and the policeman took out a note pad and pen.

"Your name is John Augustine. You live in Jean Anglais." The Inspector spoke with no intimation of a question.

"Yes, Inspector, that's my name. You know me, where I live."

"Just for the record, John, now tell me what you know about the murder."

John took a quiet, deep breath, he felt his chest expand. He looked into the Inspector's eyes. The bottomless gray of his eyes disturbed John. Take your time. Be careful, he told himself. But he looked away right after the second word left his lips.

"Two days before the man was killed."

"You mean Harry Hudson," the inspector interrupted.

"Yeah that's who I mean. I was on my way up to the Valley of Bones, to cut a bundle of grass for my cattle." Slow down, a small voice whispered inside John's head. You already said too much. "I came around the corner just before heading up the hill. Jack was moving his goats and talking to himself when I came up behind him. He was mumbling something about how the man was molesting his son, and how he going to put his cutlass across his neck." John realized he hadn't exhaled since starting his presentation. He inhaled and spoke in a more measured tone. "That's what he said, I heard him."

"Who else heard him?" the Inspector asked, and fixed John with a lizard stare.

"I was alone. I don't know who else heard him."

* * *

After John had left, Dennis Didderot sat in the room shaking his head. His prime suspect had walked into the station and attempted to inform. During the interview at the home of John and Tilly, the boy Ezekiel had sat there looking into thin air, hardly breathing. The policeman knew he should have pushed; try to speak to Ezekiel alone.

He knew John was his man, came to this conclusion based on an incident no one around Belmont and Jean Anglais could forget. About three years before, the manager of the new hotel on Grand Anse Beach, came tearing through Belmont in his car. Near Marchal's shop, the man struck and killed a little girl. "Why was she on the road? Why was she on the road?" He kept repeating those words, acting as if inconvenienced that he would have to wait for the ambulance and the police. John, Lester, and Mondu stood in the crowd gathered around the weeping parents of the child. The driver's apparent lack of remorse over the child he had killed enraged John. John jumped on the man, punched him in the face and stomach, knocking him to the ground. Mondu and a few others had to pull John off of the man.

When the police arrived, they found the man bleeding, his lip split, two teeth knocked out; he was almost unconscious on the ground. John's knuckles bled. They arrested John and let the driver go. The crowd became enraged. They marched to the police station and stood out there for hours until John was released. Afterward, no one mentioned the assault.

Inspector Didderot saw John as the only man with the audacity to take the law into his hands. He decided to approach the investigation from another angle, start with Jack and Cora as a diversion, gather more evidence, let John relax and become careless.

First, Inspector Didderot asked to see Jack Masanto's cutlass and he took it into town. The results of the test on some substance below the handle surprised the Inspector. Two days later he brought Jack in for more questions. Jack claimed the blood found under the handle came from an animal he had helped a friend butcher. The test revealed the blood to be human. A warrant was issued. They arrested Jack Masanto for the murder of the Missionary Man.

* * *

Ezekiel crouched behind a clump of bush near the standpipe waiting to hear the latest gossip from people fetching water. The boy had found a surprising use for his snooping. He came to the understanding that listening to what people say had other advantages besides the amusement of a peeping-tom. Ezekiel had learned to grasp when people were telling the truth or not.

The obsession captivated him entirely, and now that he had discovered its further use, he felt a certain excitement about its possibilities. He saw the actions of his father, the Missionary Man, Jack, and Cosmus, all tangled as one big knot. Ezekiel wondered if such a mess should be taken intact, and if so, could the confusion be settled with the use of a sharp blade. He knew the murder of the Missionary Man had saved him from some serious trouble, and he regret no longer being able to share any of this adventure with Malcolm. Ezekiel realized shadows were piling in on him. Since the murder and Jack's arrest, Malcolm seemed to be far away, unreachable but still close.

Ezekiel felt sure he knew who killed the preacher. Everyone around Jean Anglais began guessing, and provoking each other, about what they knew and what they saw. He heard them as he hid and listened, trying to figure out how all this would boil down. The things he heard sat in his stomach like a stone.

One evening, on a whim, Ezekiel decided to stay out of sight and follow his father to the Valley of Bones, to make sure nothing had rekindled between him and Monica, or to see if he had found another woman. John was picking some of the food planted after the men had helped him with the land. The valley appeared empty. He wondered if his father might be waiting for someone, the way he took his time picking the corn and looking around with expectation. Ezekiel supposed that the spirits that roamed the Valley of Bones should be crawling out soon, but his curiosity outweighed his fears. The boy hid behind the clump of trees and waited. Monica emerged near the edge of the corn and they were quarreling before she reached the spot where John stood stuffing the ears of corn into a bag.

"Did you kill the man?" Monica's neck cranked to one side.

Ezekiel saw his father become frantic, face twisted, jaws stiffened as if biting down on his teeth. John stepped toward Monica with threats in his movements, lips firm as he spoke.

"If I told you who killed the man, what good would that do? Why you here asking dangerous questions? This makes no sense."

Ezekiel thought Monica would recognize and hear the threat in his father's voice, turn and run away, but she stood firm.

"I helped you. You told me what he tried to do to Ezekiel, and I know what he was doing to Malcolm."

"Why didn't you say something, why didn't you do something?"

"Lord, have mercy on me. I should have said something sooner. But everything was so confusing. And just what I feared--"

"He paid you money, so you kept your mouth shut." John lifted his hand as if to slap Monica.

Monica looked at him, didn't flinch. "I didn't know you planned to kill the man. I worked for him, yes, and he paid me good money each month, was going to use that money to get out of this place. Where am I going to find another job, what am I going to do now?"

"If you so sure I killed the man, what you doing here with me? I could kill you too, you stupid woman. You with Lester now, okay, and you know the bad blood between us. Stay away before he gets crazy. Stay away from me, and stop asking foolish questions. You might get the right answer from the wrong man."

"You can't do anything to me, John. I'm the mother of your child. I'm going to tell Lester, sic him on your ass. You'll see. He'll come after you. Watch your back. Watch your back, bad man."

Ezekiel saw his father flail one hand, as if in disgust and walked off across the evening without looking back. Monica's threat didn't seem to worry him. The boy questioned the wicked ways of the world. Now, as he sat recalling all this, hiding in the bushes near the standpipe, Malcolm's words seemed prophetic: "Someday you might hear something you don't want to know." What did Monica mean about the father of her child?

* * *

Jack's trial was short, compared to the cases of other people accused of serious crimes in Grenada. Dennis Didderot watched with dismay. Jack said nothing when they pronounced the sentence on him for the murder of Harry Hudson. The issue of homosexual/pedophilia was discarded by the judge. The inspector had turned that information over to the defense in an attempt to slow things down, and gain more time to investigate.

"This is a murder trial. No evidence of a sexual nature will be allowed. This is not a morality play," the judge admonished the defense lawyer.

Thomas Brand, the black lawyer hired by Cora to defend Jack, had just returned to Grenada after studying law in England. This was his first case. The young lawyer had a face that pleaded for a beard, but he kept it shaved, would itch his chin time and again, leaving the impression of a nervous tic. The judge, in his black robe and powdered wig, appeared to intimidate the young lawyer. Thomas Brand repeatedly pleaded with Jack to help in his defense. Jack smiled and kept muttering about the mercy of charity and offering the last thing he had to give. The lawyer grew more frustrated each day.

* * *

Because of the death sentence, an appeal was automatic, and that didn't take long. The High Court agreed with the sentence. Inspector Didderot experienced some mixed feelings. He felt uncomfortable about the entire course of events and swore to keep his eyes opened and ears to the ground. *A person who got away with murder will always try it again*, he told himself.

When Cora informed him of John's desire to own her piece of land, the entire state of affairs seemed to pivot. The inspector felt irritated that he had allowed himself to be duped by a farmer. The presence of the blood under the handle of the machete still baffled him. He assumed some other person had to be involved, so John became his secondary suspect. Exactly how he intended to get hold of the piece of land perplexed the inspector, since both Cora and her son were still alive. Did he also intend to murder both of them?

One day before Jack's execution, Didderot made a trip to the prison. Weather was overcast. Low hanging clouds slumped over the prison, obscuring his perception as he drove up the hill, creating the illusion that the old buildings floated above the earth. He had visited the cells of condemned men before, but this one had an odd feel so the policeman wanted to be around just in case Jack made a final confession about his accomplice. Jack rested calmly on a narrow canvas cot. He stood when the inspector entered the cell. A roach on the floor scurried into a crevice in the wall, abandoning the crumb of bread it had been gnawing on.

"How do you like my pet?" Jack asked, pointing at the spot where the roach had vanished.

The policeman smiled.

The sound of hammers and saws, putting the finishing touches on the gallows, echoed up from below. Dennis Diddderot stood with his back to the cell door. Jack moved to the gap in the wall facing the yard below.

"By God! They built it fast," Jack said.

"It's ready-made, preassembled; the sections are stored in a shed on the grounds. All they have to do is put it together." The inspector spoke as if talking about a puzzle or some kind of toy.

* * *

Jack knew, by this time tomorrow, all this would be over. Yet he held on to a smidgen of hope. He looked away from the yard and the gallows; his eyes followed a thin corridor of cocoa and nutmeg leaves, toward Westerhall, and Calivigny, where he had spent good times with friends, playing cricket, football and cutting cane. His vision came back to the three men finishing the contraption in the yard below. One of them released the trapdoor and it flew open with a wicked screech. Jack shrugged. All that fuss for nothing, he thought. For the first time in his life he felt powerful. He enjoyed the idea of wasting their time. He turned and faced the inspector.

"It feels like something else," he said. "I know this is not a movie, but it sure feels like, you know, unreal." Jack looked at the Inspector. Their eyes met. Jack pursed his lips.

"If you have anything to say, Jack, this is the time. You don't have much of it left."

Jack unfolded his lips, exposing toothless gums. A mirthless little laugh escaped his mouth. "What you want to hear, man? You want me to say something that will make you feel clean, allow you to think that you didn't help send an innocent man to the gallows? Don't look here, white man; I'm no priest."

"Jack, I'm not looking to unburden." The Inspector patted his chest, smiled and threw his palm wide open. "Because I don't think you are innocent." He pointed one finger at Jack.

Jack Masanto returned the smiled and ran one hand over his face. "Well if we talking about…neither are you. We all born in sin and shaped by inequities. The Bible said something like that," Jack looked at the floor, took a deep breath.

"I had no idea you were a religious man," Didderot said. "It's a good thing."

"Let me tell you about the dream I had last night," Jack said and shuffled his feet.

"I don't have time to listen to your dreams," Didderot said and turned toward the door.

"You in a hurry to visit another condemned man? This won't take long." Jack looked at the inspector. Didderot turned and waited. A slight breeze blew through the cell. Jack began speaking with a touch of tranquility. "I was down there on the gallows with the rope around my neck. I could hear a drum, beating, and beating, perfect strokes. Only Mano could beat a drum like that. Ever heard that man beat a drum, everything just so? I could hardly wait for the next sound to reach my ears. The pauses were painful, seems to last forever. And suddenly in the dream, I became aware of where I stood, and I wondered how Mano's drum could reach me. I held my breath. That's when I realized it wasn't Mano's drum. It was the beating of my heart."

Jack Masanto moved back to the cot and sat down, didn't say another word. He could feel Didderot's glare.

"Well Jack, I'll see you tomorrow then." Dennis Didderot turned.

Jack spoke to his back. "What you coming for, to enjoy yourself?" The inspector left without a responding.

What will become of Malcolm? Jack thought. Such a gentle soul and that Cora. I should have cuffed her on her mouth a few times. Too late for that now. This old shirt will make a good noose, he thought, strong, braided, rope.

Jack recalled the conversation with Cosmus, the boy he had known since birth. That their lives could cross in this way made him wonder about fate, God and all the other miracles of the universe. "I want you to bring me a Bible. Hide a razor blade inside it."

"What you going to do with a razor blade?" Cosmus had asked. "It could take you forever to kill—where am I going to get a razor blade anyhow?"

"Don't worry about it, talk to Butcherat. The man can get anything in here, within reason of course, and for a price," Jack smiled.

"So that's already handled, right?" Cosmus asked.

"Just talk to the Rat, okay,"

Jack remembered Cosmus shaking his head and speaking like a preacher. "I've been wondering about junctions," he said. "What if I had never met Constance, would you be here?"

"What you talking about?"

"Look at it this way. The Carlyle family would still be in that house. No Missionary Man for you to kill."

Jack Masanto looked at Cosmus and smiled. "I didn't kill the Missionary Man."

"So who… killed him?" Cosmus asked.

"At first, I had three suspects, John, Malcolm, and Cora. I realized John had no way to get his hand on my cutlass. So how did the preacher's blood get under the handle? That left the only two people in the world that I love. I refused to put them in any danger."

"I hear what you saying," Cosmus said. "I don't know if I should help you. What you thinking is against the will of God. At first, I had no trust in God," Cosmus continued. "But after Maga chopped up Gimpy down in the pigpens, and they made us watch the hanging, I've come to understand how precious life is, whether it's life in here or out there."

The two men looked at each other for a moment as if they had come to a fence. But Jack spoke softly, giving a rationale that Cosmus could not renounce. "Jesus gave his life for us people that he loved, right? What's wrong with me doing the same for people who I love?"

Cosmus looked at Jack for a long time and then he said, "Wish I could argue with that."

And the deal was sealed.

That a skill taught to him by his father would come to such a sorrowful use didn't surprise Jack. He started right after dinner, wanted to get it right, and didn't want strands of rotten threads in the shirt to foil his plan. So he tore the shirt into strips, using the razor blade, and plaited those into small strands. He then braided those strands into a stout, short rope. When he was finished, he made a slipknot at one end and placed it around his neck like a tie. Jack placed the cot against a wall, climbed up to a rafter, fastened the other end of the rope and stood there for a moment balanced on the end of the cot. He thought of Ogoun's Point, and the tales of the old Africans who flew back to Africa, saw the Missionary Man walking through Jean Anglais singing to a group of kids. "All things bright and beautiful, the Lord God made them all." Darn foolishness, he thought, as he pushed the cot with his feet.

When the two prison guards, accompanied by a priest, came for Jack early the next morning, they were assailed by the stink of shit. Inside the cell, they found Jack dangling from the rafters at the end of a neatly braided cloth rope. The man had been dead for hours.

* * *

Cora felt cheated. Why did they have to keep his body? He was already dead. She would have liked to at least have a wake, have some of his friends come by the house for a shot of rum and some food, bury him with dignity. The rage of this denial absorbed her, came out of her like puss from a lanced boil. All directed at John. That son of a bitch, she thought, I'm going to put such a Zoogoo up his ass. He will die in pain. I'm sure Mama Viche won't do it, but I'll find someone, I'll find another Obeah woman to do that dirty dog.

Three days after Jack's death, Cora made the decision to sell the piece of land to John. She planned on using his own money to put the Zoogoo on him. The Obeah woman from Crochu had told her to bring three hundred dollars. She smiled a smile of sweet vengeance when John handed her the two thousand dollars for the piece of land. The next day she took the bus.

After all was said and done, Cora Masanto found it very hard to leave the place where she was born. Old memories came at her like a pack of snarling dogs, engulfed her in a tangle of grief, and cultivated bitterness. The night before she began preparations to move the house from Jean Anglais, to the new house-spot squeezed between the Mang and Belmont, Cora made a blunt confession to her son.

"You're just like him," she said. "He had no backbone. The best thing he did was end his life. He died for a crime he didn't commit. That fool, that stupid coward, couldn't kill a fly."

* * *

Realization eased into Malcolm. He looked at his mother, saw tears running down her cheeks. He thought of bolting for the door, but his bare feet remained nailed to the floor. The boy wanted to ask his mother some questions, but the food he had eaten for dinner bubbled in his stomach; he swallowed and gasped, a bilious taste floating at the back of his throat.

His mother's voice sounded far away. Malcolm thought of his friend Ezekiel, wondered what he might be doing. The wind outside ceased to blow. The only sound he could hear was his mother's croaky whispers, pitched to remain inside the house. Malcolm felt as if her voice had crawled under his skin, and dislodged something. As he listened, bits of him were leaving, and her voice continued to fill the indentations. Malcolm imagined himself outside his body, somewhere up in the rafters, looking down on two strangers.

"Vicious, mangy dog, he's the one who pointed the finger at us. Plain covetousness and spite, kissing the white man's ass," she said.

Cora caught her breath as if she might burst into tears.

"He came to the house one evening with a cutlass in his hand. I swear he wanted to attack us, started wailing about the man trying to fuck Ezekiel, and how the man is probably fucking you. I chase him away, talking like that about a man of God."

Cora nodded and took a deep breath.

"The next week, while collecting wood, I ran into the Missionary Man in the bush behind his church. I stood there with the bundle on my head and the cutlass in my hand, felt shameful repeating what John had told us. But I did. I did it. Malcolm, I expecting the man to speak about forgiveness and ignoring nasty rumors, instead, he stood there with a bold look on his face. And then he laughed at me, he laughed at me, Malcolm. He said John spoke the truth. And we can't do anything, because he had more to offer; education, a big house for you to live in, and he continued to provoke me. No one would believe us anyhow, he said, ignorant country people talking about a white preacher. He said you a son of Mithra now, whatever the hell that means. And we shouldn't think of you as our son anymore. I got so vex. My head filled up with wind, like a hurricane blowing through me, in one ear and out the other, taking my brains with it. I went blind for a moment. The bundle became light as a feather, lost all its weight and I threw the bunch of wood at him. He staggered and fell to the ground as the pieces of wood hit his face and I went after him with the blade."

Malcolm listened to his mother and counted the nail heads in the boards on the floor. He looked up at her when she went silent. Her shoulders moved with jerky motions, her hands rested palm to palm in her lap, and tears flowed down her cheeks. Malcolm felt an urge to rush to her, throw his arms around her, but fear held him back. He stood motionless across the room.

* * *

Ezekiel and Malcolm attempted to remain friends, acted as if the upheaval had nothing to do with them. They still met at the gap and walked to school with the other boys, but things felt peculiar. Ezekiel carried his suspicion and guilt like a crooked load. He found it hard to talk with Malcolm, try to get his views on the confusion in Jean Anglais.

One day they attempted to learn what had happened to the body of the Missionary Man. They went to the mortuary and spoke to an old woman who was sweeping the floor. She laughed when they asked about the body of the white preacher, and then she chased them off with the broom, shouting shoo, as if chasing chickens. Ezekiel and Malcolm assumed the body had to be placed on a ship, taken back to England. They speculated on whether the Missionary Man had a mother and a father, and friends. The boys remembered no pictures of anyone around his house, just shelves and shelves of books.

As time pass, it seemed certain kids refused to leave things alone. Schoolmates harassed Malcolm. They called him names. On the street, away from school, they composed rhymes that went like this:

> Jack Ketch said come swing with me
> Jack Masanto said whe whe whe
> Jack met Jack on a sunny day
> Broke his neck from here to there.

Malcolm stood taller than most of the other boys, and could have easily beaten any of them to a pulp. Yet he took the taunting without raising a finger, or even his voice. No one tried to protect him. Ezekiel looked on at Malcolm's sad face and wondered. Regrets and guilt held him in a tight squeeze. He started looking for ways to avoid his friend, fearing he too could become a target. After Malcolm had skipped school for two weeks, Ezekiel went searching for him.

The place where Cora and Malcolm moved their house sat off the road, down the hill, below all the other houses on the way to the Mang. Dirty water and other refuse from up top ran behind the house. Land-crabs subsisted in holes nearby, feeding on the waste that ran down and soaked into the dirt, creating nourishing juices from the decay. Ezekiel saw Cora standing in her doorway, wearing shirt and pants, rubber boots on her feet. She looked like a man on his way to work a piece of land. The woman stood there with one hand on her hip, looking cruel. He thought of walking away, but instead, he greeted her casually. "Good day, Miz. Cora, Malcolm at home?"

She looked at Ezekiel as if he were some kind of vermin.

"I didn't see him for a while, so I thought he might be sick or something."

When Cora didn't respond, Ezekiel's imagination got the best of him. What if she grabs a cutlass and comes charging at me, he thought. "Well, good day then. Tell Malcolm I came to see him." Ezekiel took two steps back, still looking at Cora standing in the doorway. He kept one eye on her until she was out of sight.

"Ezekiel, over here, this way," Malcolm's voice came from behind a hedge, near one of the other houses. He came into view wearing new blue jeans, a khaki shirt and rubber boots. In his hands he carried a cutlass, a crocus sack rolled into a long bundle and tied with a rope to form a loop.

"What you doing hiding there? Look at you, where you going?"

"I'm getting out of here on the next bus. Did you see her?"

"She looked really angry, didn't say a word to me."

"Angry? You mean crazy."

"Where you going?" Ezekiel repeated the question.

"Any place except here. I want to continue the work of Reverend Harry."

"Continue the work? What work?"

An iguana scampering across the vegetation behind Malcolm, chickens cackled from the neighbor's yard. The two friends squared of on the path.

"Spreading the word of God," Malcolm said. "I'm already doing some meetings, with people in their homes, Bible studies and so on, making my mother real__"

"Why don't you move back to Jean Anglais?"

"And do what? Live where? I need to get away. I think I'll move north, to the country. Grenville or Sauteurs, maybe."

"You don't know anybody up there."

"I'll make do. You'll see. People I know have friends and family up there. I'm a hard worker."

"I don't know what to say, man. What about school?"

"I know enough, I'll be fine. I can read, write and count. Don't worry about me. You're smart, Ezekiel. Secondary school is the place for you. Show them what a country boy from Jean Anglais can do."

"I can't help thinking," Ezekiel said. "You might be wasting something?"

"I don't know what… just wish me good luck," Malcolm said.

Ezekiel and Malcolm stood face to face, looking at each other. Malcolm began shaking his head and smiling. Ezekiel tilted his head and focused on Malcolm's crafty expression. He hadn't seen that look in a while. "What? What's the matter?" he asked. "I don't want to hear anything from that dead Roman."

Malcolm's grin continued to widen. "You remember the night behind Tante Monah's house when somebody pushed you from behind? You were so darn scared you didn't even look back. You shot off like a bird." Malcolm laughed.

"I never told you about…that was you?"

"Tante Monah saw me and assumed if Malcolm is there, Ezekiel must be also. She came to the house, shouting about Peeping Toms. I got a terrible licking from my mother. They assumed we were there to peek at them. I wanted to listen to the radio. The next day, Tante Monah went to see her sister, Olga, and took Delores with her. I snuck into her house and stole the radio, hid it in the church for a couple days, had no idea what to do with it. Couldn't play it, it would make noise, people would hear it. Finally, I smashed it up with a rock and scattered the chunks all over the place. People kept finding the pieces and bringing them to her. You remember when she buried those parts in a shoe box behind her house? I felt really bad. Everybody acted as if attending a funeral."

"That was criminal." Ezekiel laughed. "You really did? That radio was old, older than you and me. People still joke about Swallow, the first owner. They say he treated that radio like his child."

"I'm still not sure why I did it. I got that beating, but everything else, such a mess. I mean, me going down there and allowing Harry to mess with me. It felt good at first, but nasty afterward. Took my confusion out on the radio, I guess." Malcolm looked at Ezekiel, and then he lowered his gaze to his mud-stained boots. "I've got to go. The bus is coming."

"Take another bus. Let's go up the hill, see it one last time before you go, say goodbye."

"Naah," Malcolm groaned.

He picked up his few belongings, came near and slapped Ezekiel on one arm. He sneaked behind a nearby house and disappeared.

As the months went by, rumors started floating. Malcolm had turned into some kind of healer. Someone from LaDigue had witnessed him resurrecting a dead chicken, placing it under a bowl and tapped gently with his fingers. The chicken came back to life and scampered away. And there was a man from Grand Anse who could hardly walk, had to use crutches because of pain in his joints. Malcolm placed his hands on the man, said a prayer, told the man to stop eating sugar and bread, stay away from booze. The man followed his advice and now the man can dance. The rumors continued like a blaze and people fed it. They had seen Malcolm and he was crazy with religion, speaking in tongues, baptizing people all over Grenada, holding services for large crowds in the outer villages. "The police and the politicians are keeping their eyes on him. God has his hands on that one." The gossipmongers continued as if speaking about some kind of local messiah.

* * *

It took John Augustine a year to rehab the spot where Cora's house once stood. First, he removed the barbed wire fence separating the two properties. The old plum tree had grown and absorbed strands of the barded wire into its trunk. John hauled the wire away and stored it for future use. He purchased a donkey, and staked it to the spot, carried big bundles of Caapi vines from the bush and covered the ground. Three topics still dominated conversations in Jean Anglais: who murdered the Missionary Man, no one thought Jack did it, and who destroyed Monah's radio. The sanity of Cora Masanto was the most distressful. John allowed all of this to wash over him like heavy rain.

He experienced an exceptional moment the day Alma brought words that her aunt would like to speak to him. The Obeah woman had never summoned him before. What could have brought about this occasion, he thought. Mama Viche appeared relaxed and contented sitting in her wicker chair on the veranda knitting a garment.

"John, you look well for a man who should be exhausted from the snakes in your belly."

John frowned, "What you mean by snakes in my belly? You called me here to have fun with me?"

They stared at each other and the woman almost smiled. "Someone placed a Zoogoo on you, boy. I saw it, saw it plain as day."

"Mama, you know I don't believe in--"

"You may not believe in Obeah but Obeah believes in you. It's in your blood."

"If I believed in Obeah, I would have to accept that you may have done something to my son," he said.

"What reason would I have for doing anything to Lloyd?"

"Tilly thinks you hate her because of your godson, Jake."

"I hold no animosity toward Tilly. That's just her left-over guilt talking. I looked around your son and saw some inflammations in his belly. But you don't believe in any of this, you don't want my remedies. Talk to your son Ezekiel."

"Talk to him about what?"

"The boy has the gift of second sight. Right now it's kind of weak. Just wait, destiny is calling his name."

"What destiny? Leave the boy out of this."

"You see what I mean? Blind to the ways of the spirits, blind to the path forward for Jean Anglais, for the Valley of Bones and our redemption."

"I've no idea what you saying, Mama."

"Okay, that's fine. I called you here for another matter."

"Okay, okay, tell me."

"Do what I tell you and we can turn it around. If not, you will suffer."

"Mama, you threatening…you playing with me?"

"No threat from me. If you smart as I think you are, you will listen." The old woman paused and leaned back in the chair. "Bring me a young pullet, one that has laid no eggs. Dig three yams with your hands, use no fork or cutlass; don't bruise them. Then catch a large crapo, alive, and bring all of that to me. The next full moon, take a swim at ebb tide."

A contrary way of thinking caused John to snicker as he left the Obeah woman. What she proposed sounded like dinner. He had no objections to giving some provisions to the woman and her niece, but this swimming at night under the full moon, and the large frog? John brought the items to the Obeah woman three days later. When the moon became full, and the tide rose, he went down to Pandy Beach, and swam in the seawater. He thought, what is there to lose? If she is wrong, nothing, but what if she is right?

* * *

Tilly felt pleased about life returning to normal, following the confusion over the murder of the Missionary Man, and the death of Jack Masanto. The day after Lloyd's birthday, John had left for the Valley of Bones in a slight drizzle, taking Ezekiel with him. But the precipitation subsided, and Alma had shown up to take Lloyd for a walk. Tilly decided to make use of the free time; prepare food for the next two days.

She looked at the section of land that ran from the south corner of the house all the way to the hedge near the bottom road. The papaya and the avocado trees were laden with fruits. The neat symmetrical beds carved out of the ground rested in the blended shadows of the two trees. She walked across the yard toward her garden with a knife in hand. Sunlight bounced off big red tomatoes, heads of lettuce and cabbage nestled among green leaves. Herbs hedged it all: rosemary, basil, sorrel, and Tilly's favorite, lemon balm, which she used for cooking but more often for bathing. She appraised her garden with special consideration, then stooped, and put the blade to a stem, freeing the head of cabbage. It felt substantial in her palm. This one would be full of flavor, she thought.

Tilly looked down the line of flowers in full bloom, admiring how the wilted petals fell and settled on the grass. Her attention shifted from the flowers to a young woman with a small boy in one hand and a satchel in the other. They came into full view and Tilly recognized Monica, the preacher's former housekeeper. The woman walked with a small boy beside her. They took forever to reach the spot where Tilly stood.

"Good day, Tilly," the young woman spoke softly as she approached.

"Hey," Tilly replied, examining the woman and the child. The woman didn't have to say a word. Tilly knew it the moment she focused on the boy's face. The nose, the eyes, and the mouth: the spitting image of John.

"Your garden looks good. How often you have to water?"

The simplicity of the question almost jerked an answered out of Tilly, but the panic in her mind made her tongue heavy. She stood staring at the woman and the child.

Monica broke the silence. "This is Henry, John's son."

Although Tilly had already drawn that conclusion, hearing the words from the woman's mouth made her clamp her jaws. A slow rage took hold of her as she did the calculation. It produced a tang in her mouth, like biting into an unripe fruit. Her muscles shudder. Relax, a little voice whispered in her head. She obeyed and felt warmth rushing to her face. She also remembered to breathe, and she released her tongue from the grip of her teeth, ran it across the roof of her mouth and swallowed. The knife slid out of her hand and fell into the bed of vegetables.

"I've a chance for a job in Trinidad, can't take him with me right now. My parents don't want to keep him; Lester doesn't want me to bring him. What can I do? I'm afraid to talk to John. He might fly into a rage, and beat me up. You have to keep him, Tilly. He's a good boy. You're not afraid of John. I'll send for him as soon as I get settled and have Lester under control." She smiled a shrewd smile.

The words poured out of Monica's mouth and Tilly heard an echo, as if she stood in a big, empty room.

"He's your child," Tilly said. "Why you bring him here to start___? How can I be sure he's John's child? How old is he anyway?" The words sounded stupid and desperate in Tilly's ears. She wanted to reach out, grab them back, but they were out.

"Look at him. He's your husband's child, Tilly, which makes him almost yours," the woman said.

Tilly laughed.

Monica seemed surprised by Tilly's reaction, and then anger rose to her face. Her lips compressed, her eyes narrowed. Tilly stared at the young woman, searched in vain for something to convince herself that this may not be real. Tilly felt trapped between sympathy for Monica's desperation, and an urge to punch her face.

"Tilly, he is your man," Monica said. "You didn't give him what he needed, so he came to me."

"Don't flatter yourself, reaching for excuses because I don't give a shit. That's like begging."

"Well, if you want me to," Monica said.

Tilly gestured with one hand as if chasing a mosquito from her ears. She stared at Monica, searching the expression on her face, and then she looked deep into the girl's eyes, attempting intimidation. But everything turned into a blur. Monica suddenly had no face. Tilly shook her head to refocus. At thirty-seven years old, she suddenly felt aged and confused. Tilly struggled to comprehend the menace she felt from Monica, the boy, and her own violent impulse. She never wanted to be like the other women around Jean Anglais, always thinking about the competition, always worrying about the devotions of their husbands. Tilly returned to her senses, out of the storm blowing around her, to the ache of her fingernails digging into the head of cabbage.

"Girl," Tilly said. "Go back to where you came from. Take him somewhere else. There's no place here for him. You are the one who spread your legs and got your belly big."

"Tilly, what ever you may think of me, you know John is his father, and the boy belongs with his father," Monica said.

"That shit means nothing to me." Tilly turned and started pulling weeds.

Monica took two steps toward the front of the house, placed the suitcase on the stairs, and the child next to it, turned and started walking.

"No, no, no you don't," Tilly said and blocked Monica's path.

The boy stood up to follow his mother, issuing a slight whimper. Monica picked up the child, and thrust him into Tilly's arms. Her sudden movements caught Tilly off guard. Tilly instinctively grabbed the child. She stood on the edge of her garden, speechless, cabbage in one hand, the child in the other. Tilly watched Monica's rage slide into tears. The young woman backed away, turned, and ran as if all the hounds of hell were on her heels. Tilly watched Monica's back, astounded. Monica ran down the gap, and cleared the corner of the hedge, onto the bottom road and vanished.

The boy opened his mouth wide, and burst into a scream. Tears flowed down his cheeks. Tilly heard laughter from the top road. She wondered if the neighbors had listened, heard it all, and were now laughing at her. Wives are the last to know. Over five years and no one had said a word. How could that be?

"Boy, Boy, Boy__ you don't belong here," Tilly spoke to the screaming child, grasping him in her arms as he wiggled and pushed against her breasts. She placed him on the ground. Tilly walked toward the kitchen with the head of cabbage in one hand and holding the boy by the other as he tried to pull away. For an instant, she thought of just releasing his hand.

"I woke up this morning happy as a singing bird. Now here you are a little bug in my broth. Oh, Lord! Lord, Henry, you look so much like him. I'm sorry. Wait till that big-head son-of-a-bitch gets home." Tilly spoke the words through clenched teeth. A slow rage oozed back into her. She slammed the head of cabbage on the kitchen counter and felt it split in her palm.

Alma and Lloyd returned, strutting down the path from the top road. They looked jovial as if they had made an important find.

"Tilly," Alma shouted from the distance, "Lloyd knows numbers. He understands how to do calculations. Let's give him an arithmetic problem, you will see."

"Not now, Alma. You see my problem. You need to go home."

"What's the matter?" Alma asked.

Tilly turned to her son, "Lloyd, this is your brother, Henry."

"Not Ezekiel. Brother? Have Ezekiel come back." Lloyd spoke, confusion all over his face.

"Your other brother, Lloyd, you have two now."

She said it and that gave it consequence. Tilly focused her attention, plotted how she would make John pay for this humiliation. The woman watched Alma walking away, wondered what does the girl know? What did her aunt tell her? Of course, they all knew about him. To hell with all of them, she thought.

Tilly took the two boys and started towards her parents' house. The people she passed on the road seemed indistinct. She decided she could call none of them friends, because friendship was a thing you cultivated like a garden. She had developed nothing with many of them. Tilly thought of Cora, Jack, and Malcolm, and wondered if there was anything she could have done to prevent their ruination.

* * *

She walked into her parents' kitchen with the two boys. Tilly experienced a sense of dread. Coming to her mother felt dreadful. Florence stood in the middle of the room, a straw hat on her head. On her feet, she wore canvas slippers. She had just returned from working outside. Tilly introduced Henry and announced the details of his origin. Her father, Vernon Stewart, without a word, took the two boys and headed toward the door. Tilly watched his back as he shepherded the children. Their little quarrel when she had told him of her intention to marry John felt like a forecast.

"You will have your hands full with that father and son, a ready-made family," her father had said.

Tilly knew that was the extent of the blessing she would receive.

"I know. I can handle it," she had said.

"Their disposition is so opposite," Vernon had looked at his daughter, recognized her objection to the arc of the conversation.

"The boy has lots of his mother in him," she said. "And smart in an intuitive way."

"John was a willful boy, always in my office. He wasn't much of a student. Ezekiel as you were saying, that's another story all together. When is the ceremony and what do you need from me?" That was the extent of their conversation before the wedding.

In this kitchen where she had eaten so many meals and shed many of her adolescent fears, came home when her first husband Jake had lost interest. Tilly suddenly felt inappropriate, as if she had worn the wrong cloth for an occasion. She told herself this would be the last time she would bring her troubles here. Returning to teaching was an option, but she knew she would have to kiss too many asses. Remaining with John, taking care of the house and the boys seemed a tolerable choice. Tilly rushed toward a conclusion.

She sat in a chair and her mother remained standing, sometimes shifting as if nervous. Tilly saw the effort exerted by her mother, trying to mind her own business. Mother, daughter, friend, confidant and the mixture reminded Tilly of bees wax. The embarrassment of the situation knotted the muscles on Tilly's face. She saw her mother struggling to say nothing. Tilly understood that the circumstances would eventually force her mother to speak. So she waited.

"You can't say we didn't warn you, Tilly," Florence said.

Tilly smiled a tight smile; it tugged at the corners of her mouth.

"It's worth it, Mommy. All the pain, the humiliation, I just gained a son," she said. "Didn't have to walk around with a big belly or suffer through childbirth. She came to my door and gave him to me like a sack of potatoes. I will not give him back, even if that fish-face bitch comes crawling on her hands and knees. I'll deal with John in my own way." The resolve in her words came as no surprise.

"This is not what your father and I pictured for you."

"Mommy, I know you never liked him, I know you expected me to leave him and come back home. I already did that once. Remember Jake?"

Tilly looked at her mother, saw a smile on her face and wondered.

"I remember the day you told me your plan to marry John. Only one word came to me. It flew out of my mouth. I was mortified."

"I remember answering your one-word question," Tilly said.

"You said love always carry risks. And I thought, how cynical," Florence said.

"That's me I guess. Even now, I still love him. Wounds do heal."

"You sure about that? Not all wounds heal," Florence said.

The mother and daughter looked at each other for a long time, and then they leaned into each other's arms. No words passed between them. When they released, it was like the passage of a fresh breeze. They kissed, held hands, smiling at the realization of what had just taken place. For the first time, they saw each other as women, as friends. They were still mother and daughter, but a new dynamic had entered their relationship. Tilly felt punished, but at the same time she realized that she had gained some power from this miserable situation.

* * *

Tilly returned home without Lloyd and Henry, began chopping the head of cabbage with a vengeance, and throwing the chunks into a pot of boiling water. The stink of the steaming vegetable pleased her, sent her mind wondering down a dismal path. She thought of the Moritz sisters, twin girls from River Road who had killed two men who tried to rape them. The girls were arrested for murder. The newspaper printed pictures of them, along with a story of what had happened and the authority's decision to charge them. Women complained bitterly and started marching in the streets, the sisters were quietly released and not another word was said.

The number of men beating their wives and girlfriends decreased. People started saying those girls should leave Grenada because the family of the dead men might come after them. Most people assumed the girls would never find husbands now that they were known as "man killers". Tilly sat immersed in the stench of the boiling cabbage, appreciating the bravery of those twin sisters.

Tilly said nothing when John and Ezekiel walked into the kitchen. She avoided John's eyes. Instead, she looked at his old rubber boots, khaki pants tucked inside. She watched him place the cutlass in the corner, followed his movements as he sat down at the table. Ezekiel followed his father. He's no longer a boy, Tilly thought. Look how much he has grown and filled out. Where has all that time gone? She watched him as he sat down at the table next to his father. Ezekiel looked at Tilly; she avoided his gaze. She wondered how long it would take John to realize.

"What's wrong now?" John asked.

Tilly ignored the question. She placed the porcelain bowls full of cabbage and pig snout on the table in front of John and Ezekiel. The father and son ate without words. She stood across the kitchen looking out the window. The banana, palm, and mango trees swayed gently in the evening breeze. Everything appeared so ordinary, so common in the last light, but a raging volcano boiled inside of Tilly. She thought she had settled certain aspects of this thing, could handle it calmly from here, but it came back at her like a hurricane changing course for a second swipe at an island.

"Lord, have mercy, what have I gotten myself into," she whispered under her breathe.

She felt itchy, knowing his eyes were raking her back. Tilly ignored him as he shoveled the food into his face, chewing ugly. Let him grumble and wonder, let the food make gas in his stomach. She knew the moment his belly was filled he would start making demands. But Tilly refused to engage John in the presence of Ezekiel. So she waited for the moment. As the spoons scrap across the bottom of the bowls, she slid into action.

"Ezekiel, leave the dishes. Go to Grandma's house. You are spending the night. Lloyd and Henry are already down there."

"Who is Henry?" Ezekiel asked.

Tilly turned and faced John. "Your brother," she said.

She saw realization on John's face. She knew Ezekiel must be full of questions. But he stood, hesitant in his movement. She wondered if he already knew the details. Their eyes met, she watched him; Ezekiel obeyed without another word. He marched out of the kitchen.

John sat at the table, the empty plate in front of him, the frown gone from his face. He remained there, motionless, looking at Tilly as if trying to ignite some cinder.

"How long have you known?" He spoke as if that bit of information could produce a difference outcome.

"Just today, she's leaving for Trinidad," Tilly said, looking at John with scorn. "Why, John? Why? This is not good enough for you?"

Tilly grabbed her dress at the neck with both hands, tore it all the way to her navel. Her bare breasts jumped out. "Answer me, John! Answer me!"

She took two steps across the floor toward the table where John sat. Tears ran down her cheeks. He stared at Tilly, and then he avoided her face by looking at her feet. My wife, my children, my garden, my cows, she knew what he was thinking, possessions, things of value, to be protected, resources to be used. Tilly decided to change his mind about all that.

"What kind of beast are you? Doing this to me, to us, to our family?" she asked, standing on the other side of the table near him.

John sat in silence. He was completely unprepared when her right hook connected with his jaw. His eyes flew open; he lurched backward, shook his head and brought his hand up to his chin as if to keep it in place.

"Answer me, you son of a bitch, would have been better if you just chop me with your cutlass. Why didn't you?"

He came to his feet, half standing, massaging his jaw, and she drove her fist into his stomach. John grabbed the table to steady himself, tipped it, and the dinner dishes went flying across the floor. He regained his composure before she could throw a third blow, blocked it in midair and pinned both her arms.

"Let me go. Let me go. Don't touch me with your stinking..." she shouted, kicking, and flailing.

"Don't hit me again, Tilly," John said.

He pushed her away. Tilly staggered, regained her balance and kicked the bowl that had come to rest in front of her. The bowl missed John by inches, bounced off the wall and shattered all over the floor. John started to gather the utensils and the other dishes from the floor, handed them to Tilly and went back to the table, pulled it closer to the bench and sat down. Tilly stood across the room with the dishes in hand, staring at John. She thought she saw a wisp of condescension on his face. In the next instant, she pulled back and hurled the dishes at him. John ducked and covered his face.

* * *

Ezekiel heard the first sharp words and the splitting of the cloth as Tilly ripped her dress. At the age of fifteen, the boy had formed certain opinions about adults and this clash between his parents now resembled water flowing down hill. The result of all that he had witnessed between his father and Monica became a basis from which to formulate. He remembered the last time he saw his father with Monica, bickering at each other, and later seeing her in Saint Georges with a small child. He tried to figure out why he didn't put things together. She didn't live in Jean Anglais so he saw her only now and again after the death of the Missionary Man. How in the world Tilly could not have known, with all the gossip mongers wagging their tongues. Tilly must be the kind of person who others like to study, like watching a cat walking across an empty clothesline and wondering when it would loose footing and fall.

Ezekiel heard the anger and the pain in Tilly's voice, as he lingered near the garden, contemplating whether to go back, hide and listen, or move on to see this brother who was the source of the confusion. He spotted the knife Tilly had dropped earlier, picked it up, walked over to the papaya tree and stabbed it into the trunk. Nothing happened for a moment, and then white milky sap oozed past the blade and trickled down the trunk of the tree. He left the blade stuck in the trunk of the tree and walked away.

The young man moved down the red gravel road toward Belmont, past the church, the yellow house, and Mama Viche's place, his hands stuck deep in his pockets, his feet disturbed the loose gravel. He wished this could be one of those times when the future would flash before his eyes, and leave him with some comprehension of what could be.

Ezekiel found it easy to love Tilly. He recalled two times when he was the recipient of her full affection: he had a toothache and she held him, gave him the herbs, took him to have it extracted; and when that centipede bit him, she made and applied a poultice to sooth the pain and clean out the poison. He saw his father in another light, distant, frightening and selfish. Ezekiel recalled two Bible passages from Kings and Isaiah, about rulers being put to the sword by his sons. He wondered if it came down to it, could he kill his father. The situation with Henry forced him to entertain that possibility.

A warm breeze brushed across his face. Henry, the result of what he had witnessed between Monica and his father continued to fascinate him. What kind of brother will he be? He felt alone, trapped in a dense fatigue, wished he could find Malcolm with the advice of the dead Roman. Ezekiel imagined Malcolm speaking in a pleasant voice: 'The cucumber is bitter. There's a briar in the way'. A figure staggering down the road caught his attention.

Ezekiel recognized Mano by the song the man was humming. The man swayed as he moved toward Ezekiel, slurring some kind of drinking-song. The man wore a short sleeved shirt, unbuttoned and flapping in the breeze, his hairy belly exposed. Dirty dungaree pants hung on his frame, starched with dirt and coal dust. *The fool is drunk again*, Ezekiel thought, *what's new, it's Saturday*. Mano lurched, two to the left, two to the right, one forward. The rubber boots on his feet dragged and shifted the gravel.

"Ezekiel, you disgusting little shit ass," Mano shouted. "You stay away from my daughter."

He grasped at Ezekiel as their paths crossed. The boy ducked out of reach. Mano lost his balance, tilted, and regained his footing. Ezekiel reached down and picked up a chunk of gravel. He moved to the left of Mano with the stone clenched between his fingers. It felt rough and familiar. He thought of birds he had knocked out of trees, thought of the day Papa LaTouche's dog, Mayoc started barking at him, teeth bared as it charged down the gap. When the rock connected with its head, the dog whined and ducked through the hedge. It never bothered Ezekiel again.

Mano stood a short distance away. A tall slim man, blood-red eyes set wide on a gaunt face. "I'll catch you one day and thump your ass, you little pig-eating bone sucker." Mano slurred, threatening. Spittle flew off across a darting tongue. Mano licked his lips and regained the moisture. His head of sun-rust hair jiggled and bobbed as he tried to focus on the boy standing in the road. Ezekiel was angry but not a single word left his mouth. He saw Mano as the same kind of person who had made his life itchy and uncomfortable. Ezekiel rolled the rock into his palm and clasped it with the tips of his fingers like a ball.

All the boys around Jean Anglais made fun of Mano and he would threaten. The boys never spoke to or made fun of the man when he was sober. Ezekiel knew why rum and other booze were called spirits. It was as if the man was possessed by the liquor. When sober, Mano was a shy, melancholy man. He watched as Mano muttered curses, and then turned away. The words of the drunken, silly song slurred off Mano's lips again, and Ezekiel stared at the back of the man's head. The chunk of gravel felt heavy in his palm. He drew back to throw it and thought better.

Mano played the drums on weekends, when drunk. The constant repetitions would travel through the village. He played the drums on two other occasions, at village ceremonies to complement stories, and around Carnival, when he would dress as a fierce Jab-Jab, body greased with lard and smeared with coal dust, lips painted blood-red with lipstick, tattered clothes and a chain around his waist, held by the master covered in talcum powder.

The worst of these black Jab-jabs, Mano amongst them, always demanded tribute for this grotesque portrayal of their slave heritage. If you refused to pay, they would bump into you, leaving the grease and coal dust as a reminder. Ezekiel watched as the man staggered away into the distance. Mano seemed undisturbed by the presence of the young man standing behind him with a rock clenched in his fist. Ezekiel threw the rock into the trees as he walked away.

He passed the house where Mama Viche lived with her niece, Alma. That Mano would warn him to stay away from Alma seemed odd. Ezekiel knew Alma was different from most girls. Other girls laughed and giggled at stupid things, but Alma laughed at real jokes. She was the only girl in whose company he felt comfortable. The only time Ezekiel and Alma saw each other, outside of waving in the distance, was when Alma visited Tilly. Ezekiel hated going to the Obeah woman's house. The reputation of the place gave him the willies.

The house was partly hidden behind fruit trees: two mangoes, a guava, a sapodilla and a spinet. Only the toughest and most adventurous of boys dared to raid Mama Viche's fruits. The more sensible boys gave Mama Viche's place a wide berth. They all have heard stories about the fate of those caught stealing from the old woman, for instance, the boy called Slinger. She caught him in her fruit trees and worked Obeah on him: first, his voice changed to the bleating of a goat, he grew a beard and then his feet began turning to hooves. The spell lasted for one full night. Slinger went to sleep and when he woke up the next morning he was fine. Sometimes the boys would grow tired of the dangers of messing with her and just ask her for some of the fruits. Her response was always the same: "Take some and leave some, children," she would say.

Ezekiel walked down the road near the old briah and mahoe trees that had grown and stretched out, forming a canopy over the roads. To his left, just off the road, stood the wooden, white-washed church, knee-deep in grass. A lone cross rested over the entrance, the only testimony that the building was once used as a place of worship. The block house sat further into the trees across the field. The Missionary Man long dead and gone and no one came to take his place.

Ezekiel reflected on that portion of his life, on the Missionary Man, Jack, and Cosmus, still locked up in Richmond Hill Prison. He wondered if life would always be this messy. Would he always be sorry for some events outside of his control? Would bad luck always lurk around a corner? Would he always fear his father? Ezekiel made his way further down the road wrestling his demons, worried about what he had left behind between John and Tilly.

* * *

John hated the way Tilly quarreled. Those long moments of silence haunted him. When he thought she it was finished, she would start all over again, with renewed vigor, and on a different subject. They quarreled about everything: about Joan who was dead, and her son Ezekiel, about Lloyd who was not the perfect child and about Monica and her child, Henry. And as an aside, Tilly inquired about where John expected Henry to sleep. When she got around to Jack, Cora, the piece of land, and the Missionary Man, she pitched her voice low, as if worried about her neighbors and ears beyond the walls of the kitchen.

She accused him of murdering the preacher and pointing the finger at Jack. John laughed, recalling Monica's accusation, he engaged Tilly with a slanted glare.

"I've never killed anyone in my life, but don't think I won't consider it. And what you doing with a man you think is a murderer?"

Tilly stood there staring at him. John enjoyed the reprieve from her scorn.

He took in the details of the kitchen as if seeing it for the first time. Soot from coal and wood fire coated the rafters and galvanized tin roof. In the far corner, strands of sooty cobweb held a dead fly. The headlines of the magazines and newspaper pages pasted to the walls sprung out at him. Tilly had been helping him to brush up on his reading, and these headlines were his original lessons. COW THIEF CAUGHT BURYING SKIN. A magazine page sported a headline, THE MASAI LION HUNTERS OF KENYA. John distracted himself by reading the bold prints on the pages. When Tilly finally spoke again, John thought, oh Jesus Christ, deliver me.

"You hurt me, John, you hurt me bad," she said. "You held my heart in your hand and you squeezed it hard. I don't know if it's broken. What does a broken heart feel like? Will I even be able to forgive or trust you, ever? I lost something and I want it back. You had no right to thief it from me. It's all I had."

Tilly's words between her tears jabbed John on a spot where he had never been touched before. He felt it deep inside, in the place where conscience slept. At first, he thought, this happened a long ago, damage done, didn't intend to hurt anyone. John's justification went all the way to the bone, and in the next instant he felt a pang. He saw no way to repair what he had done; no way to help Tilly out of her grief and anger. Sorry seemed a stupid thing to say. But he knew he would have to use that word sooner or later. For the first time in his life he felt inadequate.

"Tilly, what I did was . . . I can't tell you what I did was right. I can't change that. I lived with it like a Loupgarou with his secret, always hoping you would never find out. I had to do favors for people so they won't get vex with me and tell you about him. I lived in hell, a hell I created."

Since he saw no way to placate Tilly, he decided to buy her the radio she had once mentioned. And he decided to focus on the three boys, came up with the rudiments of a plan: he would take the boys down to the beach at Mon Pandy for an hour each day, to exercise and swim, rain or shine, for the rest of their lives, or until he could no longer tell them what to do. He saw this as partial atonement.

Her long gaps of silence troubled John, forced him to try and douse the flame he felt floating between them. "Say something, Tilly," John said.

"No! You speak to me, John."

"Tilly, I'm sorry. I broke it off with her before she started in with Lester. I just didn't want to hurt you. I had no idea this would come back like this. She told Lester the child belongs to him and he believed her."

"Christ John, you think Lester forgot how to count to nine? Unless… too sordid to imagine. Both of you at the same time? I feel sorry for the girl."

* * *

Tilly stood across the kitchen, as far as she could from John, listening to his breathing and gazing into the expanse of foliage outside the window. The woman was searching for more options, thought of leaving John and finding her own house, could take Lloyd, and move to Trinidad, find a good job, go back to the States or even England. But where's the money for all that, she thought. She reverted to the simple solution she had conjured up in her mother's kitchen. Tilly embraced the hidden advantage in John's regret. She had traveled full circle.

"Forgiveness?" she thought. "Forgive but not forget." She decided to go one more step and open an account at the Co-operative Bank in Saint Georges. Not as a prelude to leaving John, but you never know. A slight smile flirted across her face. It hardly affected her eyes and lips, but it was liberating. John took a quick look at her face and she knew he would draw the wrong conclusion.

* * *

John thought of her complaint about a place for Henry to sleep and in that recollection, he discovered the place to begin with her again. He could work on that small portion of her discontent. Not much could be done without the assistance of his friends in Jean Anglais: Checklea, Mondu, Papa LaTouche and a couple others. They agreed to help. John started the job early one day, with Ezekiel assisting as best he could. The others joined later.

They surprised Tilly and began tearing her house apart, taking down the back wall, took care to save the nails. Ezekiel straightened the bent ones. He gathered the old boards onto a pile as the other men pulled them off with crowbars. John laughed and talked with the others as he passed around a bottle of rum, acting as if this was all so ordinary. Tilly tried to stay in step with it. She cooked food with the help of a couple other women, and they fed everyone working on the house. A truck showed up with galvanized tin and new boards, and they went into full operation with saws and claw hammers. The expansion of the section of the house where the boys slept took shape. Soon the materials that John had bought began to run low. "This, this, this won't be enough, John," Mondu said, pointing at the dwindling materials.

"Son of a bitch, I miscalculated." John hammered a nail into a piece of board. "That money in your mattress? Just a loan, I'll pay you back."

"No! No, no, that's for Cosmus. I, I, I know where you can find more, more lumber for free." Mondu pitched his voice low and looked at John. John saw Tilly listening to the conversation.

"Just a, a just a suggestion, you might not, like, like, like it, but a church with no, no preacher, and no, no congregation, you know, no, no longer a church."

John acted as if the suggestion was outrageous. He knew that Tilly had already suspected them of plotting, but this suggestion about the church, coming from Mondu, seemed so acceptable. John shook his head, and thought, people think this man is somehow stupid because he stuttered. He pretended to reject the idea for Tilly's sake.

"I don't want the police coming around my house looking for stolen stuff."

"What, what, what they going to do, scrape, scrape the paint and know one piece of board from another?"

Checklea heard the conversation and smiled at Mondu's reasoning. They recognized that crooked, little smile as an agreement to help with whatever they were planning.

* * *

The next day more lumber and galvanized tin for the roof showed up, as if by magic, and were slapped on the back section of the house and painted over in a hurry. The materials looked hand-me-down. Ezekiel had walked by the church and noticed that portions of the structure had vanished, some boards from the lower section of the sides, just below head level, a portion of the roof along with some rafters. The place looked wounded.

John didn't take the entire building, but before long other villagers joined the carnage, taking parts and adding them to their houses. Soon, just the concrete foundation, with six metal bars stood out there on the edge of the field. Eventually, even the metal bars disappeared, taken by the person who put a hacksaw to the rods of steel. Eventually, someone erected the cross in the dirt, outside of the foundation, and supported the crucifix with rocks. What remained resembled a big, flat gravestone. Ezekiel felt uneasy about the origins of the materials in the space where he now slept.

Soon after, John came home with a radio. That evening, a crowd came down to listen and admire the new fangled device. It looked nothing like the old one, and John began to explain as if he was some kind of expert on radios.

"The old one had tubes," he said, "those things that looked like bulbs. This one is solid-state, transistors."

"Aaah!" the crowd intoned and John puffed his chest, continued to clarify bandwidth, depth of clarity, and the various features of his new radio. He told them radios are becoming cheap, pretty soon everyone would own one. Tilly smiled at her suggestion from so long ago, now happening like a chicken laying eggs. John switched channels and passed the little device around with pride. It amused Tilly that these contrary situations could collide in such a way to producing this new outcome.

* * *

As the murder of the Missionary Man and the death of Jack Masanto retreated to legend and the illusory, Mama Viche decided to stir the people of Jean Anglais, pull the old substances back into the light. The old woman settled on a ceremony known as a Kanzo, not the real ritual where Servitors are moving to a more serious level of Obeah, but one modified to remove the blights left by the Missionary Man. This would also be a ritual to shout out the living, a kind of provocation to remind them of who they are. They would gather, eat food, recite stories, listen to the drums, and dance into the night, like in the old days. The only true element of Kanzo consisted of Mama Viche's decision to initiate Alma as her Legatee.

The same day that she had made the decision to hold the ceremony, she saw Ezekiel walking up the road near her house and she motioned him over. Mama Viche couldn't help but consider how much the boy had grown. Now almost seventeen, he appeared more like a man than a boy, with his long pants, polyester shirt and a book clutched in the palm of his hand. He crossed the road, walked to the house and stood at the bottom of the stairs.

"When's the last time you told a story? Not something from one of those books you always carrying around. One of your own, from inside your own head" The old woman fixed Ezekiel with a determined stare.

"Can't recollect, people don't do much of..." Ezekiel hesitated, searching for the proper word.

Mama Viche smiled, "That blasted radio, blasted Zombie. Not alive, but talking."

"When I was little," Ezekiel said, "people told stories all the time. Most of them scared me."

"You know any stories, can you tell one?"

"What kind of story? I think I can tell one."

"It's not as easy as you think. Your words must stand for something."

"I know, Mama."

"You might get the chance to tell one, if you have the courage. It takes courage to stand in front of people."

"I can stand in front of people and tell a story."

"Get ready then," she said.

The old woman watched Ezekiel as he turned his back and she appreciated his acceptance of the challenge. She sent out messages to all her friends, to people who owed her favors, and most importantly to the man who would loan her a tent for two days, just in case it rained. They all came: drummers, dancers, and spectators, they came down from the surrounding hills, came up from Belmont, even some nonbelievers from Saint Georges came to see the spectacle and listen to the stories. Mano brought his drums, all seven of them, in various shapes and sizes, made from goat and sheep skin. The instruments rested in a circle. No one touched them without his permission.

Mama Viche knew the origins of similar events, held now and again at various places across Grenada. She had attended many as a young woman. The story element of these gathering was the brain-child of a Hogan, a priest of the Obeah tradition named Henry Cox. He was a tall African man with skin so black it appeared blue. People claimed his ancestors came from a band of fierce nomads who roamed the desert of North Africa. The man spoke with his entire body, hands moving about, eyes darting here and there, dancing to the rhythms in his voice as he rendered the tale.

He told tales with himself at the center. The devil on a white horse would chase his car down the road at midnight. Everyone knew that Henry didn't own a car and couldn't drive, but that didn't matter. He told of the night he gave a ride to a La Diablesse. The demon took the form of a beautiful woman, who tried to crawl into the backseat of his car, situating herself right behind him where she could get a good grip on his neck. But he was wearing a charm given to him by Mama Viche, and that saved his life.

Henry told tales about men who dealt with the devil, those who visited silk cotton trees in the dead of night, he spoke of men who owned funeral parlors and sold expensive coffins. Those who would stand over fresh graves, waving their hands and chanting incantations, making the ground open so that they could retrieve the expensive boxes sold to grieving relatives. The man returned year after year, with many fantastic tales. Finally, they decided he was the greatest liar in the world and storytelling became the main attraction.

People from far-off Grenville in Saint Andrews and Chantimelle in Sauteurs came down for the two days, bringing food, fruits, and gathering under the big, green tent. She wondered if Ezekiel would try to tell a tale, as she had attempted to instigate, and what kind would he tell. Would he join the crowd and tell the customary yarn about something that may or may not have happened to the teller? Would he tell tales of creations of the sea, earth and air, tales of smart and witty animals, or something original, influenced by the remembered customs of the old country? Or would he cross the line and deliver a cautionary tale to the villagers? The old woman knew that only a person of respect in the community could tell such a tale, but she hoped he would come forward. She had seen him wrestling the wind, knew of his birth behind the veiled, and had surmised that he could be the one to set those poor spirits in the Valley of Bones free, the one who would be known as the Redeemer. She wanted to see if her presumptions held any credence.

Moments before the event kicked off, people jostled for the good spots under the tent. Some came for the thrill of the yarns, the drummers came to hark back, and to mate with the voices, coax sweat to trickle down skin, allow bare feet to stomp the earth. But others would just come to watch, and to secretly call on Mama Viche, without raising suspicion. The old woman looked at the children sitting quietly at the back of the crowd, amongst them Lloyd and Henry. Tilly sat up front with John and Ezekiel, looking relaxed and happy.

The old woman instructed her niece on the code of conduct when presented as the central figure in the ceremony. Any of the other girls, Delores, Anna, Margaret, any of them could have been chosen, but their time would come, in accordance with family priorities. The honor was bestowed on Alma because the people of Jean Anglais knew that Mama Viche could not live forever. If the old woman had taught the girl everything she knew, and the girl had absorbed even a fraction, she could turn out to be one of the most powerful Obeah priestesses on the island.

The event started with four drummers, Mano, Papa LaTouche, Checklea and Mondu, teasing the crowd with shallow beats, enticing a voice to join them and carry the first song. Mama Viche saw Ezekiel and the crowd bursting with anticipation, glad for the festive mood. In this song, one person sang the lead, the crowd sang the chorus and the drums became the backbone, holding it erect, making it stand up, walk and talk. She looked at Mano's hands flailing at the drum, and she recalled her sister Maureen, Alma's mother, how she would dance to the beats produced by Mano's hands on the drums. She knew why her sister became Mano's lover. It started with the drums.

Tante Monah took up the challenge presented by the drummers. She stepped up and situated her ample self, took a deep breath, and in a voice that pealed like a bell, she shouted: "Yaaa ya ya oui ya yeaaa."

The assembled joined in with the same refrain. "Yaaa ya ya oui yeaaa," And the drummers filled in with two short beats, then stopped.

Then Tante Monah continued, above the crowd, singing in a voice that came from more than her throat. The drums came back to season the voices. "Ya oui ya oui yea/ Wigme bongo talli zull yaba/ ya oui ya oui yea/ Wigme bongo talli cou bulli/ ya oui ya oui yea."

The drums blazed on, the crowd shifted from the fringes to the middle of the tent to dance, bodies moving, twisting and turning, feet stomping and shuffling through the dirt. The drums mounted, and the voices slackened to create fresh harmonies. One pleading voice called out, Tante Monah's, begging the drums to behave.

The drummers resisted, remaining in that tickling pitch. The harmony lingered along a slow lament. Bare feet pummeled the dry dirt as if to arousing spirits from a thousand years of sleep. When the exhaustion finally commanded some to cease, they sat down under the green canvas tent, ate food, drank, basking in the light of the smoky kerosene torches, as young men and women drifted off to produce the next generation.

Mama Viche allowed Alma to take charge. Before each session of story telling, they engaged in a ritual called the Silence of Sorrow. They sat quietly for some minutes with their thoughts, and then the drums would interfere, rising in tone and calling them back to the business at hand. Alma walked to the center of the tent with a stick in hand; she drew a circle in the dirt and moved away to a seat in the crowd.

John stepped forward and entered the circle to tell his tale. Ezekiel sat on the edge of the crowd with Tilly, wondering what kind of tale his father would tell. John cleared his throat: "You all know how much a La Diablesse hates cussing," he said. "I hear some of you going up the road, late at night, making all kinds of noise and cussing loud. Some people might think you just drunk, but I know what you doing, keeping La Diablesse away. I was a young man back then, coming home from a dance in Grand Anse late one night. That's when I ran into my first La Diablesse. I came over the hill, near the Faledge, and almost stumbled over the most beautiful woman, standing by the side of the road in the moonlight. She had straight black hair that ran over her shoulders and down her back. Her skin looked like cocoa tea sweetened with condensed milk. She wore a long white dress that dragged on the ground. She looked like a run-away bride. I thought it was strange that she would be standing there, in the moonlight, at that time of the night, dressed like that. I decided to talk to her anyhow. In those days, I was the sort of fellow who couldn't leave women alone. I just loved to talk to them and play Saga Boy every chance I get."

"You still love to play Saga Boy, John. What you mean by back in those days?" a voice shouted from the back of the crowd. Laughter erupted.

John frowned, waved his hand in a dismissive gesture and continued speaking. "We started walking and talking. Her shoes kept making a clack, clack sound on the road. I couldn't get over how beautiful she looked. I kept wondering how come I'd never seen her around before." A breeze blew off the sea below the cliff, and I could smell the salt in the air.

"'I live in Mon Joule,' she said as if she could read my mind. 'I live up there with my Uncle and Tante.'

"I asked her, what you doing way down here at this time of the night?"

"'I came down to see a girlfriend, but we got into a quarrel about a boy, and she chased me out of the house. Some friend, huh?'

"Thump! I stumped my toe against a big rock, real hard. Damn, son-of-a-bitch, I shouted. I had no idea that we had left the road. Suddenly a hail of laughter burst out of the night, 'Heeee! Hee! Ha! Ha ha haaa!' And the La Diablesse took off flying, straight up and away on the wind. She yelled, 'I almost had you tonight, John Augustine. You won't be so lucky next time!' The laughter sent a shiver up my spine, made goose bumps on my skin.

"I came to my senses and looked around. I was standing on the brink of the cliff, looking down on the waves and rocks far below. One step away from death. Foolish me, I should have recognized the sound of her one cow foot hitting the pavement. Feet do your duty I said and didn't stop running until I reached home. I opened the door and entered the house backward. Those spirits can follow you home and crawl right into your bed, without you knowing it. The next day all you would find is a huge lump of wet cow shit, left as a reminder that a La Diablesse slept with you last night. And you would be tired for days."

Ezekiel wondered why his father chose to go first when his tale was so short, and from the old times. The boy would have preferred a tale from Mama Viche. Ezekiel wondered what they would think of his tale, and he felt hesitant about entering the circle.

Next, a man from Grenville named Whitfield, entered the circle. He told a tale from a long time back, when men walked the sky, when they could go anywhere they pleased. But they became lazy, forced other beings to do their work, refused to take care of the slightest tasks, even refused to wipe their own asses or spoon their food into they mouths. The other spirits grew tired of them and cast them down to earth. Even today, they still haven't learned. They still try to purchase, borrow, and steal, the most important thing from each other, our labor and our time. That's why, even today, we still scorn, and admire, people who can survive without selling the days of their lives for money.

Ezekiel loved this tale. He understood the lesson of waste, greed, and not taking what you have for granted. But that one was also too short. They continued to tell tales, tales as old as the earth, tales brought from Africa in the belly of slave ships, tales so old no one could remember the first teller. Ezekiel made two attempts to tell his tale but hesitated and allowed others to go. This was the last night and if he faltered, he would have to wait for another occasion. And no one knew when that would be.

When Tilly stood and walked into the circle, Ezekiel was pleasantly surprised. He had never heard her tell a tale in front of a crowd. She began in a voice calm and modulated. Ezekiel leaned forward; use all of his ears to hear her. "Have any of you ever heard the tale of the Silent drum?" Everyone exchanged glances, as if surprised at Tilly's question. A hush fell on the gathering, tree frogs and crickets shrieked at the night. Ezekiel spoke in response to Tilly's question.

"What's the use of a silent drum? It's almost like a broken drum__ it can't talk," Ezekiel said.

Everyone nodded in agreement.

"This is not that kind of drum," Tilly said. "This drum is far from ordinary. This is the sacred drum. It's part of the legends and folklore of all African people. I'm surprised that none of you have heard of it. The silent drum is made of wood, gold, and the skin of Mangua. It stands four feet tall and was never heard in its immediate vicinity when struck, but it was heard by the ancient kings of every kingdom. It told them when it was time to meet in council at the appointed place."

"Tilly, how can a silent drum call anyone?" Ezekiel asked. He sat on the edge of the crowd near his father, on the spot that Tilly had just vacated to enter the circle.

"Shhhh." Tilly placed her index finger to her lips. "Each time the council of kings met, a different kingdom had to be the keeper of the drum. This time, King Tuango and his scribe, Manicou, came back to the kingdom of Zavimbe with the sacred drum. The prophecy said that three signs would tell when the time came to let the drum sleep. Manicou knew of the prophecy and kept an eye out for the signs. They came so fast that at first Manicou was in doubt. The first sign was the stealing of the children from the bosom of the mother while her milk still flowed. The second sign was the partition of land, which led to boundaries inside the tribes. The third sign came when King Tuango and his allies lost a great battle with foreign invaders. Zavimbe laid in smoke and ashes. There was no doubt now. Manicou saw that those three events were the signs, and it was time to let the drum sleep, as the prophecy dictated. He carried the drum across the Great Rift Valley to the mountains beyond, which are the legs of the throne of God. Manicou took the drum into the Cave of the Golden Lion. The lion yawned as Manicou approached with the drum, and he walked over the tongue into the mouth of the great beast, and they became one.

"Since the golden lion accepted the silent drum, we have been waiting for the Messiah, someone to lead us. The prophecy said that one day the Messiah would come. He'll be the one with the face of night whose eyes would shine like a billion stars. His message would be about the unity of all African people, and love for their brethren of all shades across the world. The Messiah would know the way to the Cave of the Golden Lion and the Silent Drum, and the Messiah would yawn, the Golden Lion would go into him and become one in spirit. The Messiah's voice would become the drum, and the faithful everywhere would hear the drum at the same time, and they would know with their hearts what it means." Tilly whispered the last words. "So, keep your ears and your eyes open, people."

Mama Viche saw the ceremony coming to an end, and she had something to say that couldn't wait. She looked across the crowd at Ezekiel. He appeared mystified, seemed full of questions, and wanted explanations about Tilly's Fable. The whole thing had captured his imagination, and the old woman saw what she interpreted as love and admiration between Ezekiel and Tilly, the way their eyes met across the crowd, and their shared smiles.

Mama Viche stood up from the chair and stepped into the circle. "This is a true tale," she said.

The old woman looked at the illuminated faces, and then her gaze shifted to the ground. She stood as if waiting for something to rise out of the dirt, and then she raised both feet and stomped the ground. "This history belongs to all of us who lives right here on this island. I'll use the one name by which the messenger was known. They called him Beaubrin. He lived for years among the Caribs, up in Sauteurs, before moving to this village. Beaubrin was just a young man around the time of Julian Fedon, one of the few accomplices to survive after the British put down the revolt."

Mama Viche saw Ezekiel's curiosity bubbling like boiling water. He started to crawl around the back edge of the crowd, trying not to disturb. John and Tilly stared at him as he moved off. Alma grabbed his hand, whispered in his ears, and made him sit next to her. The old woman's voice grew stronger.

"The Mysteries do strange things to the human mind. My grandmother said the old Carib woman who told her about Beaubrin was so old she looked as if she must have played with the devil when he was a boy. Beaubrin saw visions, she said, magnificent visions. One night, in the middle of one of the worst droughts to hit Grenada, he had a dream that would save all of them. Two spirits, Dambala and Mabouya, came to him. They were at war, causing the drought.

"They stood on the ground, near Sauteurs in a mighty storm of lightning, thunder, and wind, with no rain, the earth, dry as dead bones. Mabouya was angry because most of his people had been killed. That's why he allowed no rain. Mabouya knew in time, he would be forgotten and would have to spread himself on the wind. Mabouya confronted Dambala and threatened to turn the land to sand, if not allowed to strike a bargain with the Africans.

"Dambala knew fighting with Mabouya would be useless, so he struck a deal. Mabouya would have the wind, the sun and the sea, could even have the domain of dreams and take the form of birds. Dambala would have everything else: land, rain, all that grow on the land, and the imagination of the people. In exchange, Mabouya could form a covenant with us.

"Mabouya came to Beaubrin, dressed in a robe of fire, running along the ridge near Leaper's Hill. Beaubrin was young and strong then, but he had no intentions of wrestling an angry spirit. Mabouya told Beaubrin the legend of the wandering Carib warriors and asked for a sacrifice. Mabouya wanted Beaubrin to send his children into the world, all except the first born male. All off-springs must abide by this pledge. The rest must go into the world, away from this island, so they can carry a bit of Africa and a bit of the Caribbean with them. Mabouya and Dambala reside in the tamarind seeds, their essences are in those seeds. Beaubrin's progeny must take seven tamarind seeds on every journey and cultivate them in the new land. Finally, Mabouya told Beaubrin about the Valley of Bones. The land is bestowed on the people of Jean Anglais, but they must have the courage to claim it. They must follow the man with the courage to lead.

"Beaubrin decided to deal with Mabouya. Only time will tell if he made the correct deal. You see, in the realm of the spirits, there's no such thing as a good or a bad pact, because only time can show you that, and time does not exist for the eternals. Human will is their prime ingredient. The Caribs had the simplest and most beautiful of plans. Whenever a place became crowded or food ran scarce, the strongest warriors would strike-out from the home ground to capture new lands. In this way, the Caribs could have captured the world as they knew it. But then the Europeans came in ships, with guns, carrying their strange ways, bringing our captive ancestors, bringing Dambala, and here we are on this rock in the middle of the ocean."

The old woman felt dissatisfied as she moved away from the circle, believing no one else would step forward. No stories about the old Africans or those circular tales. Those might be lost forever, she thought. She felt a shudder in her joints when Ezekiel stood and came forward. She felt suddenly refreshed, as if some soft drizzle had drifted across her skin. Mama Viche saw a distinct change in Ezekiel, the way he held his body, the look on his face. She stood anticipating what he would say. He must be the one, the one destined to liberate those ancestors from the Valley of Bones, shc thought.

* * *

Ezekiel stood in silence for a time, all eyes on him. His first attempt to speaking to a crowd, rubbed his nerves raw. The young man decided to let his conscience be his guide. He began speaking in a voice that sounded like the coo of a dove: "You may want to know how I learned these things. These recollection floats through my veins, through all our veins. The blood of our ancestors conveyed them." He paused, waited for his feelings to transform.

MamaViche gazed at him, drew the night air into her lungs, took two steps back and sat down in the chair. Ezekiel wondered how far he would get before people started to grumble. He had no idea what to say. The boy decided to start talking, spit out the words as they floated to his tongue.

"You are expecting something familiar, something that speaks of flying Africans and the old days, but that's not what I have in mind."

Ezekiel saw Mama Viche perusing the gathering and everyone gaping at him with what appeared to be uncertainties. Mama Viche's gaze rested on him for a moment, and the look on her face gave him fortitude.

"I'm going to speak to you about what I see on the road we are traveling. I'm going to speak to you about my experiences with all of you."

"Tell us then. What you waiting for?" A strange voice shouted from the crowd and a collective chuckle followed. This interruption gave him time to reflect and a general idea took form.

"The now and the future, that's what I'm going to talk about," Ezekiel said. "The old times are gone and will never return, no matter how we remember them or speak of them and cuddle them. Don't get me wrong, the past is gone but not dead. In this place nothing is ever dead, nothing. Everything has many lives, in legends, in our superstitions. And don't think of me as fresh when I use the word superstition. I don't mean it in the sense of false notions or fallacies. I'm from here, a true son of this land and I'm beholden to our ways. I'd be a fool to think that these customs do not serve you. I see no difference between those who go to the Catholic or the Anglican churches downtown and those who stay home and adore Dambala or Mabouya. All of us maneuver toward the divine and the miraculous in our own ways. Faith and beliefs are the substances that keep our ancestors alive and moving among us." Ezekiel gestured over one shoulder at the backdrop of night.

"To us, even something as solid as a rock, we form a myth to embrace it, move it into our consciousness. You remember the rock that rolled down the hillside into the ocean and created a great wave that rolled all the way to Aruba? Lovely little story, but the rock never made it to the sea, it's still here, behind Mama Viche's house, buried in the earth. In our own way, we gave that rock a life."

Ezekiel nodded and smiled as if begging the crowd to agree. Everyone remained somber. This might be a good spot to inject a bit of humor, he thought. Nothing funny came to mind. The boy tried to consider what Malcolm would have said. What he would have scraped together from the words of the dead Roman. Anxiety forced Ezekiel to latch onto the lost fragment to flit across his mind.

"You remember my friend Malcolm, the albino?" he continued. "We climbed to the top of Ogoun's Point one day. Two boys on a quest like the knights of old. We climbed to the top of the mountain in search of the cave once shared by God and the devil. We found a small empty cavern. No devil inside. The devil dwells in our hearts. Words and actions have consequences, and influences. Those of us who do careless deeds are feeding the devil." Ezekiel became conscious that his words could be interpreted as a reproach to many people in the crowd. He tried to avoid eye contact, paused as if he had lost his bearings, and kept looking down. "It's so much easier to climb a mountain than to come down," he said.

"Looking at this village, from down here is a nice thing: the green grass, the blazing trees and flowering plants, birds, bees and everything, all so good-looking. But from up there," Ezekiel pointed at the mountain, "it's like seeing with God's eyes. I now appreciate this island as one complete entity, alive and smiling at me with its own face. But living things left without nourishment will die. People go away, scatter all over the world, never coming back to pay homage to the place of their birth. If we don't take care of this place and people, we call home, one day we will shrivel and die. We are not the first people to call this place home. The ancestors showed me. We all have tasks to perform in order to save ourselves and this place we call home. But first, we must start with our ancestors trapped in the cane in the Valley of Bones."

Ezekiel sensed they were loosing interest in what he was saying, so he switched his attitude to a more down to earth slant, began speaking about the Missionary Man and how he came to Jean Anglais to barter with God, twenty black souls for the chance to save his own soul. He spoke about Cosmus LaTouche and Jack Masanto, asking accusing questions, comparing the troubles of those two men to a form of slavery. The crowd shifted nervously. As he concluded, everyone remained still and silent, as if they had been chastised.

Alma came to Ezekiel smiling. "Where did you learn to speak like__? You sounded like one of those politicians. Wow!" Before he could respond, John and Tilly came close and stood one on each side of him. John looked at Ezekiel as if he wanted to slap his face.

"What you doing speaking to people like that? You think you some kind of__"

Alma moved off toward her aunt.

"Leave him alone, John. What he said was the truth," Tilly said.

"The truth my ass, what does he know about anything?" And John stormed off.

The others villagers refused to looked at Ezekiel. They milled about like ants disturbed.

* * *

Although Mama Viche appeared pleased with the places where Ezekiel had trespassed with his speech, she recognized the danger in what he had said about the past. The next day she spotted Ezekiel walking up the road past her house and she summoned him. Ezekiel felt reluctant, considering that the last time the old woman had spoken to him it led to his speech, and people appeared offended. He felt hesitant but had no excuse to reject her summons. "You are a very smart boy," she said as he stood before her. "I watched you grow since the night your mother delivered you with that veil over your head and face."

"A veil?" Ezekiel asked, grinding his teeth.

"We decided to keep this from you, didn't want you to grow up swell-headed."

"Why would I--seeing stuff, not fully understanding the difference between dreams and reality. Now I understand."

"We knew sooner or later you would hear all kinds of stories about the kings, the emperors and the gift of second sight. Your mother didn't want to burden you."

"Burden me? What's the use of this second sight anyhow? I couldn't use it to save her."

"It's not magic, Ezekiel. You can't just wave your hands and make the true world obey. I promised your mother to do this. So here." Mama Viche handed Ezekiel a brown envelope. He opened it and peeked in. A bit of shriveled tissue sat inside.

"This is it?"

"That's your veil."

"I expected something more impressive," he said.

Mama Viche smiled. "Do what you want with it. And one last thing, the speech you made at the gathering, your idle words about the past--"

"I know what I said, Mama. Only fools think they can ignore the past."

"I have a feeling you understand. That's why I'm giving you your veil and why we are having this conversation. I know your gift would give you a look at what's to come. What have you been seeing?"

"Not much, Mama. Just glimpses of this and that, now and then, always seem to be the future."

"How do you know?"

"I just know. I can feel it," Ezekiel said.

The old woman chuckled and looked at the expression on Ezekiel's face. "Our ancestors in the Valley of Bones, how often do they visit you?"

"Only once, Mama, they came to me a long time ago, mentioned something about the reasons for sustenance."

"The reasons for . . . what else did they say?"

"They ask me what I'm waiting for. Uncle Lester had told me about you telling him to feed them. So, I thought they might be asking about food."

"Lester told you about feeding the spirits, huh? That boy is so sly," Mama Viche said.

"Mama, I remember when I was little you saying something about a spirit inside of me. Is it still there?"

"No Ezekiel, it was only here to point the way. Once you were on your journey, it was easy for me coax it out and send it back to where it came from."

"Where did it come from, who was it? Was it Beaubrin?"

"Spirits don't have names, boy. It came from the Crossroads. You know that place between the living and the dead."

"Mama, I've doubts about all this?"

"Good. No one is forcing anything down your throat. Believe what serves you."

* * *

After the fête and the removal of the tent, Jean Anglais appeared gloomy and unfulfilled, as if Mama Viche had accomplished the opposite of what she intended. No one spoke to Ezekiel for days. Even his father and Tilly seemed sullen and withdrawn. The villagers acted as if he had delivered a prophecy of doom. Two days later, Ezekiel had one of his waking dreams. He saw his brother, Lloyd standing in a funnel of bright, blue light, his arms extended to the sky. Lloyd looked like an angel crucified. Ezekiel wondered if his vision had something to do with Dambala or Mabouya, and Mama Viche's story about the long dry season. He wanted to steer things, give Lloyd a warning, but he saw no obvious way to convey his misgiving without causing undue alarm. What a worthless gift, he thought.

Lloyd's difficulties held his mind in the shadows, but his physique looked robust. If he kept his mouth shut, very few people could detect his affliction. Henry just kept growing, mentally and physically, the spitting image of his father, John. The boys had pulled off a major cooperative effort: hauling water, collecting, splitting and stacking wood. They started grudgingly, right after they had returned from Mon Pandy with their father. They gained momentum as the sun rose. When Tilly did her inspection of the work and approved, the boys breathed a sigh of relief and began preparations for a knock-about in the Valley of Bones.

Ezekiel and Henry held a deep affection for their brother Lloyd. At times, schoolmates would attempt to make fun of Lloyd, and his brothers would jump to his defense. Some schoolboys would ask Lloyd to solve tricky mathematical problems, just to laugh at the way he scrunched his face before sputtering the answer. Most of them had no idea whether he was right or wrong. An incident at the movie theater became a breaking point. The three of them had gone down to see the movie, Ben Hur. Talk about a sea battle, men in chains stuck below deck on a sinking ship and a mighty chariot race. All this captivated them. They sat in the crowd at the matinee, full of expectations as the lights dimmed. Ezekiel and Henry wanted to see how Lloyd would handle his first movie experience.

The light showered the screen and the Metro-Goldwyn-Mayer lion roared. Lloyd jumped to his feet and shouted, "Mash, mash dog." The volume and clarity of his voice surprised Ezekiel and Henry. The audience roared with laughter. Lloyd enjoyed their reaction, and continued to shout those words long after the movie began, and the lion gone from the screen. Everyone grew tired of his noise, and the boys were asked to take their brother and leave. They didn't receive a refund. After that, Ezekiel and Henry resisted taking Lloyd on outings.

Tilly realized she had to do something to remedy this breach. She took all three of them into Saint Georges and bought them brand new white sneakers. In exchange, Ezekiel and Henry had promised to stop excluding Lloyd from their trips. This journey into the Valley of Bones became an attempt to fulfill that agreement.

Ezekiel and Henry had their doubts about how to handle Lloyd, but they had a conversation the day before and decided to exercise patience. Let him chase butterflies, smell flowers, and collect sticks. After all, they would still have almost the whole day. They discussed the possibility of taking Alma along, to deal with Lloyd, but decided against taking a girl. They took a machete, some matches, and slingshots. Their pockets bulged with good round stones. They planned to knock a few birds out of the trees, roast them on an open fire, eat some stolen sugarcane, suck a few ripe mangoes and wash it all down with coconut water.

Ezekiel, Lloyd, and Henry crested the ridge leading into the Valley of Bones. In a pasture below, ox-peckers hopped on the backs of the cattle, eating ticks from the hides. The young calf, which John would sell in about a year, kept chasing its mother. She kept kicking him away, weaning time. The birds took to the air and floated there as the boys walked near the cattle tether to an iron stake near a patch of grass.

The brothers headed for the field of cane. Lloyd and Henry kept a lookout for the owner while Ezekiel crawled into the field to make the selection. Ezekiel dragged out a stout stalk with the top still attached. He severed the cane-top with one blow of the cutlass. Henry picked up the top and chucked it back into the field like a spear. Ezekiel carefully skinned the bark off the stalk and chopped the naked cane into three equal chunks. The boys continued across the valley, chewing the cane, swallowing the juice and spitting the chaff as they went. They came to a mango tree just before the pasture gave way to a stand of young briah and black sage.

"Look! It's a ripe one!" Henry shouted. They stopped under the mango tree and stared up through the leaves. All they could see were bunches of green mangoes. Henry moved to one side, pointed at a branch way high in the tree. "It's over there," he said. They saw one yellow mango nestled in a bunch of green. Two wasp nests guarded any access to the single ripe fruit attached to the cluster.

"Henry, take off your sneakers, climb up and get it," Ezekiel commanded.

Henry chuckled. "You must think I'm stupid. I saw Glen try to get around something just like that." He pointed at the wasp nest, "in that Julie mango tree behind Tante Monah's house. He stretched around the hive, all stiff, and quiet, reaching for the mango. His feet slipped, and his face bounced into the nest." The boys broke into a hail of laughter. "The wasps poured out, all over him, stung him all over his face and head, some got inside his shirt. He batted at them, beating himself up, trying to knock them off. He lost his grip; tumbled out of the tree, caught a branch before he hit the ground, leaped down in full stride, hands beating at his face and neck as he ran. No way, no way." They were still convulsing with laughter as the last words left Henry's mouth.

Lloyd and Henry looked around for sticks and stones to pelt at the lone ripe mango. Ezekiel seized the opportunity to wander off, to do some exploring on his own and use his sling shot on a bird or two. He walked through the delicate mauve flowers of Shaving Brush, mixed in with the dried mass of Man Better Man, and the scorched pasture grass that concealed the crickets. The insects jumped each time his feet hit the silage. He left the grass and followed the path grooved in the earth by feet in the mud from the seasonal rain. Ezekiel's senses absorbed everything: the way the wind whistled through the trees and the cane, the chirping of birds, the shape of the clouds that drifted above, chasing the sun across the bright blue sky.

Ezekiel felt incredible, a little close to paradise. Memories of Alma added to his joy as he ducked under a branch hanging low across the path leading into the trees. He parted a clump of low hanging brush; a noise in the bushes caused him to stand still. First there was the stir of wings, and the bird flew out of the branches straight over his head and landed a short distance away, on the path. The bird, the size of a small chicken stopped, started pecking at the dirt. Ezekiel dug in his pocket, placed a rock in the tongue of his slingshot, aimed and fired. The rock struck home and the bird leaped into the air, fell back to earth, wings moving like slurred speech. Ezekiel approached, stood over the bird for a time as its wings became still.

He dashed back down the path, thrilled at his success, the kill dangled from one hand. He dashed into the pasture, and stood dumbfounded by the cluster of green mangoes his brothers had knocked out of the tree. One wasp nest rested on the ground amongst the collection of green mangoes, wasps buzzing all over. The single ripe mango remained in the tree.

"What the hell you guys doing?" Ezekiel shouted.

Lloyd and Henry ignored Ezekiel as they continued from a distance, to chuck stones, sticks and even some of the green mangoes into the tree.

"Look at this," Ezekiel said.

Lloyd and Henry turned, and dropped the green mangoes they were about to chuck. Ezekiel waved the big dove at them and then threw it on the grass near their feet. Lloyd and Henry inspected the bird. Lloyd looked at it as if undecided, tears or enjoyment. Ezekiel took a stone out of his pocket, placed it in the tongue of the slingshot, aimed up through the branches of the mango tree and fired. The fruit tumbled down and hit the ground. Henry's attention shifted to the mango sitting on the grass. Ezekiel snatched the fruit before Henry could reach it and he ran away from his brothers. A few wasps still circled near the nest on the ground. Ezekiel wiped the fruit on the side of his pants and bit into the skin. Henry stood looking at Ezekiel. When Ezekiel took a second bite, yellow juice squirted out of the corner of his mouth.

"You plan to share that, right?" Henry said.

"Go find your own." Ezekiel took another bite.

Lloyd shifted his focus from the dead bird to Henry and Ezekiel with the mango. The two boys exchanged quick glances and Ezekiel took off before they could team up. Lloyd and Henry chased him. They ran for a moment in circles trying to catch Ezekiel.

"You want this? You want this, huh." He smiled, teased them with the mango, extending it toward them and pulling it back, staying just out of reach. The teasing and laughter slowed him down and they both jumped on him. All three of them fell on the grass, wrestling for the half eaten fruit. Ezekiel lost his grip and the fruit rolled away, bits of the dry blades of grass clinging to the meat where Ezekiel had bitten into it.

They shared the rest of the fruit. The two younger boys offered the seed to Ezekiel. He declined and Henry kept it for himself. Henry gnawed on the core of the fruit until all the yellow was gone, just the white outer husk and bits of fiber remained on the seed. He took the machete, dug a hole and planted the seed near a cluster of black sage bush. They retrieved the bird and headed deeper into the Valley of Bones. They moved about, chatting and telling jokes as the sun retreated from the sky.

Ezekiel found a suitable spot as they circled back toward the entrance to the valley. He placed the bird on a log, chopped off the head and began ripping at the feathers. Lloyd went berserk

"No, no, no. Not the head!" Lloyd screamed. "Not the feathers."

"It's dead, Lloyd. We need to make a fire, cook it and eat it. It'll be good," Ezekiel said.

"No! No! You making it naked," Lloyd said. He grabbed the bird out of Ezekiel's hand and dashed into the undergrowth. Ezekiel and Henry heard him crashing through trees and shrubs. They waited, assuming Lloyd would return without the bird and they would have to go retrieve the carcass. After a few minutes and no Lloyd, they started to worry.

Ezekiel and Henry looked at each other, and then they headed into the trees after Lloyd, calling his name as they ducked into the low trees and undergrowth. After searching for some time, Ezekiel saw the onset of panic on Henry's face. Shadows had begun a measured retreated and the two boys stood at the edge of the trees without their brother.

"We can't go home without him," Ezekiel said.

"No shit. They will kill us if we do that," Henry said. "What we going to do?"

"We might need some help. I'll search some more. Go get Tilly and Daddy," Ezekiel said. "Tell them to come quickly and bring…"

Henry took off down the trail before Ezekiel could complete the sentence.

Ezekiel looked around and took a deep breath. Although he held a scant belief in the mythology of the lost souls who roamed the Valley of Bones, things elusive and confounding still subsisted on the edges of his imagination. A bird sent out a lonesome call and got no response. Ezekiel had been alone in the Valley of Bones after sunset before, but he couldn't master thc uneasiness. An educated man should not feel this way, he thought. What would Malcolm have to say about this confusion? Ezekiel interpreted the slight chill in the air as the breathing of the night. He continued to search, keeping an eye out for Henry. Companionship, such a splendid thing, he thought. He missed Malcolm.

Henry returned with Tilly, John, Alma, Mano, and a few other inhabitants of Jean Anglais. They carried flashlights, bottle torches, and they moved with haste. As he watched the glow of the lights pushing back the darkness, the depth of the situation thumped his guts. Ezekiel communicated what had happened and Tilly looked at him with blame on her face.

"Did you two do something to him?" She asked.

"You have to tell us what happened," John said.

"I see a little blood on the cutlass," Mano said.

"The blood is from the bird he got so upset about," Henry said. "Why would we do anything to Lloyd?"

"Cane killed Abel," Tilly said.

"If we killed him, we would be long gone, heading to the East of Eden, into the Land of Nod," Ezekiel responded with a smirk on his face.

"Watch your mouth, boy. We don't need your smart ass, back talk." John scowled at Ezekiel.

"Papa, he grabbed the bird and dashed into the bushes, just like Ezekiel said."

"We are wasting time, no need for blame. Let's find him first, before it gets too dark," Tilly said.

"Let's break up into groups of two. If you find him shout. He can't be too far. Alma, you coming with me," Mano said.

"That sounds like a good plan," John said, "Ezekiel, you with me, Henry, you with Tilly."

They scattered from the point where Lloyd had started off. The searched continued as a thick darkness swallowed the Valley of Bones. Lloyd's name pealed off their tongues. Tilly had warned them that loud noises would do no good. When he got upset he would only sit and rock in silence. After an hour, everyone returned to the stop where they had started off. No one found Lloyd or saw a trace of him. When Alma and Mano returned, shaking their heads, everyone bowed.

"Tilly, you should go back home, just in case he walks out of here and finds his way," Mano said. "Alma, go with Tilly."

Ezekiel had never seen this side of Mano before. He silently promised himself to never disrespect this man, ever.

After exploring the woods for the third time, the search party, which now included Mondu and Checklea, disbanded, promising to return at daybreak. Ezekiel, Henry, Mano, and John decided to remain in The Valley of Bones. They would keep a fire going, something Lloyd could see from a distance. Around midnight, a drizzle fell on them, slight scattered drops that barely raised Ezekiel's concern. But before long, a bright blue streak of lightning flashed across Ogoun's Point, and thunder followed. The lightning snaked down in long ribbons, lancing across the valley, and the thunder crashed almost immediately after, hard and loud. They decided to seek shelter under an outcropping of rocks on the ridge.

As they climbed the side of the hill in the rain, cracks of thunder echoed and diminished. In the silence, Ezekiel saw the outlines of a figure engulfed in a shaft of bright, blue light and the thunder cracked again, right above their heads. A voice rang out, mingled with the receding rumble. Ezekiel realized what he had witnessed and he knew it must be Lloyd. He took off, running toward the figure with Henry on his heels. They slipped and fell, almost lost the flashlight, got up and kept moving as the rain beat down on their heads. Steam rose from his hair when they found him. His new sneakers blown out around the soles of his feet. He lay on his back mumbling something that sounded like a prayer. Rain drops bombarded his face. John and Mano caught up with Ezekiel and Henry as they reached down to pull Lloyd to his feet.

"Don't touch him, don't touch him," John and Mano shouted in unison.

"Why not?" Ezekiel asked as they pulled Lloyd to his feet and embraced him. Lloyd screamed and recoiled.

The two men stood looking at the three boys. John and Mano looked as if something should have happened, but didn't.

"What happened?" Lloyd asked. "I saw angels, little blue angels, pulling the hairs on my skin with their tiny fingers. Oh God, my skin is on fire."

"Lightning struck you," Ezekiel said. "You don't remember?"

Ezekiel saw the damage the lightening had done to Lloyd. Besides the burned marks on his skin and clothes, the tip of his nose and ears looked injured. He sensed that something beside the injuries to his body may have happened to Lloyd. They held him close as they maneuvered him down the hill into Jean Anglais. Mano left them as they reached the gap that led to his house.

"What happened to him? Oh Lord." Tilly shouted, tried to embrace her son as he stood between his brothers. He avoided her outstretched arms. Ezekiel and Henry released Lloyd and he slumped into a chair, but he sprung back to his feet and screamed. Tilly and John began an examination of the burnt marks on Lloyd's body. "We should take him to the hospital right away. Oh Lord, oh lord."

"You should have seen it. It's a miracle he is alive. A thunderbolt struck him," John said.

"Oh my God, lightening struck him? How are you, Lloyd?" Tilly asked.

"I don't know. It feels like my skin is on fire and my tongue is no longer heavy. I see colors when you speak. Your words have color."

"John, we have to take him to the hospital, right now."

Tilly and John trudged through the molasses night with Lloyd. John felt uneasy about going to Jacob Elmo for help. Jacob came to the door after hearing the bark of the dogs and the pounding. He looked surprised to see John and Tilly with their son. He asked very few questions. He got dressed and drove them to the hospital in Saint Georges.

Lloyd remained in an isolated room in the hospital for almost two weeks, as nurses and doctors tended to his charred skin. He looked like a mummy, bandaged from head to toe. Everyone looked as if surprised at the speed at which he was healing, and the doctor appeared fascinated by Lloyd's sudden mental boost. Upon Lloyd's release, the doctor spoke to John and Tilly, gave them an account about bacteria in the gut, and the importance of the right balance, and how the proper balance worked on brain function. The possibility that lightning could rectify that balance fascinated Tilly. The doctor appeared mystified by the notion that Lloyd could now see words and numbers in a mixture of colors.

* * *

Lloyd returned to Jean Anglais disfigured, but a changed being. Everyone came to look at him and shake the hand of this man who had been struck by a thunderbolt and survived. The excitement of what had happened to Lloyd created an upbeat atmosphere around the village. Ezekiel thought about all that had transpired, and he wondered if these things could be somehow linked to Mama Viche with her Obeah powers. Could she have conjured these things, even the lightning that struck Lloyd?

Ezekiel sensed a design in all that surrounded him. He realized that his life was being slowly absorbed by Alma. Each time she came to visit Tilly and brought those books for Lloyd, he found himself occupied by the way she sat, with her legs crossed and the fleeting laughter that made her eyes glow.

He finally gained the courage to embrace this desire that had been robbing him of sleep. Instead of fighting whatever charms he presumed the Obeah woman may have placed on him, and his family, he decided to embrace them. Ezekiel arrived at this decision on his way back from a trip to deliver some of Tilly's vegetables to the Garifunas who lived on a compound near the Valley of Bones. His attitude toward Alma and how he would handle his feelings for her dominated everything. As he came down the road, he heard loud wailing from the center of the village. Instead of making his own inquiries, he went home and Tilly gave him the sad news.

Ezekiel knew there was nothing he could do for Papa LaTouche, so he continued with his plan. The evening sunshine came through the trees at a low angle. Shafts of idle light deflected the shadows cast by the trunks of briah, towering over goat weed and pomme coolee. In spite of the news Tilly had given him, he felt confident as he reached the gap leading to the home of the Obeah woman. For the first time, Ezekiel walked up to the house with no reluctance. He caught a glimpse of the old woman, her face framed by the corners of the open window and the white cotton blinds.

"Mama, can I speak to Alma please?" he said.

He spoke before she pulled the blinds open. She looked at him, and for the first time, Ezekiel stared back without lowering his gaze. Mama Viche almost smiled. The corners of her lips twitched.

"Alma!" she shouted. "Ezekiel Augustine is out here in the yard. He wants to speak to you." She said his full name as if there might be another Ezekiel. She turned to him. "Don't keep her too long."

Alma came down the stairs from the house wearing a flower print dress that came down to the top of her black and white shoes. The braids in her hair resembled a headdress, the way they hung back and over her ears. Her round face, and stubby nose, the full shade of her lips, Ezekiel almost whispered her name when their eyes met. He let his eyes move down past her neck, and when he came to her breasts, he tried to glance away and realized that he couldn't. He became aware that Mama Viche still watched them from the window.

Alma stood before him waiting. "You came here to stare at me?" she said.

"Papa LaTouche died last night," he said.

"We heard, such a fine man. He lived a good, long life. But that's not why you came here."

Her words forced Ezekiel to gauge his technique. He glanced at the window. Mama Viche was gone. "Let's take a walk," he said.

"Tante, I'll be right back."

"Don't be too long," the old woman shouted from inside the house.

"No, Tante."

Alma and Ezekiel strolled away from the house, toward the road. They walked in silence for a while, and stopped near a sapodilla tree.

"You never came to see me like this before. You not scared of Tante anymore?"

Ezekiel laughed quietly. "I feel something and I don't know what to call it. I can't stop thinking about you."

"Thinking about me, huh? I suppose lots of people might be thinking about me," she smiled.

"I want you to know--Alma, you making fun of me?"

She laughed. "Ezekiel, I know about life. I see far. I'm glad you finally opened your eyes and looked at me."

Ezekiel felt astonished by the precision of her words. It was exactly what he had experienced, what brought him to her aunt's door.

"I see you constantly, Ezekiel, in sleep, in wake. I remember how you smell when I come to your house. I contemplated stealing one of your sweaty shirts." Thunder rolled, her eyes glanced at the sky; in the next instant, clouds covered the sun.

Alma looked displeased about the weather. Big drops soaked them in less than a minute. They stood in the downpour. The water dripped off her braids and down her face. She didn't wipe one drop. Ezekiel took her hand, steered her to the shelter below the branches of the sapodilla tree. He ran his other hand over her face. Alma brought her hands up, ran them over his face and his hair.

"Coming to see Tilly tomorrow?" Ezekiel asked.

"No, Ezekiel, I'm coming to see you," she looked at him. Ezekiel felt assured. The raindrops on the leaves trounced out a soft melody. Alma spoke in a voice tinged with regret. "I should go. Tante will be vexed with me for getting wet."

"The wake for Papa Latouche is tomorrow night. You going?"

"Yeah, I'll be there. Will they let Cosmus come home to bury his grandfather?" she asked.

"Who knows, we'll see," Ezekiel said.

Alma stepped into the downpour. Wind pushed the rain now. Ezekiel watched her running toward the house, crouched over, and sheltering her face with one hands. He stood under the sapodilla tree as drops of rain came down through the leaves and hitting him. He left the shelter of the tree and started home, ignoring the rain on his head and back. Ezekiel felt accomplished as if he had put something off for a long time, and now it was about to start.

* * *

John and Mondu sat inside the house with a pint of rum on the table between them, smoothing out the final details. The old man's death presented the opportunity they had been waiting on for a long time. In certain respects, the plan appeared flawless. Cosmus had become so trusted that getting the officials to let him out of prison to say farewell to his grandfather came down to some minor bribes. John spoke to the right people, and grease a few palms with bags of fruits and vegetables.

"We'll get this one chance and no more," John said. "It has to work."

"You, you have the stuff, from, from Mama Viche and the and the papers from the fellow at the printer?"

"Right here." John waved a vial of clear liquid at Mondu. "I'll pass all of it to Rita. She'll slip it into their drinks. The moment they fall asleep we'll grab Cosmus. You sure the Pioles understand?"

"Yeah, I've, I've, I've everything on my end arranged." Mondu slapped his palms, entwined his fingers and cracked his knuckles.

"We don't need any surprises," Ezekiel said.

"Yeah, yeah, yeah man. You think, you think we come this far for me to screw it, screw it up? Trust me."

"I'm just clarifying things." John and Mondu took a shot of the rum. "You told them where to take him?"

"To, to Maturin, show him the way to Amana Del Tamarindo," Mondu said.

"Okay, Okay," John said.

"John, John, John relax. Take it, take it easy, man," Mondu said.

"I'll relax when he's off this island and way out at sea."

Mondu had been working on this plan for years. He had been helping the Spaniards from Venezuela to negotiate prices, helping them load the illegal whiskey and cigarettes they would take to the big ship anchored offshore, the ship used to smuggle the cargo back to Venezuela. They had come to recognize Mondu as a valuable resource. So when he asked them for this favor, they were happy to help.

The wake took place at the house where Mondu lived. Rita returned for her father's wake and funeral, and to see her son for the last time. She packed a suitcase with clothes and secured some cash, as Mondu and John had instructed. When the two guards from the prison brought Cosmus into the house, Rita hugged her son and thanked the two guards. Everyone gathered around, the women hugged Cosmus and the men shook his hand. They treated him like a dignitary, like a long-lost pilgrim who had finally returned home.

Mama Viche kicked off the wake with a tribute to Papa LaTouche. She stood near the table loaded with food and bottles of drinks. She carried no notes or papers. She spoke about the man from memory: "Augustus LaTouche was born in eighteen ninety, the son of Theresa and Theobald LaTouche. He lived through two wars and saw young men leave this island to join the killing over there in Europe. As a young man, he traveled to Aruba, where he worked and saved his money, came back and built two houses with his own hands. He was a friend to all. If you had a piece of ground to work, he would be there with his cutlass and his fork. Augustus had two children, his daughter Rita, who's here with us tonight and a son Septimus, in San Fernando, Trinidad, who couldn't be here. We are glad to see his grandson, Cosmus, here to say goodbye. Let's make some noise to let the ancestors know he's coming to join them."

The wake swung into full force as songs filled the air: Nearer my God to thee, When the Roll is Called up Yonder, and other mournful noises. Ezekiel and Alma joined them. The two prison guards fell into the celebration, talking, eating and drinking as if they were there for the feast. It was easy to slip them the portion. Before long, they were sleeping like babies. Cosmus looked surprised when John and Mondu approached him, stood on each side, and began nudging him toward the door. Ezekiel kept an eye on the happenings and smiled at the times he had spent chasing the mystery of Cosmus. And now here he was an ordinary fellow behind a beard, not even tall. He left Alma and followed them outside.

"What's happening? Where are we going?" Cosmus separated from John and Mondu, stood looking at them.

"Everything is set," John said.

Before John could explain, Rita came out of the house and threw her arms around her son's neck. John and Mondu stood as if irritated by this hesitation. Rita sobbed and stroked Cosmus' clothes. "Go. Go," she said. "Take this. Be free. We can both be free." She pushed the suitcase at him. "Some clothes," she said.

Mondu stuffed a wad of bills into Cosmus' palm. "Some, some cash, you'll need it"

"Take care," Rita Said. "I don't know if we'll ever see each other again, oh God!" She dashed into the house, sobbing. Cosmus stood with the suitcase in hand, looking at Mondu and John. Ezekiel came out of the shadows as Cosmus crumpled the money in his palm.

"Let's go," Ezekiel said.

"You not going anywhere," John looked at his son.

"I saw this. Three of us walked him down the road to the boat."

"What you talking about? Go back inside," John said. "Go keep your girlfriend company."

"You don't understand, Daddy."

"I understand you getting into things that's none of your__"

"Daddy, why you always so__"

"Okay, okay," Mondu said. "We don't have, we don't have time for this."

"Wait a minute. I told no one about this," Cosmus cocked his head and looked at Ezekiel.

"You told no one about what?" John stared at Cosmus.

"All those years in prison, some of my dreams about him." He pointed at Ezekiel. "Never doing anything, just watching, must be something in stock for me and you, Ezekiel."

"I'll go ahead; whistle if I see anything suspicious." Ezekiel walked ahead of his father and the others without waiting for any contradiction.

"That sounds, that sounds good," Mondu said. "Extra eyes."

"What's this? You guys think this is a . . .? I can't hide on this little island. I'm not running and hiding like a dog," Cosmus said.

"We have a ride for you, all the way to Venezuela," John said, pointing his index finger at Cosmus like a gun.

"It'll be alright. They have been planning this for years," Ezekiel said as he allowed the group to catch up.

"There you go again, interfering." John turned on his son as the tree frogs pinged in the underbrush. A dog barked in the distance and the voices from the wake floated on the night wind.

"I heard you and Mondu talking about this many times," Ezekiel said. "I saw most of it, I saw it in visions. Well, not quite visions. Most of the time, I was awake."

"What kind of mumbo jumbo? All of you must be crazy." John shook his head.

Cosmus glanced at the house in the shadows across the field. He nodded, turned and spoke as if to Ezekiel.

"My selfishness killed her; could have rejected all of her advances. But I didn't."

"It's a good thing they didn't hang you," Ezekiel said. "You sound like a man still pining, can't hang a man when he's in love."

"What do you know about love?" Cosmus said.

"I feel the same way about a girl. Well, not the same, you know what I mean?"

Cosmus smiled at Ezekiel. "When she drowned, the police already had me in the station downtown. Actually, they contributed to her death by arresting me. The responsibility for what happened to her stretches far and thin."

"Christ! We thought we were so careful." John looked at Mondu. "Cosmus, I had a fellow at the printing office put some papers together for you, just in case you need them. Your new name is Augustus, just like your grandfather's, but you from Trinidad. Practice your Triny accent."

"The police will come looking. You two might be too smart for your own good. That's why you encouraged me to keep learning Spanish. How can I ever thank you guys?"

"So Ezekiel," John said, "if you saw things about Cosmus, tell him something that only he would know."

"Well, let me see," Ezekiel said, "Jack asked you to bring him a razor blade tucked inside a Bible, and you brought it to him. That's how he made that rope to hang himself."

"How did you know? I never said a word about..."

"I saw that and more."

"Oh man! He's telling the truth, fellahs. I know there must be something regarding you and me."

Cosmus touched Ezekiel's head. John and Mondu acted as if this confirmation of his abilities amounted to nothing. Ezekiel moved on ahead sniffing out the terrain like a hunting dog. He whistled and came back to the three men, walking down the road. Ezekiel pointed at a police Land Rover heading toward Grand Anse. They stood, watched the vehicle travel down the road, and then they headed into the Mang, where Mondu's boat sat pulled out of the water.

"Ezekiel, far as you going," John said.

Ezekiel started to protest, and then he extended his hand to Cosmus. "This is for you. They say it brings good luck." Ezekiel handed Cosmus an envelope.

"What is it?"

"My talisman, my veil, I was born with a veil."

Cosmus looked into the envelope. "You can't give this to me. Is that real? I read about veils. They say sailors who possess one of these can't drown."

"And you are going to sea," Ezekiel said.

"Thank you," Cosmus said

"All this time and no one said a word to me about you and a veil. Christ. Why are we standing here blabbing? Get in the boat, let's get going, let's go," John said.

Cosmus looked at the envelope, pushed it into his pocket with the wad of money, and then he shook Ezekiel's hand. The boy helped push the boat into the water, and watched as Mondu got behind the oars. The boat with the three men moved slowly across the lagoon.

* * *

On the Carenage, near the fire station, Mondu and John delivered Cosmus into the hands of the Piole smugglers. Cosmus greeted the group in fluent Spanish, as he boarded the craft. One of the smugglers started the outboard.

"Take this, Cosmus." John handed him a paper bag with seven tamarind balls. "When you eat them, save the seeds and plant them. They will bring you luck."

"What kind of luck?"

"The good kind," John said.

"Thank you both. Mondu, you take care of Rita." The words came out of Cosmus's mouth as if he had suddenly developed a cold.

They pushed the loaded craft away from the wharf. John and Mondu watched them motor across the Carenage, into the moonlight beyond the pier, and out to the mother-ship anchored offshore, the ship that would take Cosmus and the smugglers to the eastern coast of Venezuela.

John felt a satisfaction so great it was as if he had broken Cosmus out of prison by himself. When Rita came to thank him properly for his part in freeing her son, he saw a distinct change in her manner. He recalled the time when Cosmus had told him about seeing two emotions at the same time, on his mother's face. John looked at her and saw the same thing, sorrow for the death of her father and joy for her son's freedom. She looked as if at any moment she would break out laughing and crying.

For almost a week the police lived in Jean Anglais. They searched every house more than once, day and night, hid in the bushes and followed people to see where they were going. Inspector Didderot acted like a hound dog. He regarded John as a special undertaking, following him, trying to fulfill both of his suspicions about the man. For awhile the uproar and harassment continued, but that boiled down the moment the newspaper started printing stories about the irregularities in Cosmus' conviction.

It didn't take long for Rita to quit her job in the laundry at the hotel. With the death of her father, Rita became a wealthy woman. She rented her father's house to a couple from Grenville who worked at the same hotel on Grand Anse beach. Six months later Rita and Mondu got their papers in order, climbed aboard a vessel one night and sailed away from Grenada. Rumors had it, they moved to Panama or Venezuela. From time to time, although nothing of consequence had taken place in Jean Anglais for two years, Inspector Didderot continued to drive his police vehicle through the village.

* * *

Ezekiel celebrated his birthday with his two brothers and some friends. They shared a cake prepared by Tilly and Alma, washed it down with sorrel and ginger beer; a good time was had by all, but after they had grown tired of listening to the radio, the focus of their amusement soon shifted to jokes about Alma and Ezekiel. Ezekiel heard the teasing, and he wondered why Alma looked so disturbed, hoped she didn't think he could be blabbing to his friends about their private matters, especially about what occurred three days ago.

As if to change the focus, Alma jumped into the merriment and began telling jokes about a mischievous, genius of a child, called Stubby. "Have you heard the one about the teacher who asked Stubby to spell a word? 'How do you spell crocodile?' the teacher asked Stubby? 'Kro-ko-dile,' Stubby declared, proudly. 'Wrong,' said the teacher. 'That might be true,' said Stubby, 'but you asked me how I spelled Kro-ko-dile.'" The gathering erupted with laughter. Alma laughed with them, and then she continued as if to prevent anyone from jumping in with a joke of their own. "And another time the same teacher tried to trick Stubby, ask him a question that she was sure Stubby couldn't twist into a joke. 'How old is your father?' the teacher asked. 'Ten,' said Stubby. 'Well how could that be?' 'I was born ten years ago and that's when he became my father.'" Ezekiel admired how she steered the conversation.

Three days before, Tilly had dispatched Ezekiel and Alma to pick some fresh corn in the Valley of Bones. For the first time, Alma had consented to stay for dinner. The trip to the valley was hot and muggy. Black sage bushes fluttered in a breeze that barely made the day tolerable. Birds flew in the low branches, singing and chirping. Ezekiel and Alma engaged in a tidy conversation as they walked to the valley.

"Hey, the other day, when you were playing marbles, with Punky and those others ragamuffins, I came up behind you and stood there listening," she said "You guys love to make-up stories about girls. Delores warned me."

Ezekiel looked at Alma and tried to recall what he might have said. When nothing materialized, he said, "I don't know what to think about Delores."

"You can think what you want; she's her own kind of person. Her mother beat her bad, dragged her down to see Tante. She refused to tell the name of the father of the child in her stomach. Tante said there was nothing she could do. Delores is just too pigheaded."

"So who is the father?

"She never told me. But Tante knows. Delores said she didn't want some man claiming her child, a child she carried for nine months. When all the man had to do was thrust in her, rub around for a minute and squirt a little liquid," Alma said. "I thought it might be yours."

"What!"

"She had her designs on you. She told me."

"I heard you two talking, at the standpipe. She was ranting about having no use for men and you telling her to let them win." Ezekiel paused for a moment to let Alma take in what he was saying. "And you talking about teaching me to wash clothes and do dishes."

"How did you . . .?"

"I was hiding and listening."

"Ezekiel, you rascal. What else have you . . .?"

"Nothing, nothing! Daddy told me the boys who talk the most about sex get the least."

"You didn't say much yesterday. What does that mean?" She smiled and lifted her brows.

Ezekiel felt himself slipping into a trap with this line of conversation, so he was relieved when they came to the field of corn. They stood near the stalks and stripped off the ears. The silky corn beard wrapped around their fingers, for a moment, the breeze tugging at the fine hairs, pulling them into the air with flashes of fractured grace. Ezekiel watched the little silver-yellow threads floating across the glare of the sun.

He chopped down the bare stalks, gathered them into a bundle, and carried them to the cow pen under the mango tree.

"Jesus, this sun is hot," Alma complained as Ezekiel returned.

Ezekiel threw her a side-long glance. Their eyes met. The perspiration, the glow of her skin and the conversation about Delores had generated something. He had never before imagined or appreciated Alma in this specific way. That glow reflected all over her, in her hair, down her smiling features, and the old cotton dress she wore emphasized the contours of her body.

"Let's go take a dip in the pond," Ezekiel said.

Alma looked at him, hesitation in her eyes. "Great idea," she said, after a moment.

Ezekiel carried the basket of corn and Alma followed as they took the trail through the bushes. They arrived at the meadow on the hillside, where the river emerged from the earth, between two huge rocks, into an indentation in the earth. Ezekiel placed the basket of corn under the running water, removed his shirt and walked in. The water felt cold. Alma removed her sneakers and waded in with the rest of her clothes on, and then she ducked her head under.

When she came back to the surface, the dress clung to the shape of her body. Ezekiel moved toward her, stood in a spot on the submerged rocks where the water came up to his knees, took her hands, and then he attempted to lift Alma. He had no idea she would weigh so much. As he tried again, to lift and carried her out of the water, she felt substantial but pliant. His fingers indented her skin like the feel of a ripe fruit. He looked into her eyes for some reaction as he rested her on the grass. Her steady, determined gaze confused him. He couldn't tell if they held defiance or surrender, so he proceeded. It was the first time Ezekiel and Alma had progressed this far. They had kissed and touched before, but this held another sensation. The intense look in her eyes bothered him. He continued to kiss her ears and he whispered. "Tell me if you don't like this."

"The grass is tickling me," she whispered, and giggled.

He leaned back and looked at her face. Her expression reassured him. Ezekiel ran his hand over her hair, and she took a deep, noisy breath. And then she gently buried her face in his chest, breathing rhythmic and warm against his wet skin. Everything about her became clear: eyes, ears and nose, the flake of dry grass in her hair, all became a delicate composition. Ezekiel felt powerful, tensions eased out of his body.

The sound of two approaching voices interrupted their interlude. Delores and a man coming down the path quarreling. They grabbed the corn and sprinted off into the woods, running until they could no longer hear the voices.

"Let's go back. I want to see why she's making all that fuss."

"No," Alma said. "Would you want people spying on us? No privacy, no romance."

Ezekiel and Alma circled away from the pond and back to the path. They walked slowly savoring the private warmth, allowing the sun to dry Alma's clothes. He picked the grass out of her hair. They didn't care to see anyone or talk to anyone. Ezekiel and Alma strolled oblivious to inquisitive eyes.

"Could you be someone's wife?" Ezekiel asked, looking directly at Alma.

"It depends on whose wife."

"My wife, of course."

"Well. I've had other offers."

"From who?" Ezekiel almost shouted the question.

"Jacob, Raymond, and others," Alma said.

"Jacob, Jacob Elmo? He is old enough to be your father, and he's already married."

"I told Tante about him flirting with me and inviting me to ride in his car. She laughed, called him a mongoose and threatened to send a Jumbie into his house."

"Nasty old man. I would enjoy beating his ass with a stick."

"Don't worry. You may get your chance. He's getting older and you are getting stronger."

"I don't need to get stronger, can beat his ass right now."

"I can take care of myself. I'm not some stupid little girl."

"So that means no?"

"What you going to do with a wife? You don't even have a house. You still have to finish school, find a job."

"I don't mean we have to…right now. I just want you to know, I think of us as important and permanent," Ezekiel said.

"I was joking about other offers," she said.

Ezekiel looked at Alma and smiled. "You know if we did decide to be married, say tomorrow? Jean Anglais is a good place to live and raise children."

"You getting way ahead of…at least you thought of marriage first," she said. "But children?" She laughed.

Their clothes were almost dry by the time they made it home and handed the corn to Tilly. She looked at them with a curious frown on her face. Ezekiel wondered if she could see something between them. He promised himself to secure Tilly's opinion on matters concerning Alma. He thought that would be safer because seeking counsel from his father might be risky. The man could go off on a big harangue about women and children, how they hold you back, prevent you from pursuing your ambitions. Ezekiel could only image what else his father might decide to dwell on.

* * *

No single event brought Tilly to the decision about her marriage to John. The gossip pertaining to who might be responsible for Delores' pregnancy seemed like a slog through mud. The fact that the girl was keeping her lips sealed to protect someone complicated the issue. Tilly wondered if it could be one of the young boys. When some of her neighbors slacked off from buying her vegetables and eggs, or coming to the house to sit with John and listen to the radio, Tilly appreciated how it all felt a bit strange. His affair with Monica had been many years ago, but a little sediment still lingered in her craw. Wives are usually the last to know, she thought.

When the wooden stand she had erected down at the crossroads, near Belmont, to sell her vegetables was smashed, she figured things might be exactly what she suspected. Tilly refused to bow to the rumors and question John. She didn't want to show her doubts or expose her uncertainty to ridicule if the truth should squeeze out in another direction. The day Tante Monah packed her few belongings and moved with her daughter to Crochu in the district of Saint Andrews, everyone exhaled, except Tilly.

She stood in the kitchen, watching John's back as he sat on the stairs in the sun. Why would he get himself mixed up in such mess again? Tilly wondered what plan he could be hatching, after the work on the house and the new radio. What would be left for them if the rumors about Delores were true? She settled on her decision to try and make more money from her kitchen garden, get more cash into her bank account, just in case. Tilly looked away from John and out the window. Her father, Vernon Stewart, come into sight at the gap.

Tilly knew her father was one of the few people John respected, but his wickedness had moved them apart. John simply kept his distance from the old man. Vernon had been headmaster of the school John attended as a boy. Tilly had heard many stories about the piece of leather her father would use to discipline John and his other incorrigible students. They called the strap "The Conqueror." There was a rumor that The Conquer was soaked in piss to give it more weight and sting. It came out when the boys fought. It camc out when the boys showed a lack of respect for teachers and the rules of the school, when they refused to do their homework or arrived late for classes. John had been acting as if the old man still held the power to employ that piss soaked strap.

Over time she came to regard certain conversations with father as a single strand of support, until she realized that Vernon seemed a little eager to return to some level of normality with his son-in-law, but was unable to do so, since John had remained aloof, never engaging the old man. As her father walked toward the house, Tilly knew some junctions were about to be crossed. That time she had attempted to speak to her father about John and the affair that produced Henry seemed important now. Vernon had used four words and the conversation had dissolved like dirt, into mud on a hillside in rain. "What's done is done," he had said. She remembered the looked on his face and the words that never left her lips. If thcre is forgiveness to be dispensed, shouldn't I be the one to propose? She resented the hint of usurpation implied by her father's words. Fathers, she thought, don't they retain some kind of responsibility to defend the dignity of their daughters? She knew her father would always take refuge in reason. "Since you already forgave him, exactly what do you expect of me?"

Tilly suspected this visit had something to do with the boys and she held some concerns. Although she took care of and held Henry in a reasonable regard, he continued to be a reminder. Ezekiel, on the other hand, she thought, was too docile. What kind of man would he grow into obtaining his model from men who lacked principles? I'll have to make sure my son, Lloyd, receives better moral values, she thought. As for Ezekiel, I'll ask my father to show him the way.

She looked at John, as he scrutinized her father coming toward the house, and she wondered about the clothes the old man was wearing: brown leather shoes, baggy dungaree pants, short-sleeved white shirt, and a felt hat. The only thing missing was a tie, standard attire for a trip into Saint Georges on official matters. Vernon waved at Tilly as he came within reach of John. They shook hands and swung into the cover of ordinary conversation.

"The sun is sure hot as hell. I think it's getting hotter each year," Vernon said.

"Not sure about each year. It sure is hot as hell today," John said.

"I had to cut short my talk at the school. I think everybody were kind of glad they didn't have to stand out in the sun any longer, listening to my chinwag about the virtues of education." Vernon laughed as he sat down on the kitchen stairs next to John, and placed his cane to one side.

"The boys have been spending a lot of time at your house lately. Are they behaving?"

"Oh yeah, I can still manage this," Vernon said, took up his cane, waved it.

The two men sat in silence for a moment. Tilly joined them with glasses of iced ginger beer. She waited as her father talked about the old house and the new addition, how the original cabin was almost gone, and then, as if recalling the purpose for his visit, he shifted his line of approach.

"John, Ezekiel is the kind of student teachers prayed for when I ran that school."

"The boy has brains," John said. "He listens well. Those silly questions of his though?"

"I heard about the speech he gave, made people stand up and take notice. He grasps the essentials better than some of my children." The old man glanced at Tilly.

"Why are you looking at me like that, Papa? After all, I'm only a girl."

"There was no discrimination around our house. Your mother wouldn't allow it," he said.

"She allowed you to do--"

"See John, brains and females, a dangerous combination. Let me tutor Ezekiel some more."

"What you filling his head with now?" John asked, and looked at his father-in law with suspicion.

"He shows a keen interest in history. The secondary school could have a true scholar in their midst."

In spite of her doubts and uncertainties, Tilly appreciated what her father was saying. She and John had paid scant attention to what Vernon was doing with Ezekiel and Henry. The tutoring had been going on for several months, and now Lloyd, starving for numbers, speaking about figures of many shades dancing at the tip of his nose. Tilly looked at her father stating his case, knew about his appreciation of knowledge, and she contemplated on his greatest regrets.

All three of his sons were gone. One, a musician in Nigeria; another in Canada working as a civil engineer; and the last one, his youngest son, went to England and joined the British Army. This, in particular, angered the old man. Tilly remembered overhearing a conversation between her father and her brother, Scovil. "What kind of a man decides to become an executioner? That kind of thing is for people with no prospects. I gave you all I had and that's what you choose to do with it?" They argued for hours on end and neither of them could see the other's point of view. The rupture widened between Vernon and Scovil. Tilly's little brother seldom came back to visit the family.

The other expatriates would return for visits, but it was always sad to see them depart with their families, knowing that with each passing year, with each passing generation, it became more remote that they would ever return to make this island their home. She thought of the millions of people all over the world who can trace their ancestry to the people of the Caribbean and she speculated on what would happen if one day they all decided to return to their respective island.

Tilly knew John had a secret agenda on this docket. She wished he would say something, clear the air, see if the old man would take the bait and voice his feelings about émigrés. Tilly thought of broaching the subject with them, but she decided against. Let them go on thinking they own the world. John said nothing, made no further comments or objections. Tilly felt disappointed, but she smiled at her father's cleverness, how he had skirted any confrontation with John but had handled two tricky situations with grace.

Tilly's ambition to advance her vegetable enterprise became a reality because of one observation. She had noticed how white people often try to keep away from mud and dirt. They would tiptoe around wet soil; would refuse to acknowledge food and all things organic came from dirt. She told her children to wash everything they harvested twice, to remove all evidence of where it came from. When Mondu and Rita had decided to go abroad, Mondu could not sell his boat, so he left it in the care of John. Tilly used the boat, with the help of Henry, to sell her vegetables to the yachts anchored offshore, and to a couple of hotels on the beach at Grand Anse. This became a crucial part of her plan to rescue her son from Jean Anglais specifically, and Grenada in general.

* * *

Ezekiel recognized a change in the tutelage Vernon was presenting. Before, they had only spoken of things relating to Africa, Grenada, the myths, and legends. Now they entered a more formal stage. They met three times a week, for one hour, and then it changed to two hours on school days and a flexible schedule on weekends. Ezekiel still had to do his chores, but there was always time left for play. He knew his romance with Alma had to be nurtured, so his time with her took on substance and direction.

Ezekiel felt as if a door had been flung opened, allowing him to step outside and explore. The old man introduced him to Aesop's fables and spoke to him about the great big poem by Ovid, The Metamorphoses. He encouraged Ezekiel to read sections from the various volumes. Then there came a change. Vernon started lecturing and assigning Ezekiel reading tasks from books by Thomas Hobbes, John Locke, and other political thinkers. Eventually, Ezekiel grew tired of the redundant philosophical ideas, and the double standards of those old white men. He had grasped the subtleties in the old man's approach. He saw it plain the moment Vernon started addressing the transformative tales told by Ovid and relating them to troubles around Grenada.

Often, Ezekiel would go down to the post office with Vernon, and people would see them walking in the hot sun with heavy cardboard boxes. Ezekiel devoured the books like corn porridge with brown sugar. The more the boy read, the more he embraced the belief that an intelligent mind can be a heavy load.

At first, the books arrived in small packages, two and three at a time; then they began to receive in large crates. Ezekiel surmised that the old man had started boasting to his friends abroad that he had found a kindred spirit. In the space of one year, Ezekiel indulged in several histories, some in defense of the slave trade, and some against. He was dumbfounded by the hypocrisy of scholars, who invested their money, priests, royalty, all of them making money in the trading of human flesh. The involvement of the church, through sanction and investments, forced the young man to question all religions. But Ezekiel and the old man had already agreed that religion was a man-made venture, and man-made enterprises are never perfect. In due course, they always take on the flaws of their creators and managers.

The histories were always augmented by the old man's own point of view, connecting points, engaging in critical looks at humanity and the injustices perpetuated in the name of progress. The old man spoke of the Berlin Conference of eighteen eighty-four where the Europeans decided to carve up the continent of Africa. He told Ezekiel the colonization of Africa was not as long and ancient as some would have you believe. Vernon Stewart conceded black Africans and Arabs had contributed as much, if not more than Europeans to the slave trade. And as far as the

Europeans, what do you expect from nobilities who conspired to starve their own countrymen, to get them out of the fields and into factories?

Ezekiel's interest in history began to fade as he discovered the contrary nature of the subject, and Vernon introduced him to Adam Smith, Karl Marx, and Maynard Keynes. Ezekiel felt choked by all the information Vernon was parceling out, but he remained fascinated by the way these economists wrote about labor. What it is, its value, what's more important, labor or capital? By their way of thinking, who stood to gain? Ezekiel would formulate some ideas backed up by his analysis of the past, linking his opinions to the present, and what it might mean for Grenadians in the future. The old man would listen and smile. It warmed Ezekiel's heart to see agreement on the old man's face.

* * *

Ezekiel's journey through the secondary school progressed with a degree of ease. Vernon's tutorials had moved him beyond his classmates. One night the old man went to sleep and when he was slow to rise the next morning, his wife shook him awake. Vernon appeared groggy and unfocused. Florence sent for Tilly and they took Vernon to the doctor, where it was determined, he had suffered a mild stroke.

Old age had turned Vernon into a mystic. The old man would sit and talk to the air for extended periods, in a dreamy kind of stupor, about Haile Selassie, calling him Prince Tafari, the Messiah. When engaged by Ezekiel, he would speak of an association between Marcus Garvey and the Messiah, to return the lost children to the promised land of Abyssinia, where they would be protected by Mamluks. Ezekiel knew his stories were only legends, the same kind as those created and told in Jean Anglais.

These legends could be used to bestow pride in the people, Ezekiel thought. At times, the old man would be lucid, speaking of things relevant, about politicians and government officials, what they understood and what they did not, calling them by name. At other times, Vernon would drift off into island lore: Anansi tales, Papa Bois-the strong, old man of the bush who would warn the animals when hunters are approaching; and Mammy Watta-the siren of the sea, waiting to cast her spells on greedy fishermen. Ezekiel absorbed these tales, always appraising their useful applications, to his life, to Alma's life and to the people of Jean Anglais.

Ezekiel completed the necessary lessons for matriculation in three years. He sat for his final exams and was granted a scholarship to continue his studies at the University of the West Indies, Mona Campus, on the island of Jamaica. His teachers advised him to focus on history and economics. Don't forget us when you become premier of Grenada, they told him.

Tilly broke the news to John. Ezekiel sat there and waited for his father's reaction. He knew what would happen. John had outlined a plan for Ezekiel as they stood on the sand at Pandy beach one morning.

"I'll leave you the land and the house," his father had said. "You must always take care of Lloyd. Allow no one, man or woman, to take advantage of him. He's not like you and me. He's special. You must not sell or divide the property. Do everything in your power to make it better for the next generation." Ezekiel felt mystified by his father's pronouncement, but he promised to follow his father's instructions.

Ezekiel had always been a curious person, one who would hear things and catalog them. On further consideration, his father's reasoning appeared clear. If Ezekiel left the island, he would never return, bright lights, shiny cars and other undertakings would seduce him, grandchildren would be thousands of miles away, and would come to visit now and then, if ever, as strangers. Ezekiel understood such a scenario to be unavoidable for a man with three sons.

When John refused to yield on the issue of Ezekiel going to Jamaica, and issued his decree to Tilly, Ezekiel sat, listened and remained mum.

"Tell them to give that scholarship to someone with no future, like one of those street boys in Saint Georges," John said. "Ezekiel has a future right here. I'm a man of the land. He'll be a man of the land, and of the people. Grenada needs to keep some of her good people at home."

"Sounds like you are trying to live out your ambitions through your son?" Tilly said as she placed a pot of water on the fire.

Ezekiel saw John throw Tilly a wicked glance. He could tell she wanted to scream and shout on his behalf, but he guessed her years of living with John held her in check. Tilly moved about, keeping her distance from Ezekiel and John, started dropping Irish potatoes into the pot of simmering water.

Ezekiel left his parents to their own devices and decided to find Alma. He resolved to use the promise he had made to his father as a shield. Alma stood on the bottom road with two girls. The other girls left Alma standing in the road as Ezekiel approached. They looked back and giggled.

His desire for Alma had grown beyond measure. He knew if he went to Jamaica, it would be a long time before he could be with her again. The idea of returning to Grenada and finding Alma married with a big belly haunted him. Ezekiel knew he would obey his father, so he began plotting a definite future with Alma. In the last two weeks, he had started helping with the crops in the Valley of Bones, milking, and feeding the cattle. His father's undertaking to find him a job with the Labor Union seemed to fit Ezekiel's plan. But deep down, the young man fostered contrary ideas that would have made his father frown, spit into the dry dirt, and ask his favorite question: "Boy, you lost your blasted mind or what?"

Ezekiel tried to hide behind a mask when he told Alma about his decision not to attend school in Jamaica. But he couldn't fool her. They stood in the road watching the day slid toward night. Alma interpreted his tone and posture, felt compelled to say something.

"Why would any sane woman want to marry a man who looks so defeated?"

"What you mean by--?"

"You still a young man, Ezekiel, you hardly twenty, but you acting as if.... if I can't help you to be happy, I don't want to be involved," she said. "So decide."

"Decide, what?"

"If you want to be happy or not, it's a choice you know."

Ezekiel was surprised at the clarity of her words. He had no idea that he had presented such a superficial front. Still, he refused to surrender his stance.

"This is not what it appears to be," he said.

"What you mean?"

"I'm quite satisfied to remain here with you." He looked at her and smiled.

"You can't shift this to me." Alma waved her index finger at Ezekiel. "No, no, you might be fooling yourself for now, but may have to place the blame somewhere else, later."

"I'm not going to blame you for anything. I don't want Tilly to know I'm willingly giving up my schooling."

"How is that fair to her? You are a complicated person, Ezekiel. Too much stuff boiling in your belly, figure it out." And she walked away.

* * *

Ezekiel made his way down to the beach where Florence had told him Vernon might be. The perfect time to be at Pandy Beach, no one came to this small secluded beach at midday in the middle of the week. Only tourists and people with money had time to bathe at that time of the week, and most of them congregated on the beach at Grand Anse.

He came down the path onto the beach, searching up and down the sand for Vernon. Ezekiel surmised the old man must come here to soak in the salt water, ease his rheumatism, and enjoy the harmony. He found Vernon floating in the sea like a log. A flock of gulls squawked and screamed as they plunged into a school of herring. The old man bobbed in the water, facing the ruckus, his graying head and the tip of his toes above the surface.

Ezekiel called his name. The old man swiveled and began moving toward the shore. "Tilly told me your father refused to let you go," Vernon said. "We offered to assist with money, but he said no. This bothers me. I may be responsible for this." He looked at Ezekiel. "I filled your head with all those grand ideas."

"Grandpa, you gave me a gift and I'm thankful."

"Great mind, great suffering," Vernon said.

"Only a fool would refuse such sweet anguish," Ezekiel said.

"Who can tell, great things can happen right here. You don't have to travel abroad." The old man stood next to Ezekiel. His wrinkled toes half buried in the sand.

"I already made up my mind. I understand my future is here," Ezekiel said.

"You don't sound or look like it," Vernon said.

"So many things pushed me to this point, and I just allowed… the murder of the Missionary Man, what happened to Jack, circumstance connived, life showed me its wicked face and I chose to smile," Ezekiel said.

"Oh, you believe you could have saved those people from their fate?" Vernon asked.

"I didn't try."

"You were a boy. That's why you made up your mind to remain here, like a man in jail?"

"I have other reasons for staying here, Grandpa."

"One of those shouldn't be guilt. That's not yours to carry, belongs to somebody else."

"Grandpa, have you ever felt like two people?"

"Felt like two people?" The old man frowned and shook his head.

"I mean what you see standing before you right now and a sad little boy in here." Ezekiel tapped his chest.

The old man shifted his gaze from Ezekiel. The frown on his wrinkled face softened to a smile. "Ezekiel, I've always lived my life with purpose. I charted a course and navigated my life to this unsafe harbor called old age, never allowed myself to become immovable."

"What are you saying to me, Grandpa?"

"You see those old trees at the gap near my house? Those trees withstood all kinds of weather, simply because of their ability to bend, learned to bend, Ezekiel. Learn to bend with the winds of change."

"I read all those books, took all those exams, listened to you and learned the history, the folklore, I'm not sure I can work a piece of ground, plant peas and corn, tend to a few cows and be happy. But I made that promise about the house and land, told my father I would take care of his legacy. The little boy in me wants to do that."

A ship in the inner harbor sounded its horn, long, and low. The old man waited for the noise to cease, and when it did, he still waited as if enjoying the silence. Ezekiel stood watching the hunk of rusted steel and cables as it backed away from the pier across the water on the Carenage.

"You must deal with this in your own way, Ezekiel. The legacy belongs to you. There's no one in heaven or hell who can remedy this for you; not me, not Tilly, or even your father. You are a man now. No one can tell you how to harmonize your life. Those matters are yours to deal with. As you grow older, you will see. There's Alma, there will be children. Sad as it seems, I'll die, your father will die and Tilly will die. You will be left to square the deal with the life you built."

Ezekiel looked at Vernon; saw a little mischievous smile tugging at his lips. When Vernon spoke again, Ezekiel expected a touch of humor, but instead the old man's words forced him to contemplate all that he had said before. "You said you feel like two people, who is speaking to me right now?" Vernon asked.

Ezekiel felt stumped. The silence between them hung there, and then Ezekiel smiled. "Grandpa, I'm serious and you are teasing me."

"No Ezekiel, I'm not teasing you. You are teasing yourself. You said you already made up your mind. So what's the problem? What do you hope to get out of this conversation?"

"I fooled myself into thinking words can solve problems, acted as if this language belong to me," Ezekiel said.

"Christ, boy," the old man said. "Did our academic explorations turn you into a crazy person?" Ezekiel forced a little smile, the old man remained serious. "My intentions were to teach you to think, put you more in touch with your true self, not to separate you from--"

"Grandpa, you think this started with you, but this started a long time ago. I remember Tilly saying 'People are always judged by the quality of the words coming out of their mouths. There is nothing wrong with the dialect spoken around here, but you boys should learn to speak proper English. From now on, when you boys speak to me, or anyone in this house, you will speak standard English.' We all spoke properly around Tilly, but the moment we were away from her. Can you imagine us speaking like some Englishmen? 'I say old chap, how about a spot of tea.' I could only imagine people rolling in the dirt."

"So you are swayed by what other people think of you? I've spoken standard English all of my life and no one ever laughed at me."

"You are different, Grandpa. They expect you to speak proper English. After all, you were a teacher, a headmaster. This is much more than language. The very basis of our existence is usurped by an oppressor. Everything we do enriches another culture, another civilization. I guess once a slave, always a slave, first to a master and then to a culture that refuses to recognize our contributions to its enrichment. Don't tell me you know so much, yet you have never felt or thought of any of this? I don't believe you."

"Have I ever expressed any false notions to you?" The old man asked.

"None I know of," Ezekiel said, "but you may have omitted a few things, for instance, all the lies and half-truths written in books."

"Listen to me, boy. I gave you the tools to be a thinker, figure out truths from lies, and not allow your life to be impeded by other people's half-baked solutions."

"Now that I know and understand the methods of thinking, what do I do?" Ezekiel asked.

"Let your conscious be your guide, as the saying goes. You can run away from all this, move up to the country, squat on a piece of government land, and grow your hair into dreadlocks like your albino friend. Lots of people decide to be--"

"That sort of life is not for me, Grandpa."

"Good. I didn't waste my time then. Stay away from all thankless things. There is love in this world if you have the patience to wait for it. There is peace in this world if you have the courage to seek it. All that you need, you will have to struggle to obtain. All that you accomplish is yours. No master can take that from you. The dominant culture can only borrow it for a time. And for Christ sake, there are no two of you. You may think that now, but as you integrate all you have learned, you will come to understand what I mean. You will embrace that adhesive factor, known as your integrity. That's what keeps us fully human, in spite of what others might say or do." The old man looked at Ezekiel, pointed his finger and nodded. "Being an African is not an easy task, Ezekiel. We come from a past obscured, demonized by oppressive forces. Still they can't ignore the past, no matter what. We are the Janus people, looking at the beginning and the end. We are the bridge that spans humanity." Vernon laughed, as if he took pleasure in hearing his own voice, and then his face turned grim as if he had lost the thread of the conversation.

The ship sounded its horn one last time as it rounded the peninsula heading out to sea. Froth falling off the prow almost moved Ezekiel to tears. Conversing with Vernon solved nothing. It just raised more questions, as most discussions with the old man often did. Ezekiel wanted to ask Vernon about people born behind the veil, but he decided to leave that for another exchange. First, he would straighten things out with Alma, and then seek Mama Viche's consent to marry her niece.

Three days after Ezekiel and Vernon's discussion on the beach, the old man went to sleep and didn't wake up. Ezekiel felt a mild sorrow at the death of the old man, but he felt anguish for Tilly and her mother. He thought of the old generation dying out and wondered about what they might be taking to the grave.

* * *

It didn't take Ezekiel long to gain the courage for a visit with Mama Viche. He chose a day when he was sure Alma would be gone from the house. The old woman sat him down in her cluttered living room, served him sorrel and a wedge of sponge cake. The overcast day and the state of his nerves caused his clothes to stick to his skin. Mama Viche moved about, rearranging vials of herbs.

"So you want to marry Alma?" The old woman looked at Ezekiel.

He decided to remain bold, speak and act as if he had complete control. "Yes, Mama, I want to marry Alma," his words came out with all the bravery he could muster.

Ezekiel understood his voice would not be enough to convince Mama Viche to give her consent. No matter how Alma felt, she would not marry him if her aunt disapproved. In order to get the old woman's approval, he had to move beyond the ordinary. He stood with the glass and the small plate in hand, walked to the kitchen and placed them on the counter, came back to where Mama Viche stood, and waited for her next question. The old woman just stared, searching his face, as if seeing him for the first time.

"Why you want to marry Alma?" Mama Viche asked.

"Because I'm in love with her," Ezekiel said.

Mama Viche smiled and eased her gaze. Ezekiel felt relieved when she lowered her head.

"Ezekiel, love is often not enough. You need respect, friendship, admiration, devotion. She was so small and lonesome when my sister left her with me. The girl reminded me of a little bird with wet feathers. Turned out to be a beautiful woman, didn't she?"

Ezekiel wondered if he should answer the question, and Mama Viche smiled again as she recognized his reluctance.

"That's okay. It's okay to look on her as a woman. You want to take my Alma away, huh? She is all that remains; the last of our people. I assume you have a plan to support her?"

"Yes, Mama. No, Mama, I mean I do have a plan," Ezekiel said. "We won't be going anywhere. Alma can be my wife, the mother of our children, and still be your Alma."

The old woman blinked. Ezekiel speculated on the secrets hidden behind that face and those mesmerizing eyes. He wondered if any of the stories he had heard about her might be true.

"So, what you seeing in your visions these days?"

"Not much, Mama. Just glimpses of this and that, now and then."

"Once before you said something like that to me. You still young. Your gifts will grow in time. Learn to control them and tell no one where your good sense comes from. One day you should tell Alma." The old woman went silent and her next words sounded like all business. "What's your ambition?"

"I don't know, Mama. Daddy said he is working on a job for me with the Labor Union."

"Could be a good start, could lead to many places. Keep in mind you have to cultivate friends, old and young, allow people to like you, show them that you appreciate what they have to say, treat them with respect, care for their dignity, especially when they seem ungrateful. Don't ever act superior. They will resent you."

"I know what you mean, Mama. I realize that."

"Good. You must already realize Alma is an impulsive and determined person. Think you can handle her?" The old woman didn't wait for an answer. "I hope you can keep her happy. In the eyes of some it might look as though you and Alma are hurrying into marriage, I know better. You both must promise to take care of each other. I will say this to her, also. Good luck with your ambitions, Ezekiel. And if you ever need advice, don't hesitate to come speak to me."

Ezekiel hurried out of the house. He went there prepared for more of a struggle. The slight drizzle that came drifting on the breeze hardly fazed him. Even the hard rain that fell on him, halfway down the road, didn't dull his optimism. Huge drops came pelting out of the sky on a strong wind, dislodging the loose dirt on the side of the side of the road, filling the depressions with water. Ezekiel hopped along through the mire, soaked to the bones. He jumped into the air and shouted at the rain. His feet came down in a puddle of water, sending splatters onto the grass and the low hanging leaves.

The next day, when no one was around, he cornered Tilly to tell her his good news. "You could do worse. She is a good person. All you have to do is keep her happy, give her lots of love and lots of children. When are you planning to have the ceremony?"

"Not right away. We plan to call it a long engagement. And I need to earn some money for a ring."

"You already have a ring, your mother's wedding ring. All you have to do is have it sized. It's in the house. No one has touched it in years."

"Perfect," Ezekiel said.

"Give her the ring and ask her." Tilly looked at Ezekiel. "Don't wait forever. Long courtship is not in style these days. Henry's mother has been making noise, sending money and talking about him coming to live with her and Lester, attending the University of the West Indies.

There will be some extra room in the house soon. All you and Alma need is a wooden partition."

"We can't live in your house forever, Tilly."

"That's for sure. Your father said he secured that job for you with the Labor Union. Pay attention, you can move up fast. You are smarter than most of them, and don't forget to save your money."

Ezekiel decided to take the advice of Mama Viche and Tilly. He took Alma for a walk. They walked up the top road toward the Valley of Bones and took the path up the mountain to Ogoun's Point where they sat holding hands and looking at the houses below dotting the expanse of green. Ezekiel considered how he should propose, the words he should use. He sensed the anticipation in Alma, there was no getting around her, no surprising her with anything. In the end, he took the ring out of his pocket, and handed to her, "I'm ready if you are."

Alma took the ring and just looked at it. "Where did you get?"

"It was my mother's.

"It's beautiful. Yes, Yes." She squeezed the ring onto her finger. "Look, it fits." She waved her fingers.

They planned to take things little by little. But Tilly and Mama Viche, after years of avoidance, they pulled together and surprised the young couple.

The wedding took place in Tilly and John's yard. All the inhabitants of Jean Anglais attended, including Mano. His hair was trimmed low and he wore a suit and tie. Mama Viche presided. First, she sprinkled water over the head of the bride and groom, the tears of the bride's mother she called it. Two dolls resembling the bride and groom were presented to Ezekiel and Alma. John and Tilly made short speeches wishing the bride and groom eternal happiness. Mano handed his daughter an envelope of money. He made a small awkward speech, wished them the best of luck and told them the money was for a start in life. After the ceremony, the guests ate and drank way into the night. Finally, the bride and groom retired to Alma's room in the house she shared with her aunt.

* * *

Ezekiel was no longer the little boy hiding in the bushes, his observations now held consequences. On the course of his new life and work, Ezekiel initiated one of his old schemes, collecting information and deciding if any of the words spoken held validity. By listening to the reasoning and verb tenses in which people spoke, he drew conclusions. Deploying this set of skills allowed him to place people under close scrutiny without their detecting.

Once, while riding on a bus returning from Saint Georges, Ezekiel heard a man trying to shout over the drone of the engine. "It was the most fantastic thing, saw it with my own eyes, otherwise I wouldn't have believe it. Norman was a friend of mine, died from low blood pressure. He was stretched out on his bed, eyes closed, no breath coming out of his nose. We called his name and shook him. He was dead. This fellow called Malcolm was passing by and heard Norman's wife screaming. He came into the house with those two women from River Road, the Moritz sisters, saw Norman dead on the bed. Malcolm sat down near Norman and started praying. We had no idea what good his prayer could do. The man was already dead. The two sisters stood guard at the door, saying Malcolm needed solitude to do the Lord's work. After a while, he asked for food and he remained in the room with Norman. Almost an hour went by. All of us were wondering about this strange albino fellow. But he came out of the room, told the wife her husband would like to talk to her. You should have seen her face. I'm telling you, it was the most fantastic thing. A miracle I'm telling you, a true miracle."

People from all over the parishes, from Sauteurs, down to Saint Georges, and back up to Saint Andrews, all had stories about Malcolm. They claimed his speeches were like hitting a wasp's nest with a stick.

Another time, Ezekiel and Alma were eating at the Nutmeg Restaurant, on the Carenage, when a fellow at a nearby table with a bunch of his friends started talking about a man speaking to huge crowds all over the parishes as if he was some kind of politician. All the big-wheels were referring to the albino as a menace. Ezekiel and Alma looked at each other as the particulars fell into place. "But the fellow is just a preacher, a bush man, a Rasta Man. You should see him. He claims he doesn't need a church. The whole world is his church. And those twins girls draped all over him, rumor has it, they are his wives," the man said, and his friends laughed. "I heard the fellow up in Sauteurs once, speaking about who are the masters, and who are the slaves and those people up there just eating it up. Do the politicians work for the people, or do the people work for the politicians? I know exactly what he's saying. I wouldn't be saying that out loud though. We live in a democracy, but you know… I'm sure the police must be keeping a close eye on him."

Ezekiel and Alma took a water taxi across the Carenage to a spot near the fire station, and then they walked through Tanteen to Lagoon Road. Alma seemed anxious, but Ezekiel was reluctant to start a conversation with her. On the shore at Lagoon Road, Ezekiel saw his brother, Henry, with Mondu's boat, hauled out of the water and propped on its side. Henry had been using the boat to fish with some of his friends. Now he was tossing buckets of seawater into the boat, sponging the stink of fish with soap, preparing to row Tilly with her fruits and vegetables to yachts anchored in the lagoon. Ezekiel waved at his brother as he and Alma came to the path leading up to Belmont, the same path that he had taken with his father and Mondu the night they helped Cosmus to flee Grenada. Halfway up the dirt road, Alma halted as if refusing to walk and talk at the same time.

"What are you going to do about Malcolm?"

"What can I do? I don't know…I just hear people talking." "You must speak to him, Ezekiel. If anything should happen, you would never forgive yourself for not trying. He'll listen to you."

"Malcolm is a grown man," Ezekiel said.

"They say he has little congregations everywhere. He preaches to them and baptizes some, and then disappears back into the bush. I hear he's going to be on Mon Pandy tomorrow."

"What are you, some kind of spy?"

"Only about things of worth to you," she said. "You have to go see him, speak to him. And you must go alone. I don't want to be there."

"Why not, Alma?" Ezekiel asked.

"I don't want to be in the way."

That night, as Ezekiel tried to sleep, he found himself trapped between sleep and restiveness. He saw himself on the top road with Malcolm leading the people of Jean Anglais in a procession. Ezekiel knew they were headed to the yellow block house. As they marched down the road it seemed they were walking forever. Ezekiel realized they would never reach their destination. He struggled to shout a warning, but only a growl escaped his throat. On the side of the road stood Mama Viche and Alma, shouting at the marchers: "Don't follow him, don't follow him" and Cora shouting with them in disagreement, "Follow him to hell, follow him to hell, you damn fools, the devil is waiting."

The next morning, Ezekiel's crawled out of bed with a lingering curiosity about the dream. What kind of miracle would Malcolm perform? He pictured Malcolm trying to drown people, holding them under water for too long, as they flailed and clawed, struggling for air. He imagined Malcolm releasing them, laughing, and water spewing from their noses and mouths as they cussed at him. Ezekiel smiled, remembering Malcolm's twisted sense of humor.

Ezekiel made his way down to Pandy Beach, sat on the sand under an old bayberry tree, hidden from sight by low branches, he waited. He wanted to see what was going on before he made his presence known. Ezekiel hadn't been on Pandy Beach at this time of the day since his father had stopped the morning ritual. Some spectators were already there. The rumors had spread.

Ezekiel sat watching whitecaps crash across the reef, sending gentle swells into the near shallows. Further down, at the south end of the beach, the water gradually became deeper where the ocean came up to a rock bluff. The waves swelled up, came in, and slammed against the standing rocks with a noisy passion, sending plumes of spray into the air. He sat immersed in his imagination as the power of the waves reshaped the contours of the beach.

He heard the singing first. It came from somewhere up the path that led down to the beach: "...Wade in de water children/ Wade in de water/wade in de water children/ God go trouble de water/ Who dat yonder dressed in white/ God go trouble de water/ Must be de children of de Israelites/ God go trouble de water."

Malcolm led his singing congregation onto the sand and toward the deep end of Mon Pandy. He resembled a phantom with his scalp covered with white hair and rust colored dreadlocks hanging down past his shoulders. The crowd moved straightforward down to the edge of the water. Twelve people, young and old, all dressed in white, and wearing no shoes, Ezekiel stepped out of the shelter of the low-hanging branches and fell in behind the procession. The onlookers, Checklea with his wife and children, and others from Belmont and Jean Anglais, they followed Ezekiel. Malcolm picked his old friend out of the crowd and spoke to him.

"Ezekiel, you stand with us today. I see some familiar faces from Jean Anglais. Follow me! The Bible commands us to go down to the water," Malcolm said. "I'm not saying those of you who had your heads sprinkled, as children at the Catholic or Anglican churches, will not go to heaven. But the Lord commands and I, his servant obeys. If you send your child to the store for sugar, and he brought you salt, would you be satisfied? Let us pray for all those who join us today, and for the two who decided to step closer to Jesus through baptism."

Ezekiel looked at Malcolm's congregation. He recognized most of them, and had heard stories. The only unfamiliar persons were the Moritz sisters, the twin girls from River Road. He recognized them from their photographs in the newspaper, but those blurred photographs did them no justice. Short and slender women, the blood of the aboriginal people who once lived on this island flowed in their veins. Dark thick hair framed two exact faces. One of the sisters looked pregnant.

Malcolm went down on his knees at the edge of the water, and his congregation joined him. He led them in a short prayer, as Ezekiel and the spectators stood and watched. Malcolm stood and marched into the waves. The water pushed at him, he stood like a rock. His two candidates for baptism, dressed all in white, pushed through to the spot where he stood. First, a young woman, about Alma's age, who lived in one of those houses built by the government right after Hurricane Janet, the ones people called a Janet-house. The young woman had two young children. People said she made a living by selling sexual favors to sailors on the cargo ships along the Carenage. One night a neighbor found her bleeding on her doorstep, with slash wounds to her chest and arms. She was taken to the hospital, sewed up, and she survived. The Moritz sister cared for her children while she healed, and they convinced her to join their congregation.

The second candidate for baptism, a fellow called Beye, a bow-legged little man, was a familiar figure around the rum-shops and a close friend of Mano. Beye worked as a helper on a truck hauling sugarcane to the factory. One day the truck came around a corner and Beye fell off and bounced on the pavement like a ball. The driver stopped and hauled him out of the road. He'd sustained some bruises, on the bridge of his nose and deep scrapes on the palms of his hands. They said it was a miracle he survived and he believed the talk about divine intervention. He concluded that God had plans for him. Beye ceased drinking rum and sought religious counsel from Malcolm. This baptism was his final conversion.

One at a time they moved into Malcolm's arms extended above the surface of the waves.

"In obedience to the commands of our Lord Jesus Christ, I baptize thee." He placed one hand behind the neck, pinched the nostrils with the fingers of his other hand and took the devoted back and down under the water. "In the name of the Father, the Son, and the Holy Spirit, amen," Malcolm recited. Three times, he immersed each one under the waves, repeating the litany. A woman's voice broke into the ceremony like an ax through wood.

"Boy, what you think you doing? Who the hell told you to baptize people? And making all that noise all over the place? Who gave you the right? God will strike you dead with lightning, and you tricksters trying to steal my son? You bunch of hypocrites, filling his head with all that mess. Come here, come here right now."

Cora Masanto stood at the edge of the water, hands on her hips, shouting at Malcolm and his followers. The Moritz sisters moved to a position between Cora and her son. Malcolm looked at the twins, shook his head from left to right. The girls relaxed but stood their ground.

Malcolm waded out of the water as if in obedience to his mother. He walked straight past the sisters and stood before Cora as water dripped from his shirt and pants onto the sand. His small congregation looked on as he spoke to his mother. "When I was a child I spoke as a child, I understood as a child, I thought as a child. But when I became a man, I put away childish things."

"I'll show you who is a man." Cora dashed over to a cluster of Manchineel, tore off a limb, and bolted at Malcolm, whacking him across his face, again and again. The Moritz sisters attempted to move in but Malcolm pointed his finger at them and they halted. He stood and took the blows with no defense. His congregation held fast as the leaves flew off the branches and fell to the sand. The bare stems dripped white sap. Ezekiel felt like rushing her and snatching the branches from her hand. She pulled back to hit Malcolm for the fifth time, but she stopped in midair, looking at her son as if struck by paralysis or considering a stranger. She brought her hand down to her side, still holding the bare twig, and began shaking her head.

"You just like Jack, no back bone." She turned, stomped across the sand toward the path off the beach, the branch still clutched in her hand. "You can't take my son," she shouted. "You fools, follow him, just wait and see, you fools. Blood is thicker than water."

A few of Malcolm's congregation moved behind Cora, pelting her with bits of coral, and broken shells, hurling obscenities at her. Malcolm shouted. "He who is without sin, he who is without sin among you!"

They all halted, dropping what they were about to throw, and stood looking at Cora as she trudged up the path. Moments later, they followed the man called Beye who had plans to provide food and drinks at his house.

The Moritz sisters with Ezekiel and Malcolm, they stood where the waves lapped at the shore. Red welts covered Malcolm's face. The sisters took him into the sea and began dabbing his cheeks with the dampened hem of their skirts. He flinched, waved off the two women, and he immersed himself, stayed under for a long time, and then he rose to the surface, shaking his dreadlocks. Water dripped from his head as he moved onto the shore, his bare feet collecting sand as he walked toward Ezekiel.

"Are you still seeing visions, my friend? Did you foresee any of this?"

"A little bit."

Malcolm looked at Ezekiel and smiled. "Micah 3:7," he said. *'The seers will be ashamed and the diviners will be embarrassed indeed, they will all cover their mouths because there is no answer from God.'"*

"Are you accusing me of something?"

"The hardest sums to organize are the ones that show us how to count our blessings." Malcolm said.

"I know," Ezekiel said.

"You know? You know what?" A little smile played around the corners of Malcolm's lips.

"I'm no stranger. Remember we both grew up in Jean Anglais and shared what the place offered," Ezekiel said.

"Did we really?" Malcolm looked at Ezekiel and shook his head.

"Good times, bad times, death and murder," Ezekiel said.

"Yeah, even the misery."

"You remember what we thought about those spirits trapped in the cane?"

"We were kids, Ezekiel. I can't remember what we believed," Malcolm said.

"We held on to what the old folks believed. Did what we were told. Even death and murder seemed questionable," Ezekiel said, looking down at the sand as if counting the grains.

"You sound remorseful. You had nothing to with what happened to Harry. Cora killed the man. It's her guilt, her sorrow that's driving her crazy," Malcolm said.

Ezekiel looked up and gazed into Malcolm's eyes. "What! How'd you know she killed him?"

"She told me. She did it for me. I had no idea she loved me that much and hated me the same amount." Malcolm cast his sight across the water, at the waves smelling on the surface and rolling toward shore.

Ezekiel stood as if skeptical of the revelation. "All this time, I thought my father killed the Missionary Man."

"You thought your father...why would he...?"

"I held so much bitterness toward the man." Ezekiel words trailed off.

"Stuff like that can turn your guts inside out," Malcolm said, returning his gaze to Ezekiel.

"At one time I wondered if I could kill him," Ezekiel said.

"Easy way to think about a man you believe is a murderer." Malcolm shuffled his toes, stood as if to buttress his body. "Now you have the truth. What you plan to do?"

"Well, what can I do? Alter some of my judgments, I suppose."

"We can join together, help me spread the word. There's little we can do about yesterday, all that is in the hands of Papa God."

"I can't just forget yesterday. This life is so full of nasty contradictions and the answers are always back there, in the place called yesterdays," Ezekiel said, gesturing over his shoulder.

"Doubts can only be removed by trust in God," Malcolm said.

"Trust in God? Which God is that? You mean the God of Isaac and Abraham, the white one in the gray beard? If that God wants my trust he would have to come down here, and wipe off my doubts."

Malcolm looked at Ezekiel and shook his head. "Blasphemy, brother, that's what I'm hearing. You lack faith. You must place your belief in God and know all will be okay in the end."

"Is that what you did, what you doing? One of your women look pregnant, and everybody saying it's your child."

"That's true," Malcolm said.

"So why did you allow Harry to mess with you? He tried some stuff with me, grabbing at my penis, talking about power and all that shit. I ran like hell and told my father."

"You told your father?"

"Yeah, that's why I thought he killed Harry."

Malcolm raised his index finger, waved it at Ezekiel and began to sermonize: "Our past creates who we are in the present. Harry's words about power, power to lead, power to rule. I accepted all that. In later days, as I roamed and meditated in the bush up in the country, it all became clear to me: 'Whatever happens to a man has been waiting to happen since the beginning of time. The twining strands of fate wove both together, your own existence and the existence of the things waiting to happen'."

"Another quote from the dead Roman, I presume?"

"You might say that," Malcolm said.

"Your ability to forgive comes not from Jesus but from a dead Roman emperor? I don't know what to think about you."

"Words to thoughts: that's another kind of power, our ability to control our belief. We are our imagination."

"That's just avoidance, man. In other words, don't judge" Ezekiel threw both his hands up. "Just bury everything inside?"

"Not really," Malcolm said. "At first, I acted that way. Just delivered what they wanted, taking special care of some, speaking to them about God and the Bible. I did that right, and they came, gave me money, food and everything else."

"Sounds as though you were just a swindler," Ezekiel said.

"That's before I understood. One night, I heard the voice of the dead Roman, clear as you are speaking to me right now. *'Accept the things to which fate binds you, and love the ones with whom fate brings you together. Do so with all your heart, rejecting your sense of injury and the injury itself disappears. To live happily is a private power of the soul.'* I had no idea I was injured," Malcolm said. "That's when I discovered the road I had to walk. Two days later, Inspector Didderot pulled up beside me as I was walking along, motioned me over; told me Harry left me the place in Jean Anglais and he handed me a piece of paper."

"Really, I didn't realize," Ezekiel said. "You haven't been to Jean Anglais in a long time. Alma and I tried to invite you to our wedding. But we didn't know where to find you."

"I heard you two got married. I haven't even looked at the house since he told me."

"The church is gone," Ezekiel said. "Well, not quite gone, but__"

"What you talking about?" Malcolm asked.

"They scavenged it, took it apart, piece by piece. The church is now all over Jean Anglais."

Malcolm laughed and laughed, threw both hands over his mouth as if to stifle the joyful noise. The twin sisters looked over at him and started laughing also. Ezekiel laughed with them.

"But the house, that's still there, right?" Malcolm swallowed the laughter.

"Yes, the house is still there. And it looks like you going to need it. You can't live outside with a new baby," Ezekiel said.

"Two new babies, her sister will be showing soon," Malcolm said.

"Malcolm, you scamp," Ezekiel said, extending his palm and slapping Malcolm on his back. The gesture reminded Ezekiel of old times.

"Those two have always shared everything, starting in the womb. They shared a placenta. Sharing a man is nothing." Malcolm looked at the two women standing and smiling in his direction. "I'm having a little problem getting the house."

"Why? It's yours, right? He left it to you," Ezekiel said.

"You remember Bleak House, by Charles Dickens?" Malcolm paused for a moment. "When you inherit stuff, you inherit more than the objects. You inherit the courts, lawyers, judges, taxes; your benefactor leaves you with a burden he no longer has to carry. I have a lawyer called Brand, working on it. He is doing it for free, said he still feels guilty about Jack."

"Such a terrible thing, those bastards trying to thief what he left you," Ezekiel said.

"I've been all over Grenada," Malcolm said. "Village life on this island is beautiful but hard.

"Just like Jean Anglais. Some nice things did happen up there, didn't it?" Ezekiel asked.

"You know what I mean? You and Alma are the perfect example." Malcolm glanced at the two women standing and waiting. "I've got to go, man, before they eat all the food Beye prepared."

As Ezekiel and Malcolm moved apart, the two women came toward Malcolm, linked arms with him, one on each side and they walked down the beach toward the path. Ezekiel felt mesmerize by the whole experience. Although he didn't comprehend all that Malcolm had said, and suspected some naivety, the conversation still seemed to pulsate. Ezekiel thought of the vibrations of life in Jean Anglais, especially Mano's drums, and the traditions of the people, the approach of rain, birds pecking at ripe fruits in the trees, and the shifting winds. He followed Malcolm and the two women off the beach wondering why those images suddenly held such charm.

* * *

Ezekiel felt a certain approval from his job first job and the encounter with Malcolm, in some way, added satisfaction. The money the work placed in his pocket, the pleasure he found with his wife. For the first time, he saw his purpose not as something strictly for self, but extending to others; those living now and those to come. This approach to life radiated something energetic, an effect that pushed him to speak with authority, to the cane-cutters and other working people about the true value of their labor, and how as a group they have more power than as individuals.

The young couple had moved out of Mama Viche's house and settled into the section of John and Tilly's house that Henry had vacated when he moved to Trinidad to join his mother. Lloyd had just completed his secondary education and there were all kinds of banter about his ability to see mathematical theorems floating before his face. Just another fantastic fable like all the others told in Jean Anglais. But somehow this tale managed to escape in tact, seeping into the ears of two doctors from Miami, Florida. Lloyd's encounter with lightning added a certain enchantment to his emerging mathematical abilities.

American doctors came running, wearing thick glasses, they poked and prodded Lloyd from head to toe, tried to fool him, tried to determine if he was some kind of fraud. In the end, they invited Lloyd to come to an establishment in Miami where he could hone his skills in the areas of discrete and experimental mathematics.

John flew into a rage. "I'm not allowing those people to do experiments on my son. He will be no monkey doing tricks with numbers for them. They can call it what they want, pretend it's not disobedience with numbers." And he went on. The restricted nature of any procedures, the money and education Lloyd would receive the medical attention to his burns. All this made no difference to John.

The fracture between him and Tilly widened. Tilly spoke about all the suffering she endured; about raising the child he had produced with another woman and the unsaid rumors about him impregnating Delores.

She came to a decision, her usefulness in Grenada was over, everybody grown, her parents deceased, and the people of Jean Anglais with their constant chitchat. She packed her belongings and moved with Lloyd, into her parents' empty house. A month later, Tilly departed with Lloyd for Miami.

John continued the routines of his life, acting as if Tilly's departure with Lloyd made no difference. Alma took over the management of the household, and Ezekiel worked as a representative for the Labor Union, traveling all over Grenada, organizing secret meetings with workers, increasing the enrollment in the labor union and growing dues. Things were going well until the morning John didn't rise for his trip to the Valley of Bones. Ezekiel went into his father's room and shook him. John appeared drunk; he complained about a headache and his vision in one eye, tried to stand and fell to the floor. He had suffered a cerebral hemorrhage.

His left side, dead as stone, his mouth twisted into a curious, permanent frown, one eyelid drooped. Some friends came to see him and left with embarrassed looks on their faces. Ezekiel wondered if they felt responsible for his paralysis. None of them came back for a second visit. They would inquire about his health as if expecting him to recover. None of them came and sat with him. Ezekiel assumed it might be because they didn't want to look at his unmoving face, and slack eyes, one hand barely moving. Tilly came home from Miami, stayed for two weeks and went back to be with Lloyd. She claimed he lacked common sense, and needed guidance in dealing with the simplest of things.

John started groaning the day after Tilly left, tears dribbling from one eye. Ezekiel grieved at his father's condition. John needed help going to the lavatory, assistance to wipe his ass, and he would frequently piss the bed. Taking care of him fell mainly on Alma. She did the chores, changing him and washing the sheets, washing his clothes and feeding him. She did all this with no complaints.

Then John stopped eating and started shedding weight. The once strapping man who always walked with a swagger now lay in bed, bony-faced, wasting away. His groaning made it difficult to sleep. John looked as if one day he would melt into the sheets and vanish.

Alma came home one evening after a visit with her aunt. She looked troubled, and Ezekiel decided to expel any nonsense the old woman may have planted in Alma's mind.

"What's the matter? Your Tante prying?"

"You should have told me, Ezekiel."

"Told you what?"

"That you have the gift of second sight, born behind the veil."

"You think I believe in all that superstition?"

"If you don't believe in the myth about Caulbearers, why did you give Cosmus your veil?"

Ezekiel looked at her, wanted to explain Palcal's Wager to her, but she was shouting before he could formulate.

"You see, you see. You don't trust me?"

"That's not the reason," Ezekiel said.

"Tante would like to speak to you."

"What about, what does she want?"

Ezekiel went to the old woman house. She offered him a glass of ginger beer, a slice of sponge cake, and then she pointed to the same chair where he had sat the day he came to ask for Alma's hand in marriage. Mama Viche sat in a chair directly across from him. Her dress hung down, covering her ankles. A bandana wrapped around her head, she sat erect and alert, as if ready for business, but her eyes looked gloomy. Ezekiel braced himself.

"I know you heard all the rumors about your father and Delores," the old woman said. "Your father had nothing to do with that. That's the work of the Mongoose."

"Duncan Elmo is her baby's father?"

"He gave Monah the money to move to Crochu so his wife wouldn't find out. But that's not important. I called you here for something else."

"Not important, Mama? Tilly left him because of the rumors."

"She didn't leave him because of one thing. She left him for many reasons. A person's life is made up of many pieces. One piece, true or false can tip the scale, for better or for worst."

"I can't believe this." Ezekiel looked at the floor, shaking his head.

"What I'm about to tell you may sound cruel. It's just your duty. What you must do."

"Mama, I'm doing my best. Things are kind of--"

"It's time you let him go."

"Let him go where?" Ezekiel raised his head and looked straight at the old woman.

"John is a natural leader. His destiny is to lead the lost spirits out of the Valley of Bones. Such an unruly soul, you can't allow him to die in the house. His spirit must be set free to travel with his ancestors."

"I don't understand what you saying, Mama."

"You must take him away from the house; let him die in peace, in the bush."

"Are you suggesting?"

"That's what he wants. One generation makes way for the next. The one passing must be willing to pass." The old woman stared at Ezekiel.

"Why would he want to die alone?"

"We all die alone. People can hold your hand, sob, and wail, but we go down that road alone."

"How do you know what he . . .?"

"He came to me in a vision, told me to tell you."

"I want to believe you, but . . ."

"Okay, you can keep him there, and watch him suffer."

"He isn't suffering, Mama. He may not be able to talk, and can hardly walk, but . . ."

"He's in no physical pain but for a man like him, a man who thought he controlled everything. Can you imagine? You grew up in his shadow. You know him."

"He made life miserable for many people."

"Are you trying to punish him for his misbehaviors? Careful, boy, you never know what the future will bring." Mama Viche shook one finger at Ezekiel.

"Mama, I'm not trying to do anything to the man."

"Well, you have to do this. Think of his dignity, think of how you would feel, pissing the bed, your daughter-in-law wiping your backside and feeding you like a child."

"Once a man, twice a child, they say." Ezekiel tried to laugh.

"Okay then, okay." The old woman leaned back in the chair. "The consequences belong to you."

"So what do I say when the police come asking questions?"

"He's a crippled old man. No one will ask questions if we carry out his wishes. You must take him to a secluded spot in the Valley of Bones. Make him comfortable, and leave him with this." She handed Ezekiel a small vial of liquid as if the decision had already been made. Ezekiel took it from her hand. "Don't look back. If you look back his spirit will follow you home and remain in the house, causing all kinds of mischief, all kind of confusion that even I won't be able to remedy." Mama Viche paused and fixed Ezekiel with a halting glare. "The next day, go back and take the body home."

"Is that all? Is that all you have to say to me?"

"I think so, for the time being. Now go home, kiss your wife and decide."

Ezekiel walked home slowly, full of doubts about what the old woman had suggested. At the house, he took Alma's hand and they went outside, out of earshot of John, and sat under the plum tree where John had told the story about the Shadow Man, so many years ago. Ezekiel told Alma all that her aunt had suggested and the purpose. She hugged Ezekiel and remained silent for a long time, her face buried in the arm of his shirt, and then she spoke. "Caring for your father is not a hardship for me. I don't want you doing anything to hurt your heart. We both have long lives to live."

The next day, Ezekiel dressed his father and helped him onto the back of the donkey. They set out for the Valley of Bones in the evening as the sun went down, hoping to pass no one on the way. Ezekiel walked flanking the animal, balancing his father. A steady, fresh breeze pushed on them as the donkey carried John up the grade. Before they entered the Valley of Bones, Ezekiel looked back at the city of Saint Georges in the distance, with the sun hanging near the horizon to the west, a bright orange orb surrounded by jagged clouds. He knew none of this would ever be the same. They moved on toward the Livi-Divi tree on the ridge, where the lightning had struck Lloyd. Ezekiel tethered the beast to the tree and helped his father to dismount. Ezekiel shouldered his father's weight as they moved into the bush, and he wondered how he would get John on the back of the donkey after he was dead.

They came to a stand of rocks hidden from sight by thick brush. He assisted his father by holding his hands and lowering him to the ground. Ezekiel watched him squirming against the rocks and dirt, as if seeking comfort, and then John made three delicate motions with his half-dead hand as if giving his son permission to leave. Ezekiel stood looking at his father. John's lips were moving, puckering in and out as if trying to spit words. Ezekiel reached into his pocket and took out the vial Mama Viche had given him. He removed the stopper and pressed the vial into his father's palm, then helped him to lift the little bottle to his lips. He watched as the fluid seeped out. At the last moment, Ezekiel turned away.

He started to walk as an owl hooted in the distance and for one instant Ezekiel felt an urge to turn around for one last look. At the tree, he unhitched the donkey and rode the beast back to Jean Anglais, obeying the advice of Mama Viche. Ezekiel said nothing to Alma about those last moments with his father. They sat in silence as he contemplated what he would say to Tilly, Lloyd, and Henry. In this unusual moment, he came to understand his father had completed his plan. His three children existed where he wanted them. Ezekiel realized he was expected to follow the same arrangement. He knew he would never leave Grenada. With his marriage to Alma and her connection to Jean Anglais and her aunt, there would be no emigrating to make a new home.

The house felt silent and ambiguous when they went to bed. An hour later, Ezekiel laid there listening to Alma's breathing, and he wondered if she was sleeping or engaging in regrets of her own. His mind flipped from one fragment of contemplation to another. Eventually, he fixed on the dead: his mother, Vernon, Jack, Papa LaTouche, he wondered if his father might be amongst them yet. Then he focused on the travelers, those who fled Jean Anglais: Tilly and Lloyd in Miami, Monah, and Delores in Crochu, Mondu, Rita and Cosmus in Venezuela, Lester, Monica and Henry in Trinidad. Ezekiel found it hard to continue the list, understanding they had all gone astray. These people would never be together again, never at the same time in Jean Anglais. He settled on the comforting thought that one day, Malcolm might have the opportunity to return with his common wisdom, inherited memories and his phantom mentor.

Toward morning, Ezekiel found himself wrestling with images of a young boy walking up a road. It took him awhile to grasp the memory from so long ago. As the association became clear, it brought to light another time and place: a young boy caught in a momentary gust of wind and an old woman smiling at him from her porch. And that triggered recollections of men in trucks with loudspeakers and the wish to be of use like those men of influence. Now as he rehashed the details, they came back to him as little bolts of radiance.

Those intermingled impressions forced him to appreciate the circumstances his father had produced, and he scoffed at the notion that fate could be so barefaced, carrying him inside the Labor Movement. Ezekiel wondered how long it would take him to reach the top of the movement. Would the members see him as a country boy, one of their own, a person who resisted the lure to join the skeptics, a person worthy of their trust, one of those who remained at home and kept the fire burning? Ezekiel shook his head as the extent of his ambitions soared in his brain.

Ezekiel decided not to wait for the sun to rise. He climbed out of bed, trying not to wake Alma. The air held its chill as he headed to retrieve the remains of his father. He unhitched the donkey, saw Mano standing in the weak light on the top road and he knew Alma had involved her father.

"Your wife came to see me yesterday, said you might need some help this morning."

"I wish she didn't get you__"

"She told me about the old woman playing God again," Mano said.

"What Mama Viche said to me makes sense, not in the way she might be thinking," Ezekiel said.

"I see what you mean. Waiting for death is very wicked, especially for a man like your father."

They found John leaning against the rock as if sleeping. He looked pleased. Ezekiel and Mano carried him out of the bush. At first, they thought of loading him onto the donkey face down, but they hatched another plan. They lifted John onto the back of the beast, removing all debris from his clothes and hair and Ezekiel climbed on to, embraced his father while Mano led the animal. Ezekiel and his father almost fell off twice, but he kept things in balance and made it off the hillside. Down in Jean Anglais, Alma stood watching her father and her husband handling the body as if it still held life. They placed John in his bed and he belched like a man who had just eaten a good meal. The man is dead but here he is creating a bond between Mano and me, Ezekiel thought.

The undertaker came and carried John's body away, and his eldest son began making the rounds, informing people about the death of his father. He told them there would be no wake, and he saw disappointment on their faces.

That night, as Ezekiel rested in bed next to Alma, a curious vision danced before his eyes. He saw the Valley of Bones with no cane, and several big cisterns rested on the hillside, and many beds of carrots, potatoes, and other vegetables spread out across the land. A vast garden tended by a group of people bent over in the sun. At first, Ezekiel struggled to make sense of things: pipes running from the spring to the cisterns, and the water coming down through thin hoses to the fields through the force of gravity. Those observations made his heart swell.

Before his eyes, the vision tracked backward. He saw red-rot and wilt infesting the cane, and a huge conflagration as Duncan Elmo burned the fields to get rid of the blight. When Duncan tried to replant the cane, Ezekiel asked the union people to not work for Duncan. He saw the man forced to sell the land and Ezekiel was there with cash in hand to buy the Valley of Bones. He wondered where the money would come from and how much of this vision would come true. He thought, seeing all this was good enough for now.

Ezekiel had no idea that death could be so troublesome. Tilly and Lloyd came home, Henry came back from Trinidad dressed like a Saga-boy, and they all went to Powell's funeral home and made the arrangements for John's funeral. The undertaker told them not to worry about anything. He would take care of all the details including the death certificate and digging the grave. Ezekiel was shocked when the mortician handed him the bill. He showed it to Alma and she laughed. The undertaker wanted to be paid before he placed John in the ground. Tilly pulled a wad of bills out of her purse and paid.

Neighbors came to offer condolences and deliver various quantities of food. John's family sat at the table in the kitchen as Alma dished and served the food. As they ate, Ezekiel spoke to them of his plans for the Valley of Bones, and how he intended to put things in motion. He told them of the blight he saw coming and how he would purchase the land from Duncan with a bit of duplicity. All he needed was cash.

"Boy, you two have all the talents. You Lloyd, with your numbers, and you Ezekiel, the mastermind, sounds too interesting for me not to be involved," Henry said. "Count me in. But I don't have a lot of money or anything. I'll do what I can."

"Don't worry about the money," Lloyd said. "Worrying about money is one way to make sure it never comes to you."

"You sound as though you have a plan to get some big money," Henry said. "You plan to rob a bank?" He laughed.

"Lloyd, you raising Ezekiel's hopes; there is no guarantee you will win any of those prizes," Tilly said.

"What prizes?" Ezekiel looked at his brother. "What you doing up there in America, going to the horse races?" He laughed and looked at the others seated around the table as if inviting them to join him.

"Lots of monetary prizes up for grabs in the field of mathematics," Lloyd said. "I intend to win some of them. Right now, I have by sights on two, the Collatz Conjecture, and after that, the Hodge Conjecture." Lloyd spoke and sat up straight as if to challenge their trivial concerns.

"You mean like the Nobel Prize?" Ezekiel asked, trying to inject a level of seriousness back into in the conversation.

"There is no Nobel Prize for mathematics. But there are similar prizes, called Field Medals. I saw one of them. On one side of the medallion was the words *'Rise above oneself and grasp the world.'* That's what I intend to do. Grasp the world." Lloyd clinched his fingers into two fists and shook them.

"Ezekiel, your brother has high ambitions," Tilly said.

"You should think more on the particulars of your plan," Lloyd said. "Who will have title to the land?"

Ezekiel glanced at Lloyd, and he felt proud. He looked at the scars left on his face by the lightening strike, saw the repairs attempted by doctors, and he wondered if Lloyd saw his scars as a small price to pay for his new abilities.

"No one person will own the land. The land will belong to all of us," Ezekiel said.

"Okay. But Duncan won't just give-away the land. He will want money. And who will keep the books? After all, it's a business, right? And when you have disputes who will settle them?" Lloyd spoke and threw his palms open.

"Alma will keep the books. As for disputes, I'm not going to think about trouble right now. When and if, I'll deal with it," Ezekiel said.

"You kind of like your father," Tilly said. Ezekiel shrugged off her comment.

"That's not true," Alma said. "He's nothing like his father."

"I am not accusing your husband." Tilly smiled at Alma, delighted in the way she had jumped to Ezekiel's defense.

"Interesting venture," Lloyd said. "You know the government wouldn't let you operate taxes free? And they will find faults, come up with names for you and the people of Jean Anglais."

"I know we will have enemies," Ezekiel said.

"Lloyd, you sound as if you should come home, help run the operation," Henry said.

"I can see the whole thing, structure, measurements, calculating the ratios of success or failure. Figures are the key, everything depends on mathematics, but I can only give advice. No one would take orders from me?"

"Lloyd, the smart and the reasonable, that's who will pay attention to you," Ezekiel said.

"Well, seems like you guys have everything covered except for one. I think I'll join the police or army. You fellows may need protection one of these days," Henry laughed.

The conversation collapsed into a series of jokes, and without additional discussion, Ezekiel's family promised to send him a few hundred dollars each month to help with his project. He felt appreciative of their offer, but he wondered how long it would take to accumulate the thousands of dollars he knew he would need to execute the plan.

All of the inhabitants of Jean Anglais, and most from Woodlands, Belmont and Grandanse, came to the funeral of John Augustine. Ezekiel felt delighted when he saw Malcolm standing in the crowd. After they eulogized John, the attendants stood around the grave in small groups, watching the coffin being lowered into the ground by Henry, Lloyd, Ezekiel, and Mano. Ezekiel released the rope to Mano the moment the coffin reached the bottom of the hole, turned and walked away. He saw Tilly covering her face with her palms and Lloyd and Henry leading her away. They left Alma standing alone. Ezekiel's eyes came to rest on Mama Viche, Cummins, and two other government officials standing off to one side, old guards who had been in and out of government for many years, now here to bid farewell to one of their foot-soldiers.

Cummins approached Ezekiel, as two men began shoveling dirt into the hole. "Huge boots to fill," he said. "His absence will be felt all over this island." He looked at Ezekiel as if expecting some kind of response. "The Labor Party would like you to take his place," Cummins continued, "Be our point-man in Jean Anglais and the surrounding areas. You are well positioned for that, with your work in the movement."

Ezekiel nodded.

But he had other things in mind. He knew he could never be a subordinate like his father. Ezekiel watched Cummins walking away from the gravesite, and he came to the awareness that one day he would have to challenge this man for his seat in government. The idea intrigued him. A hand tapped on his shoulder. He turned and there stood Malcolm. For the first time in their lives, they hugged, and then leaned off and shook hands. In his uniform as if on some kind of official duty, Dennis Didderot shuffled toward Ezekiel and Malcolm. He stood watching the two grave-diggers complete their duty.

"Well it's done," the policeman said.

Ezekiel and Malcolm looked at each other and then at Didderot. The words came out of their mouths in unison. "What's done?"

"The death of the Missionary Man, as you folks called him, and Jack. All that's finished. You two don't have to keep your secrets anymore."

"What secrets?" Malcolm asked.

"There is nothing left to hide," the policeman said. "Your mother burned her house to the ground and is in the asylum. Remember, I was the one who told you about the property the preacher left you. I could have kept my mouth shut. Let the government declare it abandoned, allow Cummins or one of his cohorts to pay the taxes and get title to it."

"Nice of you to do the right thing?" Ezekiel said.

"There's nothing left to know," Malcolm said.

"Don't worry, this is no whodunit. I solved the mystery a long time ago," the policeman said. He stood looking at Ezekiel and Malcolm as if waiting for a reaction. "Allow me to take you two under my wings," he said finally.

"We don't need your protection," Ezekiel said.

Dennis Didderot ran one fingers under his nose and smiled. "What you do is dangerous, Ezekiel, moving money from one pocket to another with your union activities. They will come after you one day. You Malcolm, you have something to loose now, how you going to protect your family? Both of you are naive and defenseless against the forces of inequality."

"The lord is my protector," Malcolm said.

"That's all well and good, but a man in the police station with his ears and eyes open, he could be the hands of God."

"Why all of a sudden?" Ezekiel asked, looking at Didderot, searching for hints on his face. "You are choosing to help us. Why."

"I've my reasons, always lived here, my entire family was nourished by land," the policeman said. "You fellows are Grenada's future. All I'm doing is taking a hand in our future. I'm not going to sit near your house or follow you around, but one day when you need help, I'll be there."

Dennis Didderot waved one finger at Ezekiel and Malcolm, tightened his lips, and walked away.

Ezekiel and Malcolm stood looking at the policeman's back. "What you think he might want in exchange for his benevolence?" Malcolm smiled.

"Who knows," Ezekiel said. "I see this as a double edged blade, cuts both ways."

"Yeah, I see. Don't make much difference if we accept or not."

"He will come asking for something one day."

"He did tell me about the house. I owe him for that."

"Yeah, I suppose."

"We moved in two days ago," Malcolm said. "The place is a mess, sitting empty for so long. Rat shit, bird shit, feathers, dust all over the place. Once we give it a good scrubbing, we'll have you and Alma over."

"That sounds good. I've a plan we should discuss."

"A plan for what?" Malcolm asked.

"I'm going to buy that piece of land in the Valley of Bones and turn it into the biggest garden in the world."

Malcolm looked at Ezekiel and laughed. "How you going to work all that land alone, planning on a constant maroon? That could take lots of manpower and produce lots of food."

"Exactly, a collective, everybody earn a share of the profit, can do what they want with it."

"Where are you going to get the money to buy the land any how?"

"This is still in the budding stages."

"Similar to my plans for our church, I'll take my time rebuilding it, a little each day." Malcolm winked as if inviting Ezekiel to agree. "We can use it for worship, story telling, and our own school for those too young to attend regular school."

"We are troubled by very similar questions," Ezekiel said.

"Where there is a will there is a way," Malcolm said.

"Money doesn't fall from trees, Malcolm."

"Prayers, faith and conviction, Ezekiel. As a matter of fact, money does fall from trees. See all those ripe mangoes on the ground." Malcolm nodded his head. "We are neighbors again like old times. We can help each other. Count me in on your venture," Malcolm said and walked off.

Ezekiel felt optimistic about the situations in his head and the particulars of his life. He contemplated the expanse of food growing in the Valley of Bones; everyone making a decent living from working the land as a group, selling the lettuce, the tomatoes, the yams, potatoes and other provisions to the hotels on Grand Anse beach, to shops on the two sister islands, Carriacou and Petite Martinique to the north, and the island of Trinidad to the south, all this felt tranquil. One day, maybe even the Venezuelans with all their oil money may want to buy boat loads of these provisions

The last of the attendees moved away from the gravesite, leaving Ezekiel to ponder the demise of his father. Alma came and took his hand. They started walking away as the last of the mound of dirt filled the grave. Mano followed them to the old house. Alma left the two men in the yard near the plumb tree and went into the house.

"You heard the news?" Mano asked.

"What's happening?"

"Most of Duncan's cane is lying flat on the ground. Some kind of blight infested his field. People saying he is kind of broke, scared he might raise the rent on their garden spots. He had a deal with your father, didn't he?"

"Any deal they had died with the old man. But they are other ways to deal with Duncan."

"I know. We can kill him. His wife and children might be easier to deal with."

Ezekiel laughed at the idea.

"What you laughing at? I'm serious," Mano said.

"I'll let you know when I have a better plan," Ezekiel replied, looking at his father-in-law and wondering.

Where will the money come from? How to approach Duncan about purchasing the land? Ezekiel shuffled these obstacles and formulated an arrangement. First, he decided to talk to the fellows he grew up with, his own generation, Marsden, Kenneth, Nisbet, Punky and Eamon. Those guys have girlfriends, thinking about marriage and would need a way to make money; might be predisposed to better arrangements than their fathers had.

Ezekiel visited the bank in Saint Georges to arrange a loan. In an air conditioned room, he sat with a man dressed in a suit and tie. The man seemed far away, sitting behind a big mahogany desk. Ezekiel thought he might have to shout for the man to hear. After stating the amount he would need and his intended use for the money, the banker told him he would have to put up his house and land in Jean Anglais as collateral. He decided to give the banker's proposal some thought before acting on it.

Next, he went to see Cummins, see what kind of support he could expect from the ruling labor party, his father's old compatriots. Ezekiel sat in the office, in the same place where his father had come seeking help for Cosmus many years ago. The old politician sat behind a desk with his feet propped up. Ezekiel looked at the sole of the man's shoes, thought of standing to get a better prospective on the older man's face. But he remained seated and outlined his plan. A smile surfaced on Cummins face and broadened as each word left Ezekiel's mouth.

"...That's how I see it taking shape."

"You remember the story about the fight between your father and Duncan, and the deal they made?"

"Yeah, actually it's kind of legendary," Ezekiel said.

"Well, your father and everyone else thought they had pulled off a major coup. But Duncan only acted in his own interest. Who would cut his cane if the people of Jean Anglais went hungry? Starving people can be dangerous." Cummins took his feet off the desk and leaned toward Ezekiel. "They say you are one of the best labor organizers we have out there. You are an educated man. Did you study some economics?"

"Adam Smith, Karl Marx and so forth, the classics," Ezekiel said.

"No, no, no. That is macro economics. Micro is the other half, deals with money, banking, insurance and mortgages." And Cummins continued to speak, gave Ezekiel some interesting, but strange information, an approach to acquiring the Valley of Bones that sounded attractive and risky.

"Duncan owns the land, but it's more complicated than you realize. He has a mortgage on the place."

"So he owes some money to the bank, nothing complicated about that."

"Not some money, lots of money. The money he used to modernize his house, buy his car, send his kids to school and maintain that high lifestyle. He thinks he owes the money to the bank but the bank sold the mortgage to the Carlyle family a long time ago."

"The Carlyle family? Those people who lived in the yellow brick house?"

"The very same, daughter who had that love affair with Cosmus LaTouche and ended up dead."

"Why would they want to own the mortgage on the Valley of Bones? You think it might be for some kind of vengeance for what happened to their daughter?"

"Nothing like that, it's strictly business. Every time Duncan sells the cane and pays the bank, the family collects their share with interest. On top of that, he owes a great deal of taxes on the land," Cummins said. "If you go down to the treasure and pay the taxes you would have first dibs on the land in the event of a sale, and there will be a sale the moment those white people realize his crop failed. They won't let their money sit idle, producing no income."

"How does all that work and how much does he owe, in taxes I mean?"

"He owes about five thousand in taxes. You can acquire what is known as a tax lien on the land. He would have to pay you with interest if he or the bank decides to sell the land. You go down there and pay the taxes, get the receipt and paper work, first step toward owning the Valley of Bones or replacing Duncan as the overseer."

Ezekiel found the whole affair intriguing. He stood at the treasury with the money he had received from Tilly, Lloyd and Henry. At the last moment he changed his mind, thinking a tax lean might be kind of underhanded. His heart pounded in his chest as he left the Department of Revenue. He couldn't reconcile giving them all that money for a few sheets of paper. Instead of taking a bus home, he decided to walk, intending to formulate how he would discuss his uncertainty with Alma.

* * *

Two months after John's funeral, Ezekiel woke in a determined mood. His father-in-law Mano was lending a hand with the cattle which gave Ezekiel time to concentrate on his work in the Labor Union and ponder his new station in life. He had a notion that it might be time for the partitions to come down, make the place his own. After all, if Tilly and Lloyd did return to Grenada they would not chose to live in this house when her parent's place sat empty down the road. Ezekiel sat eating breakfast with Alma, watching her pick at the salt fish and bakes, sipping on a cup of ovaltine. He was speaking about his plans for the house when he noticed a smile on her face.

"We shouldn't remove the partition," she said.

"Why not? It's time we treat this place as ours."

"We'll have to share this house with a child."

"Well yeah, eventually," he said.

"Not eventually. We are going to be parents." She spoke and looked into his eyes.

"How far along are you?"

"About three months. Tante thinks it's a girl."

Ezekiel thought of jumping up and throwing his arms around her, but he remained seated, dabbling at the salt fish in coconut oil with a piece of the fried dough. He placed the food in his mouth, and smiled at Alma. She smiled back and they remained silent throughout the rest of the meal.

One day, Alma and her aunt returned from a trip into Saint Georges. They came walking toward the house followed by a boy with a cardboard box balanced on his head. Ezekiel looked at the old woman leaning heavy on a cane and he wondered how she became this old when people all around her were dropping like flies. The two women approached Ezekiel without words and he took the box from the boy, watched as Mama Viche fumbled in her pocket and handed the youngster two coins. The boy turned and walked away.

"How is your scheme working?" the old woman asked Ezekiel.

"Time will tell," he said. "This all takes time."

"What you expect time to tell you?" the old woman threw him a severe look.

"Tante, I told you about his plans. What else you want to know? Dealing with things like that doesn't happen overnight," Alma said. "It does take time."

"Time, time, both of you talking about time, I know about time," Mama Viche said.

"You sound as if you telling him to make haste," Alma said.

"Oh nothing like the wind." The old woman waved one palm. "Ezekiel, have you seen the light?"

"What light, Mama?"

"Your father's light, the glow revealing the way out of the Valley of Bones. I've seen him guiding the lost."

Ezekiel mounted the stairs and entered the kitchen. Alma followed. He rested the box on the table, stood trying to make sure his response didn't betray his doubts. Mama Viche remained outside looking at them as if she had forgotten something.

"Mama, I know you expect me to claim the Valley of Bones in the name of the people. I'm working on it."

"At first, I thought your father would be the one to fulfill the promise. In the spirit world, nothing is as it appears to us mortals."

"I remember your story about Dambala and Mabouya," Ezekiel said.

"Keep that one in mind. You came from great lineage."

"I know, Mama. I know the lineage."

"Not many of us get the opportunity to reach back so far. Don't wait too long, Ezekiel. Time waits for no one." The old woman walked away.

Ezekiel and Alma sat at the table with the box between them unopened.

"She wants you to snap your fingers and get things done," Alma said.

"Yeah, I know. Of all people, she is the one who always counsel patience."

"Kind of advice is always easier to give than to follow," Alma said.

"Yep. Not the kind of thing you can hurry. She knows that."

They knew the care package came from Tilly and Lloyd. Alma began pulling on the tape. She took the merchandise out of the box, one item at a time, admiring and putting them aside. It contained three maternity dresses, two pairs of blue jeans and a pair of rubber boots for Ezekiel. Some dried goods completed the contents. At the bottom of the box, Alma found a large brown envelope. She handed it to Ezekiel. He tore into it and gazed at the one-page letter as Alma took out the last of the items.

"Well I'll be...This is from Cosmus," and he started reading:

Dear Ezekiel,

Condolences on the death of your father, he was a good man. If not for him and Mondu, I may not have made my escape from Richmond Hill. I'll never forget my debt to him and the people of Jean Anglais. My life in Venezuela has taken some amazing turns. I'm working as an interpreter for an oil company. Keep this information under your hat. I'm still a wanted man. I learned from an old schoolmate, who now works in the police department that Didderot has been promoted to commissioner of police and still keeps a file on me. He is quietly seeking my whereabouts. Have you red the novel, Les Misserables by Victor Hugo? I can relate to Jean Valjean. I hope, one of these days, Didderot fills his pocket with rocks and jump into the water on the Carenage like Inspector Javert. Only then will I be able to come home. I frequently travel to the United States, New York, Miami and other cities around the world. I see Tilly and Lloyd often and have heard of you intention to start a farming cooperative in the Valley of Bones. You will be amazed at how Tilly is raising money, cooking food and inviting academics from Lloyd's work, speaking to them about your project. You should see how they open their check books to contribute to your cause. This has inspired me to do the same. You are a wise man. Besides water, there's nothing as important as food and air. If you were a Venezuelan and the Government took your advice, they would have avoided what's known as Dutch Disease. I'm sending you fifty thousand U.S. dollars. Use it to further your project. My mother has an account at the Royal Bank of Canada in town, from the rents on the two houses. She will be willing to make you a loan if you have the need. The people of Jean Anglais and Grenadians will benefit immensely. I'm also returning your veil. Let's hope it serves you as well as it has served me. Take care.

You friend, Cosmus.

Ezekiel removed the veil from the envelope and held it up to the daylight. Alma stood with one of the dresses from Tilly in her hand, and gazing at Ezekiel.

"This alters the whole thing," Alma said.

"Not really. I've always known things would take a good turn," Ezekiel said. "Now I have over a hundred thousand dollars."

"Did you see this in a vision? That Cosmus would . . ."

"Not really. All of that is gone. Yesterday I went to the valley and just stood there looking at the wilted cane and I felt lost. It never crossed my mind that Cosmus would enter the equation."

"How can a man with your gifts ever be lost?" Alma smiled at Ezekiel.

"Many roads to walk and many corners to turn, one can go the wrong way."

"Not you. Take a wrong turn I mean. And that is good, right?"

"Not really. I can't see anything any more. I'm powerless to envisioning the future," Ezekiel said.

"Don't worry," Alma said, "the moment you witness the future, it's no longer the future any how."

"I see what you mean," Ezekiel said.

Similar ideas had inhabited his thoughts before the letter from Cosmus and the return of the veil. Those inklings started on the day he stood in the Valley of Bones scrutinizing the wilted cane. All that seemed isolated now, far off in another quarter. Ezekiel felt pounds lighter. Telling Alma about his inability to deduce the future had lifted a weight from his shoulders. But other events swirled around Grenada.

* * *

Some of the young men he had recruited to the side of the Labor Movement now appeared to be bullies, harassing people who dare to speak out about the faults of the ruling party. A fellow from Belmont called Suey became their foremost example. The prime minister's men from the outer villages, calling themselves the Mongoose Gang, cornered Suey and almost beat him to death because he dared to say something negative about the government. Ezekiel decided to separate himself from the labor movement after witnessing the brutality exacted on Suey. And then Alma went to see her aunt and returned late one day with a girl child wrapped in a blanket. With the money in hand to make an offered to Duncan on the land, Ezekiel plunged forward.

He approached Duncan with fifty thousand dollars as a down payment. Duncan's quick agreement caught Ezekiel by surprise. With papers signed and all terms agreed upon, Ezekiel began clarifying details with the villagers, explaining exactly how the co-op would work and benefit all of them. Some people remained resistant to the idea, but eventually everyone came to a consensus. In the midst of the political turmoil around Grenada, Ezekiel moved ahead with his plans as if matters outside of Jean Anglais and the Valley of Bones had nothing to do with him.

One warm Saturday evening, Mama Viche invited Ezekiel and Alma with the baby to her house for dinner. Alma carried the child lashed to her stomach as if they were still one. The house looked spotless, as if the old woman had worked for days putting things together, tablecloth and the bouquet of flowers adorning the dinning table added a special touch. With Alma's help, Mama Viche served a meal of callaloo, pig snout and dumplings. Not much was said during the meal but after the spoons scrapped the bottom of the bowls, the old woman began speaking in a deliberate tone.

"Thank you both for giving the child my name. I missed that sounds after people stopped calling me by my real name." Mama Viche smiled.

"We thought long and hard about calling her Sybil. But we kept coming back to it," Ezekiel said. "And then we found the combination."

"We knew we had something when we said the name Sybil Maureen Augustine," Alma said. "Your name and my mother's name came together beautifully."

"Beautiful," Mama Viche reached out and stroked the head of the sleeping child. "I can be at piece now. There is a totality to this now."

"What are you saying?" Ezekiel and Alma asked the question in unison.

"This is the sum of a life," she said.

"What you mean by that, Tante," Alma said.

"I have to go now. I'll wait for all of you at the crossroads."

"You sound as if you going on a holiday, Mama?" Ezekiel looked at the old woman and smiled.

She didn't smile back. "There's a feeling in my heart," she said. "It's time to join the ancestors."

"I made the deal with Duncan. The Valley of Bones belongs to us now."

"I know. That's all I wanted to see. I can now rejoice with the ancestors as they leave the Valley of Bones. You did well. Now it's time for me to bargain on your behalf with Papa Legba and Guede."

"How can you…? You can't just decide to go away, you can't just leave us, Tante," Alma said.

"My time here is over. It's time that you take my place. Remember all that I taught you."

"You have many years ahead of you, Tante. Stop scaring me, okay," Alma said.

The old woman looked at Alma and smiled. "If it were only so. None of us can remain forever, girl. Just keep me in your heart. There is a sponge cake in the bread box. Let's enjoy a slice."

They left the old woman's house with heavy hearts and doubts. The next day when no one saw Mama Viche sitting on her porch, people called on Alma. They found the old woman stretched out on her bed, eyes closed and a big smile on her face. She died in her sleep just as she had predicted. Ezekiel and Alma made arrangements for her funeral and laid the old woman to rest.

The first year of the co-op turn out to be a huge success. The rains came on schedule and the crops grew. Ezekiel and the people of Jean Anglais reaped the harvest and sold most everything for more cash than anyone in Jean Anglais had seen in their lifetime. Duncan Elmo appeared pleased to receive his share of the money and the government allowed the co-op to import two rototillers, duty free. The political turmoil around Grenada grew, and the Mongoose Gang became more violent. Malcolm had started speaking out against the actions of the Government and the Mongoose Gang. Inspector Diddderot saw Alma walking on the Carenage with her baby. He went to her as if to admire the child, instead he slipped her a note. The Mongoose Gang had a plan to silence Malcolm. The people of Jean Anglais sharpened their cutlass and arranged for two boys to remain near Malcolm's house, blow the conch shell if they see men coming for Malcolm.

Four members of the gang showed up. First, they set the half built church on fire and waited for Malcolm to come out of his house. When the people of Jean Anglais emerged from the bushes with their cutlass the four ruffians backed off, but not before shouting threats at Malcolm. That night, Malcolm snuck out and caught a vessel leaving for Trinidad. The Mongoose Gang stayed away from Jean Anglais and went about their brutal business. Three months later, Ezekiel went to Malcolm's house to check on the women and children and there sat his old friend. He told Ezekiel big things were about to happen, took him to a room and showed him a stack of weapons.

Malcolm had aligned himself with the group called The New Movement. They were rejected by the governing party, refused to let them place candidates on the ballots for the upcoming election. Leftists the old politicians kept calling them. After the election, which was easily won by the ruling party, the old prime minister left on a victory trip to Canada. The members of The New Movement brought out their weapons, took over the radio station and all government buildings, attacked the Mongoose Gang, killed some and placed others under arrest. The police remained in the station and took no part in the coup. A week later Inspector Didderot moved to Barbados with his wife and children. Malcolm became the voice of the Movement, making announcement over the airways as Radio Free Grenada.

For the next three years, things were good for the people of Jean Anglais. Their collective fed into the philosophy of The New Movement and the people now ruling Grenada funneled small sums of cash into the enterprise, allowing the villagers to buy a truck to transport their produce to market, and to the vessels for export. The New Movement tried to replicate the scheme in other places on the island with minimal success. It didn't take long for the Movement to turn on themselves. Ezekiel and Malcolm scrambled to be on the right side of the upheaval. But as things fell apart inside the New Movement, the people of Jean Anglais began to whisper: No matter how many times a snake sheds its skin it still remains a snake. The two friends stayed out of the confusion and concentrated on the farming as the jails and camps overflowed with so called enemies of the people.

It didn't take long for the Americans to send soldiers to restore the old regime. The prime minister gave an order to confiscate books with Leftists leaning ideas. The police went to schools, libraries and to the homes of people formerly associated with the New Movement. They came to Jean Anglais, and ransacked Malcolm's home, seized the speeches of Fidel Castro, took all the books by C.L R. James and Eric Williams. In Ezekiel and Alma's home, they seized some papers on crop rotation written by the Cuba botanist Frere Leon. Alma hid most of their books.

Rumors started circulating about a jamboree to be held at Queen's park. Ezekiel and Malcolm had plans to attend, but Alma refused to be anywhere close to such a fiasco. The same evening she scheduled a meeting with Malcolm's twin wives and a couple other women from the village to clarify the bookkeeping system of the collective.

To impress the Americans, the prime minister had the police bring all the books confiscated to Queen's Park. He gave a rousing speech, shouting about foreign ideas brought to Grenada and how these things should be weeded out and burned. As they dowsed the large heap of books with kerosene and lit it, Ezekiel couldn't help but wonder at the stupidity of the whole debacle. Can ideas be burned out of the minds of people? The two friends stood watching the flames devour the books. Supporters of the government shouted and screeched at the joyfulness of the occasion as they threw wood at the fire. The flames crackle and spark as if the ideas in the books protested.

Ezekiel and Malcolm moved away from the heat generated by the flame and the crowd; saw a range of emotions on faces illuminated by the orange glow.

"I've a little money saved to start rebuilding the church," Malcolm said.

"The co-op will contribute. Since we will be using the building for meetings and community events," Ezekiel said.

"That sounds good. These crazy two-faced loupgarous trying to kiss the American's asses, lord have mercy."

"Be careful what you say. Never know who might be listening."

"I don't give two shits about donkey ears." Malcolm said.

"Very little difference between the men who ran Grenada before, during the revolution and now," Ezekiel said.

Malcolm looked at Ezekiel and smiled. "So, when you going to do it?"

"Do what?"

"Stop feeding people's stomachs and start feeding their minds. When will you throw your name in the hat?"

"One task at a time, Malcolm, one mission, Mama Viche once called me the deliverer."

"You see what I mean? Even the old woman knew. The people of Jean Anglais, Belmont and Grandanse will vote for you."

"It depends on what the ruling party offers them."

"Join the ruling party then. That way, whatever is being offered is being offered by you."

"Sounds like hypocrisy."

"You are the one who wants to be political. You know what the word stands for?"

"Not really. But we can't get away from it, can we. I'll have to take a closer look at its origin," Ezekiel said.

Malcolm smiled and looked at the sky as he made the sign of the cross on his body. "We have been lucky so far."

"No." Ezekiel said. "It's a game and we played it well."

"A game, huh? Some people took the ultimate stake in that game."

"I don't think any of them saw it coming," Ezekiel said.

Ezekiel and Malcolm stood looking at the old prime minister and his cohorts, some people prancing about in a festive mood as the flames licked at the night air.

"How many revolutions have we had on this island?" Malcolm asked.

"Many of them, big and small," Ezekiel said.

"Those guns I showed you in the house, I didn't give all of them to the fellows who overthrew the government. I hauled two cases up the mountain and buried them in that cave on top of Ogoun's Point."

"What are you going to do with guns? You are a man of God, Malcolm."

"I'm not the kind who turns the other cheek. There are times when God sends a man with a sword or a gun. You see, Jean Anglais come about through revolution."

"I suppose it was." Ezekiel said with a puzzled look on his face.

"Only three people know about the guns, me, you and your brother Henry."

"You trying to tell me God condone violence?"

"Who said anything about violence? I'll keep those weapons dry and stored. Maybe not today or the next, but we might find the need to protect what's ours."

"What makes you think that?"

"Food, Ezekiel, food. We know how to work together, and produce lots of good food. Think it will end there? Food is power, right up there next to cash money but they can't eat money."

"You are beginning to scare me, Malcolm."

"Good. Makes you think."

"Yes it does."